Last Memoria
Book One in the Memoria Duology

RACHEL EMMA SHAW

For everyone who helped make this dream possible.

CONTENTS

Her memories rub against my own, wearing them away. They taint me with the very essence of her, her hopes, her dreams, her interpretations, showing me the world through her black and obstinate eyes, exposing the darkness she always warned was there.

You can see for yourself if you would think the same in my shoes. I will share her memories with you as she did with me, then you can decide if you wish you had never known them.

CHAPTER ONE

Stolen memories crawled through Sarilla's mind, distorting the gale-whipped trees around her. Past fought with present until gone was the heavy drumming of rain on her skin. Forgotten was the fresh scent of the autumn downpour. The road cutting between the gnarled trunks of the Deadwood forest disappeared, as did the stationary wagon and the attached mule as it stomped uneasily in the muddy puddles. Even Sarilla's brother and the threat of the pursuing soldiers slipped away, but that was the trouble with stolen memories. You could never trust them once they were yours.

She no longer stood in a forest. Instead, sand from the eastern plains lashed at her skin, drought embattled grasses wafting about her legs in a warm breeze that lingered after sunset. The tang of summer filled her nostrils, so real she could have sworn she breathed it in. The dry, aching thirst attacked her throat as she fought to push the memory down. She needed to remember where she was, but instead of the present, another memory sprang up in the place of the eastern one. Cold flames silently licked the air, the memory's creator having apparently neglected to pay attention to the crackle of the logs and the touch of the heat.

Push it down. She needed to focus on the present. She had been in a forest, hadn't she? Either her control was slipping or the memories were too numerous to restrain anymore. She had known it would happen one day, just like it had to her mother.

Some nights she dreamt of burrowing her nails into her skin and drawing the memories out. She would pull until she was free, then cast them into the fire to be sure their corruption couldn't spread. Already they had wormed so deeply inside her that there were days she couldn't remember who she was upon waking.

Focus, Sarilla. The wagon. Rysen. The trees.

The memories faded as she fought to hold on to the image of the dark-haired man climbing down from the wagon. He greeted her brother pleasantly, but something didn't feel right. It was the present, wasn't it?

She turned about, searching for the telltale signs of a memory. Empty grey spaces of missing details the creator hadn't noticed. Absent senses that made an imperfect but beautiful whole, always unique to the creator in ways that made their memories fascinating to examine. But there was nothing. No imperfections. No lies. It was the present, not the past.

Trees. Mule. wagon. Her brother removing his glove, revealing the black tips of his fingers-

Real! It was real! Present, not past.

Rysen clapped his hand to the back of the wagon driver's neck, smiling even as the marks began to spread.

She must have made a mistake. It couldn't be the present because Rysen wouldn't do that. He knew the risks. Soldiers were searching the Deadwood for them, and he wouldn't do anything to draw their attention.

The stranger's face blanked as black rippled across the back of Rysen's hand, the vine-like marks snaking up his fingers, spreading a little more with each memory he stole. His eyes flickered as the bumps of his pupils moved under his lids, his mind scouring the stranger's memories.

Present, not past.

"Rysen, don't!"

"You want to spend another night in the rain? I'm sick of all your complaining."

More memories flooded her. The press of plush down. The soft caress of smooth sheets. They were her memories this time, though she wished they weren't since they made her miss the palace. She pushed them down, wishing she could forget them entirely.

"Only idiots sleep well with an army of soldiers after them," she said, managing to get the memories under control enough for the forest to reform about her.

Something moved behind the wagon and her gaze locked on the fright-wide eyes peering back at her as cold flooded through her chest.

There was a witness to Rysen's crime.

Moving silently so as not to alert her brother, she sidestepped the puddles, manoeuvring so she blocked the boy from view. If Rysen saw him... She couldn't let that happen. The child looked barely old enough to know who he was. If Rysen took his memories then it would mess him up for the rest of his life. She had seen it happen enough to the adults she had stolen from.

"Ry," she said, holding a finger to her lips and motioning for the boy to stay quiet behind her. "We need to go. We can't linger here."

"Not yet," Rysen said, his eyes still shut as he shifted through his victim's memories. "He's got a surprising amount in the old noggin."

"I don't care. We need to get out away before anyone sees-"

"He's got loads of use in here, Sari. He even knows how to start a fire. I'll give you the memory."

"I've enough already. I don't need his too."

Didn't he realise how bad the memories were getting for her? Each one made it harder to fight through to the present. She used to know what each contained back when there were only a handful beside her own. Now they were a forest of vines she didn't even know where to begin pruning. So much knowledge filled her that finding anything of use was quickly becoming as difficult as locating a lost grain of sand in the desert. Perhaps she already knew how to start a fire and could have saved them three miserable nights camped on sodden patches of moss, trying to catch a few meagre hours of rest as they shivered against rotting tree stumps, but she hadn't even tried examining the memories to find out. It was hard enough keeping her mind clear as it was. If she delved any deeper, she might not be able to break free again.

"Suit yourself," Rysen said. "Though don't be complaining to me when…"

His hand stilled on the man's neck.

"Ry?"

"He's not here alone."

A denial rose in Sarilla. It was on her lips, but what was the point? Rysen had already seen the truth in the man's memories.

He opened his eyes and turned, trying to see behind her. "It's Callon, right?" he asked, raising his voice so it rang through the trees. "You help your father, don't you?"

The boy nodded, the motion jerky as his entire body began to shake.

"You went for a kip in the back," Rysen said. "You must have been tired. You've been on the road since before dawn. Look, your father's tired too. Why don't you come over here and help me get him back atop the wagon?"

"Ry. Stop it! Let's just go."

"We can't leave. He's seen us. We've at least got to clear the last few memories-"

"He's just a child! I mean it. Leave him be. He's already frightened out of his mind."

"And I can take that from him. Be serious, Sari. We can't leave him with those memories. He'll alert the soldiers."

"He'll have to find them first. Please. Let's just get away from here."

Rysen glared at her for a moment longer, then sighed. "Fine. Hey, Kid!"

The boy flinched, looking ready to race into the forest, eager to exchange the threat of Sarilla and Rysen for the dangers awaiting those who ventured off the road, but she couldn't let him do that. He would lose far more than his memories in the Deadwood, though some might call that a better fate.

"Ry... Leave him be. He's terrified-"

"Fine. Look kid, we're going now," Rysen called. "And your father's still alive. Try to remember that when you're setting the soldiers after us, alright? I could have killed you both-"

"Rysen!"

"Alright. Alright."

Rysen shut his eyes, the black marks on his hands rippling one last time as the creeping invasion reversed. He released his victim and the man dropped, his eyes glazing over with the usual black haze of an overloaded mind.

Which had Rysen given him? They had to be ones he didn't mind handing over to the imperfect care of an imperfect mind. Probably those of someone else he had stolen from. Some other inconsequential victim. The Gods knew he would never hand over his own.

Grabbing his arm, she pulled him away, muttering under her breath as she picked a path along the muddy road. Out of both of her siblings, she loved and despaired of Rysen the most. Their sister wasn't old enough to know where the line between right and wrong was when it came to memories, but Rysen should have figured it out years ago.

Her footsteps squelched as she trod the thick mud coating the road. Her ruined footwear held almost as much inside as clung to the exterior. The dull throbbing in her feet pounded with every step, making her glad it was too dark to inspect the damage.

Light glimmered through the rain up ahead, signalling the presence of something other than trees for once.

"Is that a town?" Rysen asked.

"Don't even think it. They'll be too many people."

"Just a quick stop. We can wait out the rain."

"It's been raining for three days."

"Then it should finish soon."

She raised an eyebrow and cast a quick, sceptical glance skyward to the rolling grey above. "Does it look like Cursen's going to stop pissing on us anytime soon?" she asked.

"Look. My feet are about to rot off, I'm so cold I'm shaking and I've been walking funny this past day from chaffing." Rysen's forehead crumpled as he pleaded and she stared at the short, black locks above.

He looked almost normal with his hair cut like that. Like one of them. Until a few days ago, his hair had hung to his eyebrows, but the white tips were too distinctive and he cut them so no-one would realise who he was.

A memory from before filled her mind. One of Rysen laughing, his hair flicking in a white swarm as he threw his head back with mirth. He hadn't laughed like that in a while.

The memory faded and the Rysen of the past was replaced with the far wetter version standing before her, his good humour lost along with the white of his hair. Instead, rain trickled down his forehead, dripping from locks licked together by the water. He swiped them aside, blinking the worst of the downpour from his vision.

"Fine," she said, too cold to continue arguing. "An hour. No more. We can't afford to linger."

He hurried in the direction of the town before she could change her mind.

Rainwater poured from the thatched roofs, splashing down and pooling between the cobbles paving the streets. A dog stared miserably at them from the post it was chained to, but the streets were otherwise deserted. Apparently only beasts and those on the run could be found outside in a storm.

The town was an old one. It had the feel of history about it and likely had existed since long before the nation of Valrora formed a century ago. You could see it in the wear of the cobbles and the style of the houses, which were too ramshackle and looked nothing like the sleek and slender ones built in the capital over the last hundred years.

Sarilla had seen other towns like it before. She had seen many things in the memories she had taken over the years.

Laughter burst from a tavern nearby as a door swung open, blaring the chatter of voices and the chinking of mugs out into the storm. Sarilla hurried inside and heat blasted her, but she was so cold that she barely felt it. The rain had soaked her dress, making the garment cling heavily to her, the fabric so tight that it was likely never coming off again. It would take days to dry off.

The wind and rain continued to batter the windows, but she relished the sound since it signalled that, for the first time in days, it wasn't coming down on her. She was out of the forest. She wasn't being pissed on by the Gods, at least for the time being.

Her enjoyment fled at the sight of the soldiers lounging inside the tavern, the small room almost bursting from how many were crammed inside.

This couldn't be happening. Cursen couldn't hate her that much.

Turning to suggest they find somewhere else to spend the night, she stilled as Rysen brushed past her, weaving his way through the room, dodging stools and soldiers alike. He sat when he reached an empty table, looking back and frowning as he spotted her in the doorway.

Reckless idiot.

"In or out?" a voice asked, dragging her attention from Rysen to the mean-looking man glaring up at her and gesturing to the open doorway.

"Good question," she murmured, stealing another glance about the room.

"Then shut the damn door while you ponder it!"

He shoved her aside, putting an end to the draft. She tensed as his arm brushed hers. Too close. Memories surged through her. Her own this time. Each filled with the heady rush that came from delving into another's mind. Temptation taunted her, goading her to reach out and touch the man's skin. To make the connection and let her mind-

No. She couldn't. She had promised herself she wouldn't. Not again.

Muttering under her breath, she made her way over to Rysen, all too aware of the many eyes following her as she passed between the soldiers, expecting them to grab her at any moment, having figured out that the fugitives they searched the Deadwood for were hiding in their midst.

CHAPTER TWO

She fought back the urge to pull up her hood as she edged through the tavern. It didn't matter that her hair was bound back by a scarf or that the light was too dim for anyone to notice the intense black of her irises, which were too dark to be the product of even the murkiest brown.

The sodden fabric of her skirt stuck unpleasantly to her backside as she sat and the fire's heat blasted her, but she was too strung out to enjoy the sensation. It didn't matter that she was close enough to the flames that her dress would have caught fire if it wasn't rain drenched.

"Happy now?" Rysen asked, amusement and reckless humour dancing in his voice.

He flashed her a grin and she scowled back.

"No," she muttered, wiping away the water droplets clinging to her arms before rubbing her gloved hands together furiously.

"Shall I get us a drink?"

He glanced at the steaming mugs on the next table over before diverting his gaze to the bar and the woman serving behind it. You couldn't see much about her from the dress and the headscarf she wore tied at the nape of her neck, but that didn't seem to matter much to Rysen.

"I don't think it's wise," Sarilla said, referring to both his fetching them a drink and to the flirtation he was no doubt entertaining. "We shouldn't linger here. We're not exactly-"

Either not listening or choosing to ignore her, Rysen had already stood and was making his way over to the bar. Sarilla squeezed her eyes shut and muttered a quick prayer to Forta under her breath, praying for strength enough not to kill her brother as she watched him go.

He returned a few minutes later, two steaming cups in hand and a flirtatious smile still plastered to his face.

"Ry, we don't exactly have funds to splurge," she said, taking the offered mug from him, grateful for the warmth even though it took a while to feel the full effects through her leather gloves.

Sensation would have returned to her fingers more quickly had she removed the gloves, but not even Rysen was enough of a fool to do something so stupid. Even his reckless nature had its limits.

Her gloves almost reached her elbows and were as fine as anything she had ever worn. The riveted black top layer created the impression of a mosaic of white vines where it revealed the lighter layer underneath, the stunning effect a not-so-subtle reminder from Renford of what she was. What he made her be. He could have gifted her with any pair, but he had chosen those, a set of gloves that hid her shame from no-one.

If she had money enough, she would have already spent it replacing them, but she never had even a copper to her name. None of her family had. Gods knew where Rysen managed to get the small pouch of coins he had with him since leaving the palace.

Holding the mug under her chin, she breathed in the sticky-sweet steam rising from it. Was it alcoholic? She couldn't tell, but she hoped not. A roomful of soldiers was hardly somewhere she wanted to let her guard down.

It wasn't like anything she had ever drunk in the palace, yet the tangy fragrance still triggered a memory she had stolen from one of Valrora's less well-off nobles. He was likely long dead now. Renford's punishment was always swift.

A tide of other memories swarmed on the heel of the last. She lost herself in them. They were the works of lazy artists, each containing only the details the painter cared to include. Unlike memori memories, those she stole had been made by people who couldn't fully capture the present. It gave their memories a unique character that was disorientating to explore.

Rysen. The soldiers. Focus, Sarilla. Focus.

Fixing her gaze on her brother, she followed his across the room, unsurprised to find it on the barmaid again.

"Ry... you look like a thrice drowned rat."

"A handsome thrice drowned rat?" he asked, running his fingers through his hair and shaking off some of the water.

"It's not going to happen. Please don't get us killed by trying."

"A little flirtation isn't going to hurt anyone."

"We need to get out of here. That man over there is already watching us too closely for my liking."

"You never like anything."

"That's not true. I like lots of things. I liked the comforts of the palace. I liked being warm. I liked not having to worry about the rain and the mud and empty stomachs and-"

"Seriously?" Rysen stared at her incredulously. "How

13

can you even think like that?"

"More easily with every day we spend trudging through the Deadwood."

"This. This is exactly why Da never confided in you about the plan. I won't let you go back to that cage, Sari."

"I love you, Ry, but you're an idiot if you don't see that we'll be caged wherever we go. How could you let him talk you into this?"

"Da didn't talk me into anything. And stop blaming him for this. He saved us"

"Saved us? Like this is any better. We're lost, half frozen-"

"For the last time, we're not lost."

"Then where are we going?" Rysen didn't answer and she clenched the mug, her frustration getting the better of her. "Please tell me. I've a right to know."

He raised a sardonic brow, sipping his drink and grimacing at the cloying sweetness he sent tumbling down his throat. Good. If he didn't like the taste, then hopefully he wouldn't drink much of it. Alcohol played havoc with memories, and they were in enough danger as it was.

"Fine," Sarilla muttered. "Keep your secrets and I'll keep mine."

Rysen rested his gloved hand on hers. "I wish you wouldn't. You think I don't know what's been going on with you? I don't need to take your memories to see through your eyes."

He ran his fingers comfortingly along the leather, staring at it as if he could see through to the skin below.

Her throat constricted as she stared at his hand, absorbing the sensation. Was it possible to be starved of touch?

"Ry..."

"I know. I won't push you to tell me about it. Just..."

14

know that I'm here whenever you need to talk."

She nodded. It was the only answer she could give. Thinking about everything that had happened with Falon was too painful, even now.

"Please tell me where we're heading. They're my family too."

Pain flashed across Rysen's face as he sighed.

"And I wish that was enough for me to trust you again."

Withdrawing her hand, she sat back, fighting against the crumpling sensation in her chest. A nearby soldier cheered as a young recruit followed a smiling girl out the back of the tavern, laughter and mocking jibes assailing them as they went. Others nearby discussed everything from the weather to comrades dead on the march. From the sounds of it, you would think they had already lost half the army on the journey from Dranta, more than a few having stumbled upon graves in the Deadwood, a price you might have to pay for venturing into the trees for a little privacy. It was why Sarilla and Rysen had stuck to the road so far, no matter the danger the soldiers posed.

The forest was littered with the graves, areas where the ground was ready to cave in, its foundations unsteady and riddled by the tunnels spreading out from the capital, the memori who created and maintained them having been driven away a hundred years before.

"Between the graves and blackvine," a soldier said, "it'll be a wonder if half of us make it to Arvendon."

The comment earned muttered agreement from his fellows.

Blackvine. Ebony venom. Valrora's bane. Whispering death. It had many names. Sarilla had heard it called by all of them in the stolen memories she had, although she had never known it reported so far west.

The conversation lulled as a portly soldier swayed his

way onto a tabletop nearby. He sloshed his mug and the froth dribbled onto his companions. They yelled drunkenly up at him, telling him to get down, but the man didn't seem to notice.

"It's time we show them who these lands belong to!" he called, his words so slurred that Sarilla had a hard time making out what he said. If he was still sober enough to form memories then studying them would be a headache in itself.

"It doesn't belong to the blackvine," he said, swaying dangerously and almost tumbling off the table. "And not to the memori! It's ours! I say, once we take back Arvendon, we finish off those scum once and for all!"

His words triggered a memory to rise in her mind, and soon the soldiers about her were no more. The chill stabbing through her body faded as the heavy smoke from a poorly burning fire filled her nose, the char thick in the air and making it hard to see the young boy as he grinned, waggling his hands as if they were erupting from the ground.

"And then the memori sent the blackvine to kill them all!" he called, throwing his arms in the air before falling backwards and pretending to die gruesomely, clutching his head, his eyes rolling back as the memory maker squeal, tripping over her little legs as she wobbled to hide behind a chair.

"I've told you not to tell that story!"

A woman wearing little better than rags marched into the room, her expression even more scolding than her voice had been.

"You know it distresses your father," she said, looking as if she was fighting back tears. "And look at that fire. I told you to keep an eye on it!"

She picked up a poker and stabbed at the logs,

muttering under her breath as she did.

"He's not my pa," the little boy said, staring at the doorway the woman had burst through, his fists curled at his sides.

"What did you say?" the woman asked, her voice cracking as she turned to face her son, the poker still in hand.

"I said he's not my pa!" the boy yelled, screaming the words at the doorway. "He's not my pa! He never came home! The memori killed him-!"

Cheers echoing through the tavern jolted Sarilla from the memory and she cursed herself for letting her mind wander, stilling as she caught sight of Rysen's clenched jaw as he stared at his mug, looking as if he didn't see it.

"What is it?" she asked, searching his face. "What's wrong?"

He blinked, dragging his mind back from wherever it had been, something clearly worrying him.

"Nothing."

"You're about as good at lying as Lya," she said, casting her mind back to what had been happening before the memory took over.

The memori. The blackvine. Arvendon. The soldier had been talking about travelling to the old city on the rocks.

"Were you planning on taking us through Arvendon?" she asked, watching Rysen carefully.

"No."

"Then why... Wait, is Lya going that way?"

Rysen didn't answer, but it didn't matter. She could read it in his eyes.

"I told you this was a bad idea!"

"Stop worrying. I'm sure she's fine. Da will keep her safe."

"She only met him a few months ago. She must be

terrified."

Rysen bristled, seeming to take her snipe personally. "That's hardly his fault."

"No, but everything that's followed has been." Lowering her voice, she said, "Look at us, Ry. We're scattered across the country, ready to be picked off. There are soldiers everywhere-"

"With any luck, they'll be gone long before any siege starts."

Sarilla stared at him, disbelief crashing through her. "When has luck ever been on our side? We were born under Cursen's ire, not Forta's protection. His good intentions will end up getting us killed-"

"Getting who killed?" a voice asked.

Sarilla stilled as the soldier stopped beside their table, leaning over her. She hesitated for a moment, fighting to manipulate the fear from her face before turning towards the man.

"No-one," she said, trying to smile and knowing she wasn't succeeding.

Where was that memory? The one from Renford's dead ex-mistress who had been stealing from him, always looking so innocent as she did. It had taken Renford years to see through her deception and order Sarilla to search out the truth in the woman's mind. If she could just remember the tricks she used…

No! She couldn't afford to get lost in the memories. Not in a room full of soldiers.

Still, the look she gave the man must have worked. He seemed to forget his question as he stared at her, leering in a way she wasn't used to being directed at her. Nobody ever flirted with a memoria. His doing so was either a sign of her disguise being effective or of his level of intoxication.

"You should be thanking us, you know," he said. "Where would a wench like you be without strapping soldiers like me keeping the monsters at bay?"

"Where indeed?" Sarilla asked as she turned to Rysen. "Time to go."

"You'd leave me so soon?"

The soldier's hand caught her headscarf as she tried to slip past him. A white cloud billowed down about her face as he accidentally wrenched the fabric off. Panic filled her as her all-too-distinctive feature became all too visible. She yanked her hood up and tugged the headscarf from the soldier's limp grasp, searching his expression, but he didn't seem to have noticed anything was amiss, probably too drunk to realise what the sight of black roots leached to white tips meant.

They needed to get out of there. Forget the rain. Forget the mud. They couldn't risk staying any longer.

She turned to go, but the soldier grabbed her arm, pulling her back. Before she could shake him off though, Rysen moved behind the soldier and fear coursed through her as Rysen's ungloved fingers reached for the back of the man's neck, his black marks pulsing their poison.

He couldn't. There were too many soldiers.

"Ry, don't-!"

Too late.

The soldier's gaze lost focus, blanking as Rysen rifled one memory after another from him. A sweet satisfaction suffused Rysen's features as the black branches on his fingers thickened, spreading as more of the soldier's memories seeped into him. The sight was more goading than she could stand. It tempted her to do the same, taunting her with the urge to press her hands to the man's neck. To feel the rush of memories-

"Ry, stop it. Let him go."

19

Blinking through the heady rush of memories, her brother released the soldier and took half a step back, blinking as he adjusted to the new memories assimilating inside him before glancing her way.

"I had to."

"You didn't though, did you? That's supposed to be the point of all this."

She was drawing attention to them. They had to get away from there. She could scold Rysen as much as she wanted as soon as they got out of there.

Forcing back down all the anger and frustration that had been building over the last few days, she turned her back on him and slipped through the crowd. Rain still lashed at the windows, but she didn't care. Not even the prospect of another drenching could make her want to stay in that soldier infested tavern a moment longer.

"What did you do to him?"

She stilled at the angry voice ringing through the tavern behind her, causing the chatter of the other soldiers to die. Dread filled her as she spun back around, already knowing what she would see.

Everyone stared at the dazed-looking man in their midst, but her gaze flew to Rysen. He was further from the door than she was and her stomach twisted as he tugged off his other glove, his smile widening as he did.

"Care to help?" he asked before grabbing the nearest soldier's arm.

She didn't move. She couldn't. There had to be at least twenty soldiers in the tavern. He wouldn't. He couldn't.

When she didn't answer, he said, "Suit yourself. Just bar the door on your way out."

Was this what he had wanted all along? An excuse to let loose and steal the memories from anyone he wished, all under the guise of self-defence?

No-one stopped her as she fled. They were too preoccupied with the attacking memoria to notice the one fleeing.

She slammed the wooden door shut behind her as she hurried out, hoping to block out the frightened screams from the other side. An acrid taste forced its way up her throat as someone muttered a fervent prayer to Forta through the wood, bargaining over his fate. Still, she clung to the door, not letting him out, holding on until the pounding stopped.

It didn't matter that she wasn't the one taking the memories. She was just as bad as Rysen.

Mud squelched from the alley to the back of the tavern, and the young soldier from before stumbled into a patch of light beaming through a window. His armour flashed and Sarilla caught sight of his breeches hanging untied about his waist as he grappled for his sword, straining to see the cause of all the commotion through the window.

"You should run," she said to him.

The boy jumped and swung his blade in her direction, holding it with none of the practice that Renford's palace guards had always demonstrated.

"What... What's happening in there?" he asked, his voice shaking.

She could tug off her glove. Press her fingertips to his skin. Give in to her cravings as Rysen had.

Heat spread down her fingers at the thought of letting the soldier's memories flood into her. She could experience the rush once more, lose herself in the intoxication of another's life, but then what? Then she would be everything Renford believed her to be and worse.

Every memory she had stolen in the palace had been because Renford demanded that she do so. If she stole any now, then it would be at no-one's behest but her own. She would be a monster of her own making, which was far worse than anything she had ever been before.

Clinging to every shred of willpower inside her, she ran, needing to get as far away from the temptation as possible. She raced across the cobbles, continuing on even as they ended and the road became the same dirt track as those they had been following through the Deadwood for the last three days. The mud hampered her progress and her feet sank deeper with each step, but still she hurried on, only stopping when one of her boots got stuck and her foot slipped out. She fell, landing with a splat and a shriek of frustration.

She was too far out of town for anyone to hear her beside the Gods. They would be listening. Of course they would be. She was too much a favoured fool for them not to.

Rain lashed at her as she retrieved her boot from its muddy tomb, droplets dribbling down her face and washing away the worst of the muck.

She had to go back. Rysen would be looking for her. That or…

No. He would be alright. He always was.

She needed to find him. As much as she hated what he had done, she couldn't hate him. He was her brother.

In danger of being washed away by the rain, she pulled herself up and traipsed back into town, hating every step that brought her closer to temptation.

When she got there, the streets were busier than they had been before. People bustled about, gathering outside the tavern, their torches struggling to stay alight in the rain as they stared warily at the soldiers wandering around in a daze.

How many memories had he taken?

There was no sign of Rysen anywhere. Had he been

caught? There had been so many soldiers in the tavern. Surely he couldn't have robbed them all of their memories?

She turned to seek him out and walked headlong into the young soldier from before, his slack-jawed face lacking any sign that he recognised her.

It wasn't the same soldier. Not anymore. This boy lacked parts of himself that had made him who he was. That was the true destruction of their ability. Rysen might not have killed the soldiers, but he killed the people they had been.

A startled cry echoed off the buildings and rang down the street. Sarilla spun about at the sound, watching as the townsfolk shoved each other aside, forming around something in the middle of the street, each eager to get a better view.

"Kill it! Kill the memoria!"

CHAPTER THREE

The cart wobbled as she scrambled atop it, throwing her arms out for balance as it lurched beneath her. She peered over the heads of the crowd to the figure being held down in the mud, their white hair splayed out and splattered with muck. Relief flooded through Sarilla at the sight. It wasn't Rysen. Time, not the Gods, had stolen the colour from the old woman's hair, not that the crowd seemed to care about that detail.

The frail woman tried to scramble up, but someone kicked her back down, forcing her to keel over. She pleaded and Sarilla tried not to picture Rysen in the old woman's place. To hear his screams in the woman's stead.

Unable to watch any longer and eager to escape before the mob realised there was a true memoria in their midst, Sarilla fled, desperate to find her brother and get away from the town.

Where was Rysen? He wouldn't have left, not after having refused to flee the palace without her. He wouldn't abandon her, not in some backwater town in the middle of the Deadwood forest.

She searched street after street, moving through the town and checking everywhere Rysen might be hiding, but he was nowhere to be found. Had he left without her? Perhaps he was waiting outside the town?

A man wheeled a cart around the corner of the otherwise empty street Sarilla stood on. The red rind of the fruit piled atop the cart glistened, slick from the rain and all the more lustrous for it.

Goaded by days' worth of hunger, she made her way closer, pretending to trip as she reached the cart and throwing her hands out to steady herself, grabbing an apple even as she apologised to the carter for her clumsiness.

Starvation gnawed the pit of her stomach and she could already taste the crisp tang of the first bite, but a hand grabbed her wrist as she moved to pocket the apple, making her drop it instead. Mud splattered as it hit the ground, peppering her dress with even more muck.

"You'll have to ask nicely before I let you take a bite," the carter said, his grip tightening on her wrist.

He chuckled and Sarilla winced as he revealed a mouth full of yellow teeth. Bile rose in her throat as he raked his gaze over her, but she couldn't get free.

"How about a trade?" he asked. "My apples for a squeeze of yours?"

"You'd need better apples for that. These are as rotten as your breath."

She yanked her arm back in an attempt to shake him loose, but the man only rolled his jaw in a way somebody with all their teeth never could, his eyes narrowing to thin slits as he squeezed her wrist, causing pain to shoot up her forearm. She whimpered and to her surprise, his grip slackened, his gaze losing focus in an expression she recognised all too well.

The man fell, slamming into the cart and cascading yet

more of his goods to the ground as Rysen appeared behind him, black marks rippling across his ungloved hands all the way to his knuckles. The marks had grown so much. She could have sworn they were no further than his fingertips back in the palace. How many memories had he stolen in the tavern?

"It's a good thing I found you."

"I was handling him fine on my own," she snapped, glaring at Rysen as she plucked a few apples from the cart and stowed them in her pockets.

"Didn't look that way to me."

"I'm surprised you can see anything real through all those memories you've stolen."

Rysen raised an eyebrow and glanced deliberately down at her gloved hands.

"It's been a while since I've seen you take those off, but don't pretend you've nothing to hide under there."

"Don't change the subject. You had no right to steal his memories!"

"But you do to steal his fruit?" Rysen asked, scooping an apple from the cart and biting into it.

"I only take as much as anyone else is capable of stealing. Memories are different. Taking them is what makes us the monsters they think we are."

"Sari-"

"And who cares if I rob a few apples. I'm not taking anything precious-"

"Sari-"

"All you're doing is making them hate us more. Did you see what they did to that woman back there? And that was only because they suspected-"

"Sari! Argue with me later. Right now, we have to go."

He grabbed her arm and gestured over her shoulder to the gathered townsfolk who were watching them with a hostility that hadn't been directed her way since the palace.

"I'll deal with it," Rysen said. "Head for Arvendon. We need to warn Da and Lya that the army's heading their way. I'll catch up with you."

"What? No. You can't. We need to get out of here."

They would have to hide in the forest, graves be damned. It was safer than staying in the town.

"It's fine-"

"Please, Ry. Don't do this. We can be better."

"That's him speaking. Don't you see? This is what Renford's done to you. He's twisted everything and convinced you up is down."

"He hasn't-"

"We are what we are, Sari. What's wrong is that you can't accept that!"

He didn't get it. He didn't see what he was doing to those people.

Dragging in a deep breath, Sarilla steadied herself for giving her brother the ultimatum she prayed he would heed.

"Do this and you lose me," she said, watching his eyebrows crease, furrowing his forehead in two deep grooves. He searched her face, seeking but finding no sign of her resolution weakening.

"Fine," he said with a sigh before taking her hand in his and squeezing her fingers. "Come on. Let's go."

They hurried away from the onlookers, darting down the less populated streets as they made their second break for freedom in three days. The edge of the town was in sight when Rysen's grip tightened on her hand once more and the clanking of armour filled the air. As she turned to see which way it came from, Rysen pushed her down behind a stack of barrels piled outside a small home.

"We won't make it," he said as she opened her mouth

to protest. "Wait for my signal."

He ran back in the direction of the soldiers and she watched in horror as he drew their attention his way. The soldiers formed a ring about him, their blades pointed at his neck and only a hair's breadth from slicing his throat open.

Rysen glanced her way, urging her to do something she couldn't understand, then realisation hit and a chill coursed through her bones.

He wanted her to attack the soldiers. He was banking on her coming to his rescue, believing that she would put aside her scruples to save him. He needed her. He had an unshakable belief in her.

How like Rysen. How defiant. How trusting.

How foolish. She had already let him down once before. Now she was about to do so all over again.

She couldn't break her promise to herself, not even for him. Didn't he see that? In breaking her out of the palace, he had given her a chance to be better. To do better than she had been capable of as Renford's favourite memory thief. Now Rysen wanted to wrench that away from her and she couldn't let him, no matter how much it hurt.

More soldiers trudged through the rain, joining those already ringing Rysen. Silver adorned their shoulders and sleeves like creeping vines, but Sarilla didn't need to see the adornments to recognise them as the king's guards. She would have known who they were even if they had been naked, so used was she to the contempt they had always looked upon her with. If they were there, then Renford was too.

Why wasn't he in Dranta? He hated leaving the palace.

Renford the Ruthless. How many times had his subjects called him that in the memories she had stolen over the years? Nobles whispering it in dark rooms while plotting his downfall, despising him for not doing more about the blackvine threat and for the pet monsters he insisted on keeping in the palace.

She needed to get as far from him as she could, already feeling the urge to go to him begin to rise in her. She could throw herself at his mercy, beg for everything to go back to how it had been, back when she could take memories without dwelling in guilt because Renford was the one making her be the monster she was.

No. She couldn't go back to that, not now she had a chance at goodness.

She tugged at her gloves, checking her marks were still out of sight even though Renford had no idea she was there. The habit was impossible to resist in his presence. It didn't matter that he wouldn't be able to see her through the barrels, she still couldn't bear the thought of seeing his disgust in her again.

She muttered a curse as she caught sight of Rysen's ungloved hands. Would Renford notice how much the marks had grown? Of course he would. He saw everything. Every reluctance. Every hesitation. He would see Rysen for the threat they all were.

The grey streaking Renford's dark-brown hair seemed more widespread than it had been only a few weeks ago, the purple stains beneath his eyes so much darker than they used to be. Had he slept at all in the days since they had left? Or had fear over what his pets might do to his kingdom been keeping him awake?

Indecision paralysed her as she watched his approach. If she went to Renford and begged for her brother's life then he would take them both back to the cage they had grown up in. He would force her to steal memories again, using her and demanding that she be what they both hated. She would always be a monster under his protection and she couldn't go back to that. Not now she had tasted freedom.

Rysen's face paled when he spotted Renford. He shot a panicked glance her way, warning her not to show herself. His eyes filled with fear, but not for himself. She didn't know what hurt more, that she was losing him or that he still believed she hadn't enough strength to keep from throwing herself back into Renford's keeping.

"Bring him," Renford ordered before marching back down the road, his guards falling in step around him and leaving the others to deal with the memoria they had caught.

The soldiers hesitated, seeming unwilling to move any closer to Rysen. With some difficulty and a lot of manhandling, they eventually managed to truss him up and drag him down the street.

Sarilla hurried down the streets after them, plans already formulating in her head on how she might get her brother back, but she discarded each in turn. When nothing even halfway feasible occurred to her, she elected to remain close enough that she would be able to act swiftly once she figured out what to do.

She followed the soldiers as they took Rysen to a camp outside the town where Renford's army was gathered, busily packing their tents and dousing their fires. She gazed longingly at the leftover porridge the soldiers dumped onto the ground, her stomach growling at the waste.

The soldiers' deep-green uniforms blended with the forest behind them as they hefted their packs onto wagons and hoisted pikes onto their shoulders. The weapons tore through the foliage above, cascading leaves onto the men marching beneath as they broke camp. She tailed the army down the road, keeping out of sight as best as she could as they marched through the evening.

Her feet soon began to ache and although she did her best to ignore the pain, relief filled her when the army eventually stopped for the night, setting up camp along the roadside as they raised a sea of light-brown sheets atop their pikes for shelter. A few soldiers braved the trees, hesitantly leaving the safety of the road to scout the nearby forest, each soldier following the route carved by the man ahead as they attempted to minimise their risk of falling into a grave.

Needing somewhere to wait out the night, Sarilla took to the forest too, picking careful steps through the undergrowth, half expecting the ground to give way beneath her at any moment. It didn't and she thanked Forta for her favour, adding another prayer to Cursen for his forgetting about her for one blessed moment.

The Deadwood was even eerier than it had seemed from the road. Everywhere you looked, you saw the evidence of the damage the memori had inflicted during the thousand years they had lived in Dranta. They had cultivated the trees to the advantage of the memori, tricking them to grow in unnatural ways, no matter the ill effects they caused the rest of the foliage.

The canopy was nowhere near as dense as it was in the areas of the forest surrounding the capital. Those few who braved the frequent threat of graves in those parts had memories of a canopy so thick that you could barely see a twinkle of sunlight through the leaves above, even in the depths of winter. In some stolen memories she had acquired over the years, she had seen how the effects of the memori's manipulation grew far less extensive the further from Dranta you travelled, but it wasn't so where the army had chosen to camp for the night. The forest floor was strewn with branches that had died from the lack of sunlight reaching them and crashed to the ground.

Cracks and thuds echoed between the trees in an erratic rhythm as yet more fell, sometimes taking an unlucky animal with them. Several trees were no more than rotting stumps of jagged wood, their upper half insect riddled and buried by moss as it rotted somewhere nearby.

She found a still-living tree with overgrown roots large enough to offer shelter and curled up in its crook for the night, wrapping her cloak about her as she tried to stop shivering and worrying about how the soldiers could happen upon her at any moment. Insects kept crawling across her and they soon chased away all other worries, although they didn't much help her get to sleep. When she did eventually manage it, it was a fitful rest, one broken a short while later by the screams tearing through the forest.

She opened her eyes to the sound of armour clanging in the distance and a low whisper murmuring through the air. She might have mistaken it for the wind stirring the canopy, but instinct warned her otherwise. Blinking, she rubbed her eyes as she peered through the dark, trying to make out what was going on. Orange firelight flickered far off, casting strange shadows into the forest that seemed to warn her to stay away. Was it Rysen? Had he tried to escape and got into trouble?

She pushed up, clinging to the tree bark as dull thuds shook the ground and more screams filled the air. Creeping closer to the edge of the camp, she stared at the nightmare unfolding before her.

Gone was the discipline of earlier. Grown men shoved each other aside, some running towards the screaming while others fled the other way as something dark writhed between the trees up ahead. Sarilla stopped dead at the sight. Fear flooded her as she stared at the leafless black vines reaching between the foliage, whipping through the air, each one thicker than her arm and latching onto anything unfortunate enough to get caught in its path, coiling snake-like about trees and soldiers alike, engulfing everything in its reach.

Blackvine.

Soldiers hacked and stabbed at it, trying to fight it back as it crept through the camp, undeterred by the efforts to contain it. One of the soldiers faltered, his sword missing as he sliced at a tendril reaching for him. The vines wrapped around him and his face slackened as he screamed, clutching his head and looking like he would rip it from his shoulders if he could. Black sludge leaked from his eyes as the vines encircled him further, coiling until he was swallowed up entirely.

Where was Rysen? Had he tried to escape and been caught? She knew Renford. He would put Rysen to the sword rather than risk loosing him on his subjects again.

Heat scorched her as she dodged campfires and remnants of evening meals, desperate to find her brother.

The army was decimated, most looked to have fled, but some had been consumed by the darkness. Those remaining yelled defiantly as they threw themselves at the blackvine, not seeming to realise it was as unslayable as the night, claiming them one after another, swallowing their defiance whole.

Everyone was too distracted to pay attention to the lone woman in their camp. All except one, that was.

A pair of pale-blue eyes locked on Sarilla's from across the camp. Renford's gaze made her feet freeze up beneath her. She couldn't move, not even as the blackvine reached for them, coiling through the darkness.

CHAPTER FOUR

She wanted to run to him, to the man who was more of a father than her own had ever been. There would be safety in his barbed protection, her keeper and persecutor all rolled into one. But the security he offered came at a price she couldn't afford to pay again. She was better off enduring life without him than being the source of his disgust once more.

It was more than needing to prove she wasn't the monster he believed her to be. How could she go back to the palace when just the thought of its black stone walls triggered memories she wished she could rid herself of forever?

One rose in her unbidden, dragging her away from the forest and all the dangers within as fingers brushed back her hair from her shoulder. Whispered words tickled the back of her neck as she fought against the memory, pushing it back down. It was too painful to relive, but the one that rose in its place was almost as bad.

Her mother's gaze was distant as she wandered the corridor, uncaring as she stumbled into people and furniture, unable to see through the memories overflowing inside her. Would Sarilla end up the same way, too protective over what she had stolen to let the memories go, even as they drove her to madness? It would be so easy to get rid of them, but how could she do that when some of the memories inside her were all that was left of the nobles Renford had executed. Perhaps it was only guilt over the roles she played in their deaths, but she couldn't be responsible for the destruction of their legacies too.

Something snapped through the air in front of her, giving Sarilla the jolt she needed to pull her mind out of the memories. Blackvine tendrils surged out the forest, latching onto everything stupid enough to linger in their path. They landed between her and Renford and she jumped back, ignoring Renford as he yelled for her to stop.

Too close. Time to go.

She shot a final, desperate glance about the camp in the hope of catching sight of Rysen in the chaos, but he was nowhere to be seen.

Had he already escaped? Between Rysen and the blackvine, there wouldn't be much left of the camp come dawn. Was it too much to hope their numbers were decimated enough they could no longer attack Arvendon?

Turning her back on her brother for the second time in as many days, she ran, praying to both Gods to keep Rysen safe.

Vines lashed at her heels as she raced into the forest, Renford's shouts for her to come back following her all the way. The light of the campfires behind dwindled a little more with every stride through the undergrowth. The dense canopy above soon blocked out the starlight as she raced through the trees.

Fear of the blackvine drowned out any worry over graves waiting nearby, but as her foot caught on an exposed root and her momentum sent her sprawling, she thought for a moment that she had stumbled upon one. She crashed into a tree and gripped it tight, scraping her face on the bark as she fell, fighting back the desire to escape into memories where she was safe and warm, with no need to fear the blackvine.

Pushing herself up, she continued on, blundering through the forest even when all was quiet about her except the crunch of leaves under her boots. Only the piercing, stabbing in her chest made her stop, exhaustion spearing through her as she collapsed against a tree, unable to remain upright any longer.

The rough bark scraped her back as she slid down, dragging in gasps of crisp air to keep from passing out. It seared her throat, aggravating the burn from her flight.

Leaves rustled overhead and a bird chirped somewhere in the gloom, merrily ignorant of the horrors unfolding nearby. Did its presence mean she was safe from the blackvine, at least for the time being? The noise was comforting and she clung to the reassurance of not being alone. It helped keep away the fear of the darkness reaching between the trees.

She was lost. Lost and alone, except for the bird.

Exhaustion weighed on her, but she couldn't let sleep pull her under. What if the blackvine came for her while she slept?

She strained her ears, flinching at every whisper of wind through the trees.

It was a long time before dawn broke through the canopy in a patchwork between the reddening leaves. By that time, Sarilla was near delirious with a need to rest.

Food. Water. Dry clothes. A fire. All were rapidly reaching the point of imminently essential. The only problem was that she had no idea how to procure any of them. She didn't dare delve into the memories inside her to learn anything of use since she might not be able to break back out if she did.

She had to try. If she didn't survive the forest, then there would be no-one to warn Lya. No-one to rescue Rysen.

Reaching into the part of her she usually fought to keep shut away, she let the slightest of trickles loose from behind the dam. A man and woman riding horseback along the coast, their bodies swaying with the motion of the beasts beneath them. A pale woman gazing up at the stars through a small gap in the rocks. A frightened child reaching out to hold her mother's hand. A traitor with lying eyes who stood waiting before Renford.

None of those were helpful to her.

A whispered promise of treason on an early spring morning. A hand holding hers as false promises filled her ears. A surge of sunlight through a leaf.

Her mind caught on the last memory. It was different from the rest since plants had nothing so coherent as memories, but they did still feel. Though they might rely on different senses to other living creatures, they still noticed the effect of time, still felt changes to their environment through senses that creatures too dependent upon sight and sound failed to notice. The pull of the ground. The closeness of moisture-filled air. The draw of north. The cold touch of winter and the dry heat of summer. Though blind, they still knew where light came from, still felt vibrations rumble through their leaves.

Even lost in the forest, there was still a way for Sarilla to find Arvendon. The only question was, could she bring herself to use it?

The canopy was so thick that she couldn't tell east from west. Besides wandering until she lucked upon a town, city or ocean, there was only one other option.

Her fingers twitched at the idea, already anticipating the wonders only one touch away. She had promised she wouldn't steal memories anymore. Did it matter that the memories she contemplated taking didn't belong to a person?

Anticipation surged through her as she tugged off her glove. Not even the sight of the black lines pulsing across her pale hand and up her arm could douse it, although it did make her stomach churn. How many memories were stored within? Thousands? Ten times that? Far more than Rysen had ever stolen, but that was unsurprising since he had never been Renford's preferred pet.

She used to think the marks resembled delicate lace gloves, but now she recognised them for what they were. What beauty they had was woven from a thread of suffering and corruption.

She hovered her hand over the tree trunk and closed her eyes, trying to ignore the guilt as she touched the bark. The rough texture was an unwelcome change to the soft lining of her glove. She shut it out, along with the griping of her stomach. They were distractions of the body and had no place where her mind was going.

"I'm sorry," she murmured to the tree as she hesitated, its life pulsing beneath her fingers in an intoxicating surge.

Liquid gold rushed her as she made the connection, her mind floating on its current. She longed to dive in and let it take her away from her bleak reality, where all thoughts of the blackvine and Renford would plague her no more. Gone would be her fears for Rysen and Lya, along with the bittersweet memories of Falon that would haunt her until she died. In the tree's memories, she might escape all that. She could lose herself and be Sarilla no more.

Untying her tether, she let her mind loose in the foreign

tides, her world compressing into that one addictive vein.

Drawing her awareness down through the tree, she opened her mind to the sensations flooding through its roots.

Cold. Dank. Dark.

There. She could feel the fungus living in the soil, a sleeping giant that connected all the plants above in a fine, fibrous mesh through the dirt. It pulsed with life. The only thing more impressive than its size being the sheer ignorance of so many to its existence. It linked the plants above, brimming with warnings of plagues, droughts and infections that travelled faster than any messenger bird and were more complete than any missive. It was a network of life and Sarilla knew how to traverse it.

Through it, she could experience everything the vegetation above did. Their prosperity. Their pain. Sensations she didn't even know how to put words to, but knew they existed.

It was easy to locate what was left of the army through the telltale vibration of marching men. Renford must still be alive then. No army could retain such an order after the death of its leader.

She had to get to Arvendon before them.

Searching further, she sought out the signs of Arvendon. Trees fell here and there throughout the Deadwood, severing suddenly from the nexus as they crashed to the soil. When it happened a lot in a small area, it was a sure indication of a nearby settlement. She found the signs of a much smaller one between her and Arvendon. A town perhaps? If she made it that far, she might be able to steal some food at least.

Committing the location of the town to memory, she shivered at the rush trickling into her hands, incorporating with the black already in her. When it was done, she started the trial of withdrawing her mind from the nexus, forcing herself to leave behind the feast of sensations and return to her reality, feeling so much more alone than she had before.

Shoving her hand back inside her glove, she hid the evidence of her crimes as a shiver wracked her body, blurring her vision. She squeezed her eyes shut until the dizziness passed, then staggered to her feet, gripping the tree for support before setting off towards the town. She stumbled through the forest, her cloak wrapped tightly about her. It might not be raining, but she still couldn't get warm.

Hours might have passed before she saw the wooden cottages through the trees. She managed a few more steps, but the dizziness she had been fighting back overcame her and she collapsed.

Cold invaded her bones and fever laced her waking dreams as she lay shaking in the dirt. Her teeth ached as she clenched her jaw against their chattering, barely noticing when the strong hands gripped her and hauled her off the floor. She tried to open her eyes to see who had her, but the light was too bright and far too painful. The effort soon exhausted her, then darkness claimed her and she knew no more.

CHAPTER FIVE

Muffled chirping pecked away, cracking the sleep encasing her until it broke, unleashing the memories. They jostled inside her, warring among themselves and forcing her to fight through just to remember who she was.

A soft bed in Arvendon. Delicate fingers playing in her hair. It was nice, comforting, but it was far too incomplete to be one of hers.

A child playing outside and looking to her with an expression of such unadulterated joy.

The lash of thunder off a southern coast, the force of it ripping through the air... No, not hers either.

Trees. The Deadwood. Blackvine.

In a rush, it all returned to her.

Renford. Rysen. The soldiers who took him away.

Light beamed through the window beside the bed she lay on. She held up her hand to shield her face and startled at the sight of her marks. Where were her gloves? Who had taken them off and why hadn't they killed her the moment they realised what she was?

She glanced around the cottage, trying to get a grasp of

her surroundings. A small fire burned in the far corner of the room and a pot simmered above it, permeating the room with the rich scent of stew. No food had ever smelt so mouth-watering. Eager to fetch herself a bowl, she made to rise, only to pause as she noticed that she wore a nightgown someone else had dressed her in.

Her clothes were neatly folded on a rickety-looking chair by the bed, her gloves resting atop the pile. She grabbed them, wincing as the sudden motion made the room spin.

Moving more slowly this time, she raised the gloves, hesitating as the fresh fragrance assaulted her. Gone was the stench that had perforated the fabric for the last few days. It was a far cry from the delicate, floral hint she was used to in the palace, but still made a refreshing change.

Moving more gently this time, she donned the gloves, glad to hide the evidence of her crimes once more. Dressing stole what little strength she had and when she finished tying her cloak about her neck, she sank back onto the bed, needing the world to stop spinning.

"Starvation will do that," a croaky voice said from the doorway, startling Sarilla.

She spun in the direction of the speaker, eager to see who it was who had saved her. And why whoever it was hadn't treated her with the contempt everyone else levelled at her kind.

The old woman had a moustache of wispy white hairs and veins that protruded from her hands, but she moved almost in defiance of her appearance, manoeuvring through the room with a strength that belied the mottling of liverworts and the age hunching her spine.

She ladled the contents of the pot into a bowl and shuffled over to Sarilla. Although the liquid sloshed, it didn't spill, which was all the more impressive because of the woman's cloudy white pupils, so murky that there couldn't be any difference between day and night for her.

Sarilla offered a quick prayer of thanks to Forta for her favour in sending her a blind woman as her rescuer. Had she not, then there was a good chance Sarilla wouldn't have woken at all.

Moving aside so the old woman could perch on the edge of the bed, Sarilla tried not to flinch as the woman grabbed Sarilla's leg, her deft movements filled with a surety that was surprising for a blind person. She hauled Sarilla's left foot up to inspect it, and Sarilla had to fight to keep her stew from spilling onto her freshly cleaned clothes. Her protests died as she caught sight of her feet. White skin peeled away, leaving uneven welts riddling her soles. She gasped, her stomach churning at the sight of the ruined appendages.

"Oh, stop you're fretting. They've not fallen off yet," the old woman said, grunting and running her hands over the other one too, before making a face at the smell. "Though another few days and it'd be a different story."

"How... How did they get so bad?"

Sarilla had known they couldn't be in good condition, but she hadn't expected that. They reminded her of the hands of one of Renford's nobles after he had been left to rot awhile in the prison before his execution. The way his flesh fallen from him...

"You mean you didn't notice? And you stinking worse than a week-old carcass? My poor son was retching just from carrying you in here."

So those had been the strong hands lifting her.

"Will... Will you give him my thanks? And to you. You saved me-"

The old woman's lips twisted and she grunted something unintelligible. "You think I did it out the kindness of my heart? I'm blind girl, not daft. What were you doing in the forest alone, anyway?"

Sarilla cast about for anything that wasn't a lie since the truth would only lead to more scrutiny. Hiding from the king. Fleeing the country. Escaping to a place nobody knew to fear memori.

"I… I was lost. The blackvine…"

"Ahh… Got your family, did it? Well, now lass, bad things happen. You might as well get used to the fact now."

"Excuse me?"

"You're from Dranta, right?" she asked, surprising Sarilla.

"How did you know?"

"I'm blind girl, not deaf. Your accent's as distinctive as a cow in the chicken coop. Oh, Bettle will be going crazy knowing I have you here. I'll draw the tale out nice and slow. Make her wait to hear every detail. Just imagining her coming to me for gossip for once… If she can choke down her pride for long enough that is."

"Bettle?"

"Go on then, girl. Out with it. I want details so don't keep me waiting. Remember that you'd be dead without me."

"There's not much to tell. I was travelling with my family when the blackvine set upon us."

The half-lie came naturally to Sarilla and caused the old woman to snarl almost gleefully.

"Got 'em all, did it? But you must have others back in Dranta? How big a reward do you think they'll be offering?"

Sarilla stopped spooning stew into her mouth, staring at the woman. "A reward? For what?"

"Payment for my keeping you safe. It's been a lot of work for a woman of my age."

"And I thank you for having looked after me, but there won't be a reward."

The old woman rested her hand on Sarilla's glove and stroked the leather.

"Come now, Girly. No reward? And you wearing clothes as fine as these...? If menfolk spend this much dressing you up, then you can be sure they'll be wanting you back. Now tell me. Who is it? Father? Husband? Brother? Whoever they are, I'm sure they'll be only too grateful for your return. Men are always so predictable-"

"I'm sorry to disappoint you, but- Ow!"

She winced as the old woman's grip tightened on her wrist. She tried to pull her arm free, but the woman held tight.

"Listen, Girly. I'm blind, not a fool."

"Nor am I," Sarilla said, knocking over her stew as she scrambled off the bed.

The old woman seethed, the hot liquid scolding her skin even as Sarilla backed away from her towards the door, throwing it open, eager to get away from that place.

"Jaik! Jaik! Get in here!"

Grabbing a pair of boots as she passed, Sarilla hurried outside, her cloak flapping as she hurtled down the street and into the forest. Heavy footsteps chased after her own as her legs wobbled beneath her, but she kept running, pushing on through the pain and dizziness as she tried to ignore how Jaik's footsteps grew louder behind her.

Her throat seared as she dragged in her breath, throwing herself behind a tree and sucking in a quick gasp as a large figure hurtled past her then disappeared between the trees. Leaves rustled in his wake. How long before he realised his mistake and returned her way?

She strained to hear the crunch of leaves underfoot, startling at every snap, her heart thundering in her chest as she battled to not take off her glove. The man passed close by twice but somehow didn't spot her. Eventually, the forest quieted, but Sarilla was still too terrified to move.

Tugging off a glove, she lay her palm against the tree behind her. She had to get to Arvendon. How long had she been unconscious for? Enough time for the army to have reached the city? Anything could have happened to Rysen and Lya during that time.

It was easy to find Arvendon in the nexus. Even though she had never visited, she knew the shape of its lake by heart, just as she did the rocks the city was built on. She had walked its streets in others' memories countless times, crossing rope bridges and climbing spiralled staircases.

Arvendon. The place she least wanted to visit, but the one city she needed to go to.

Would he be there? It was where he had been heading, but that had been half a year ago. She didn't think she would be able to bear seeing him again. Not after everything that had happened.

She located the city with ease. She wasn't far away. Redonning her glove, she slipped her feet into the old woman's boots. They were too big, so she stuffed them with handfuls of dry leaves, tying the laces tight before she set off.

It was long past dark when she reached Arvendon. Light glimmered across the rippling lake. The sight filled her with emotions that weren't her own. She was going home, but it wasn't her home she was going to.

An image from within the city filled her vision. One of Westral Lanlethe's memories. She didn't know the name of every noble she had ever provided evidence against, but Westrel's memories always stuck in her mind. He was one of the Arvendon conspirators, gentlemen and ladies of the eastern city who had gone so far in their treason as to send an assassin to Dranta, hoping to replace Renford with a king less prone to using his memori on his subjects, and more ready to drive back the blackvine invading Valrora.

A cold, spring breeze stroked his face in the memory as the evening light speared across the treetops. He watched the day's final assault against the night from an upper window, the Deadwood spreading out before him. It was a strong memory. Stronger than most she stole. It was vivid because Westral was attentive while forming his last memory of Arvendon, but it was hard to know what parts of the memory were real since nostalgia fabricates as much as it offers clarity, particularly in those who knew their days were numbered.

Shaking her head clear of the image, she refocused on Arvendon, on the city walls rising from the rocks and surrounding the towering buildings as they speared the night's sky. Stars twinkled on the lake stretching around the city. The prospect of trekking around it made her want to weep. Her legs already ached, but if she sat, then she wouldn't be able to rise again.

Drawing on what little strength she had left, she followed the shore around the lake. Lights crowned the city wall like dawn creeping over the horizon, revealing the shadowy figures moving about atop it. Had Arvendon always had guards on patrol? She didn't think so from her stolen memories, but perhaps it was a new precaution against the blackvine.

As she passed a patch of reeds, she spotted a small boat tethered to the bank, the rope mooring it tightened and slackened with the lapping water. Thinking to spare her feet the rest of the walk, she scrambled inside, almost toppling into the water in her haste as she tugged the peg free from the bank. She wrestled the oars into place and used them to push off, manoeuvring the boat out of the reeds and cutting a zig-zagging path through the water. She kept having to glance over her shoulder to correct her course, unable to keep the boat going straight.

She was about halfway across when cold filled her boots in a rush and she yelped, startling as she looked down to find water sloshing into the boat, flooding in faster with every moment. At the rate it was pouring in, it wouldn't be long before she would be swimming the rest of the way to Arvendon.

"Why won't you let me catch a break?" she yelled skyward, cursing any God who was listening.

"You'll have to let me know if they give you an answer," an all too familiar voice called behind her, making her start. "But I'll be affronted if they do. They've always ignored me."

No. It couldn't be him. She had imagined his voice. A memory. That was it. It had to be because he couldn't be there. Not even the Gods would throw her path back together with his in such a cruel way.

Laughter danced across the water behind her as she twisted, needing to see the truth for herself. The other boat drifted across the lake towards her, its oars raised as it silently skimmed the surface, the three shadowy figures within watching her.

As it gently bumped against hers, Falon grabbed the side of her vessel, docking them together without recognising her.

Pain tore through her as she stared at him, all the love she had once felt rising back up inside her and making her heart break all over again. She was a stranger to him. The months they had spent together no more than a story he had never been told.

CHAPTER SIX

The man she loved no longer existed, but still the Gods taunted her with the dream she had once cherished more than her own life. The only place that man existed was in her memories. His memories were gone forever and he could never get them back.

Seeing him was as painful as she had known it would be and she cursed the Gods for bringing it to pass. She needed to get away. Not just because her heart felt like it would break from her chest, but because there would be no sympathy from him if he realised what she was. If any of the men in the boat figured out the truth, then there was no telling what they would do. Knowing her luck, they would probably tie her up and throw her in the lake for the fish, that or hand her in for the reward Renford had no doubt offered for her recapture.

"I didn't come out here for a theological discussion," she said, wrangling her oars back into place and trying to row away from them.

"If you don't get out that boat, the only discussions you'll be having will be with the Gods, so they'll all be theological." Falon held his hand out to her in a familiar way that triggered a dozen memories too painful to relive. "Get in," he said as she tried to force the memories down. "We can drop you off at the bank."

"Does it look like I'm heading that way?" she snapped, jarring an oar against their boat as she tried to leverage hers away.

"I did wonder," a man holding the oars said. "You weren't exactly heading in a straight line."

"We were putting bets on which way you were trying to go," a third man said, making her start.

His laugh… She recognised the sound. Why did she know it? No. Not her. Someone else knew him, but who? Whose memories had she heard it in?

"We?" Falon asked over his shoulder to the man, his derision distracting Sarilla until her boat gave a sudden lurch beneath her, the bow quickly sinking.

She scrambled out of her boat, her leg catching on the ledge and Falon grabbed her, keeping her from falling into the lake.

"Woah! Watch out. It's a bit cold at this time of year for a late-night swim."

He flashed her a grin that caused her insides to twist, but it was the small frown creasing his brow as he gripped her arm that made her shiver.

"Thank you for your help. If you could just turn about and drop me off at the city, then we can all be getting on about our ways."

"Sorry, Lady, but we're not going back. Forta won't help us escape twice," Falon said as the other man eased the oars back into the water. "We'll drop you off at the shore."

"But-"

"What he means," the strangely familiar third man said,

"Is either sit down in ours or sink in yours. Now come on, let's go. We're losing our lead-"

"No! Wait!" Sarilla called. "I'll take my chances on my own if you won't help me."

"You're not going far in that-"

"Leave her, Havric," the familiar man said. "If she wants to drown, then let her get on with it. We've delayed long enough already."

The man with the oars, Havric presumably, resumed rowing as Sarilla stared at the rocks the city sat atop. She wasn't so far away. Surely she would be able to make it the final distance. She had enough memories of people swimming to know how to do it. She would be fine so long as they didn't overwhelm her and make her forget where she was for so long that she drowned.

Standing, she placed a foot on the edge of the boat.

"I wouldn't if I were-"

Falon swore as she jumped. Water splashed up, rushing past her face as the heart-stoppingly cold liquid filled her ears, silencing the world until she was alone in the darkness. Needles stabbed her skin and she fought to return to the surface, but her clothes dragged her down instead of up. She sank deeper, kicking and slapping the water ineffectually. Her efforts became more panicked the further she drifted down. Her throat burned and her lungs cried out for air as her head began to spin, her vision darkening.

Something dropped into the water beside her. The muffled splash and the bubbling of air to the surface seemed very far away as hands reached for her through the blackness. They wrapped around her chest, trying to pull her up towards the surface, but still she continued to sink, their combined kicking as ineffectual as her own had been.

The hands moved from her arms to her neck. They

fumbled for a moment, then a heavy weight shrugged from her. Whoever had her dragged her upwards and her head broke the surface. She hauled in a desperate breath, her throat burning as she clung to Falon, his dark hair sticking to his forehead as droplets dripped down his face.

"Like I said, bad idea. You alright?"

She tried to say yes, but between her numb lips and the chattering of her teeth, the noise didn't sound much like anything.

"Who goes for a swim in a cloak like that, anyway? Were you trying to drown yourself?"

She stared at him for a moment, his words slower to process in her frozen mind. Her cloak? She patted her hair, panic returning as she realised why she hadn't drowned. She needed her cloak! If he saw what she was, then he would hate her for it.

She tried to push off him and dive back down into the lake, but he grunted, his grip tightening around her and stopping her from doing more than splashing at the water.

"Rescuing you would be a lot easier if you stopped trying to kill yourself-"

"You don't understand! I need my cloak. Let me go. Please! I have to get it!"

She kicked, wincing as her foot hit something. Falon groaned as he reached for the side of the boat and the hand Havric held out to him.

"It's a gift to the Gods now," Havric said as Falon dragged her around to face him.

She watched helplessly as his eyes widened, finally seeing what had been hidden beneath her hood before. His grip tightened and his expression hardened as he realised what he had just rescued. Agony tore through Sarilla as eyes that had once been filled with love looked upon her with disgust. She was a monster to him. That was all she ever would be.

The muscles in Falon's neck twitched as he clenched his jaw, disgust written in every line on his face. He pushed her from him and icy water splashed her face as she struggled to stay afloat. Her sodden dress still weighed her down. Her head dipped under the water again. She grabbed wildly at the side of the boat, clinging to it as Falon's top lip curled before he turned his back on her and hauled himself out the lake.

Her chest tightened as she clung on, struggling to breathe. The cold compressed her lungs as she fought another unbidden onslaught of memories. His contempt. His hatred. It was all too much.

Her numb fingers slipped against the wood. She couldn't hold on for much longer. A part of her wanted to let go since there would be no point in Falon's hating a dead memoria. Better that than face him looking at her like that again.

Rysen. Lya. She had to keep fighting for them. She glanced over her shoulder at the city. It was so close. Could she make it?

The boat slipped out of her grip and she sank with a splash.

A hand grabbed her by her dress and hauled her back up out of the water. Another hand joined in the effort and Falon and Havric soon pulled her into the boat. They dumped her unceremoniously in the basin before quickly moving away from her.

The familiar blond man watched warily from behind them as Havric sat back down, picking up the oars like they were weapons he might use against her.

Falon glowered down at her, his jaw flexing. Without saying anything, he pulled his shirt off and wrung it out. The water hit Sarilla and the bottom of the boat in accusing splatters.

"No need to sink ours too," Havric said. Not taking his eyes from her, he rooted through a pack beside him and handed Falon a dry shirt before passing her a blanket. "Change out that dress or you won't make it through the night."

Too cold to argue and too tired to care about modesty, she stripped her wet clothes off and exchanged them for the blanket. Except for her gloves. Those she kept.

She clung to the blanket for warmth, but it didn't calm her teeth's chattering or stop her body's convulsing. Her lips were so numb that she couldn't even protest as Havric rowed her away from Arvendon, their boat slipping silently across the water.

If Falon was cold, he made no sign of it. He didn't even shiver. He just kept his glare fixed on her, looking ready to lynch her.

When they reached the bank, he jumped over the reeds and pulled the boat close enough for the others to clamber out. If they intended to leave the boat there, perhaps she could turn it about and get away before they could stop her? They likely wouldn't think it worthwhile swimming after her. The lake was too cold for that.

She shifted closer to the oars as they took their gear, the boat dipping as they moved about. The oars were within her grip when someone picked her up roughly and dumped her on the cold grass by the lakeside.

Falon climbed back into the boat and picked up her sodden dress before wringing it out and throwing it at her. He rooted about in a pack before throwing her a shirt she could have fit into twice over. Slinging the pack onto his back as if he had a vendetta against it, he jumped back onto the bank and kicked the boat out towards the centre of the lake.

"Hav, lend her a pair of trousers. Mine won't fit, even with a belt."

"Please," she said, curling up and tugging the blanket tightly about her, hating how weak she sounded. "Let me go. I need to get to Arvendon."

"Why should I care what you need?" Falon asked as Havric searched his pack.

Finding what he looked for, he offered her the garment along with a strip of rope. Sarilla stared at the items, but she didn't reach for them.

"We should kill her," the third man she knew she recognised from somewhere said, all traces of his earlier humour long vanished.

"She stays alive. For now. No matter how much I want to repay her for that late-night swim."

"But she's a memoria."

"And that's what's keeping her alive."

"I'd advise you to get dressed," Havric said, dropping the trousers and belt in front of her. "The alternative is walking the Deadwood forest naked."

The Deadwood? They were leaving Arvendon?

Tipping the water from her boots, she scrambled into the shirt and trousers, eager for their protection against the cold night. They hung off her and the rope made little difference in pulling them tight. She wrapped the blanket back around her too, already missing the security of her cloak.

"We should go," the blond one said nervously as he glanced along the bank. "I'm not dying because of a mongrel memoria."

His voice was even more familiar without the merriment of before. She knew him from a memory, she was certain of it.

Like a stone triggering an avalanche, the memories of

him flooded her mind. Cedral. Cedral Lanlethe. That's how she knew him.

"Let's go," Falon said, starting into the trees. "They'll be after us."

She couldn't go with them. The Deadwood took her further from her family and they needed her. She didn't hesitate. She darted along the shore and disappeared into the forest. Pain spiked her blistered feet, but she ignored them, knowing only that she had to keep running.

Arvendon wasn't far. She could make it.

Her lungs burned, but she ignored the stitch in her chest, forcing herself on as branches slapped her face, slashing her skin. She dodged between the trees, only spotting the dark shadow jumping out at her from behind a tree when it was too late.

Falon blocked her path and she stumbled, falling and hitting the ground hard. Starlight danced through the leaves above as she fought to regain her breath while Falon's face swam into focus above her. Without saying a word, he scooped up the corners of the blanket, pulling her up too and swinging her onto his back in the makeshift sack.

"Let me go!"

He set off, jolting her with the movement and she rebounded off his back with each step, forced into a tight ball. Her confines soon grew hot and damp from the lake water drying off her hair. Cedral's muted laughter reached her through the blanket as Falon continued, heedless of her discomfort and the trial to her dignity.

She could hear their conversation, but the noises were meaningless in the muffled dark of the blanket. A tear rolled down her cheek at the thought of how Lya and Rysen needed her, but she couldn't even move her arm enough to wipe it away.

Falon laughed derisively at something Cedral said, the sound so unlike the laugh she had used to know. The thought of it triggered a memory to rise and the damp heat of her cage inside the blanket disappeared, replaced by the fresh tang of spring in Dranta.

A warm breeze wafted the plants growing about the window. Unlike the overgrown foliage on the black stones of the memoria city that had once existed there, those plants on the white stones Dranta was built atop were neatly kept. Since it was one of her memories, she could see every vein on the leaves, the curl of each budding flower. It wasn't the plants she focused on, instead on the man watching her through the patterned divide separating the windowsill where they sat facing each other, their backs to the walls.

"You're not afraid he'll make you steal their memories?" Falon asked, his attention fixed on her, his fingers stilling as he toyed with the hilt of his blade.

"Renford's no need of me. Not while he has my mother."

Sarilla's words rang through her mind even though she wasn't speaking. Her memory. Her words.

"And what about when she's gone. If you stay, he'll use you. He'll make you steal their memories in her stead."

"You don't know that. Renford's not as bad as you think he is."

"Isn't he? Holed up in here, interrogating his subjects when he should be out defending them from the blackvine. I think I've enough measure of our king already-"

"You shouldn't say things like that." The view of the memory shifted as she had glanced about, checking there was no-one within hearing range. "Don't give Renford a reason to suspect you too. I couldn't bear it if anything happened to you."

A soft smile transformed his face as he put his hand on the divide between them, waiting as she pressed her own to the other side.

"It won't. Trust me," he said, adjusting his hand so their fingertips lined up, the grill between them preventing them from touching.

As she relived the memory, she startled at the sight of her unmarked fingers, the pale skin absent of the black that lingered with stolen memories. Had she really been so untainted only a few short months ago?

The memory was so bittersweet that it was too painful to relive anymore. Forcing her way out, she pushed her mind back into her dank reality inside the blanket, grateful for the darkness as she cried for everything she had lost since being that naive girl.

It wasn't just Falon who had changed. Sarilla had too. And she was covered in the evidence of her crimes to prove it.

Nobody could ever love a monster.

CHAPTER SEVEN

"See," Falon said as he stretched, his muscles popping as he groaned. "I told you she hadn't suffocated."

"I could have," Sarilla grumbled where she lay in the spot he had dumped her. "I only didn't because I bit a hole in the blanket."

"You did what?" Cedral scowled at Sarilla and picked it up, searching for the damage and sticking his finger through the hole when he found it. "My mother made me that! What sort of feral beastie bites holes in other peoples' things?"

"Beasties who need to breathe."

"Animal."

"Kidnapper."

He stormed off, muttering to himself. When he was gone, she glanced about, more than slightly surprised to find herself staring at something other than trees. She was in a small but serviceable cabin. There was an abandoned feel to the place, but it was still a luxury in comparison to where she had been staying lately.

Falon followed Cedral out of the cabin, leaving her

alone with Havric as he concentrated on starting a fire, seeming so intent on the task that hope of escape flared within her like a rekindled flame. Creeping up, she made her way towards the door.

"I wouldn't if I were you," Havric said as she grasped the handle.

She wrenched her hand back, scowling at him, but he wasn't looking in her direction. She was about to say something, but the door opened and a cool breeze whooshed into the cabin, bringing an irate-looking Falon with it. One bushy black eyebrow rose as he stared at her.

"Are you done?" he asked, sounding more irritated than angry.

"With what? I wasn't doing anything."

"Sure, but I'd rather not spend half the journey chasing after you while you're not doing anything, so if you don't mind…"

He hefted her up by the back of her trousers, being careful not to touch her skin as he carried her to the bed and dumped her on it. She shrieked as he grabbed her gloved hands in his, pulling her wrists together. Rope in hand, he paused, staring at the leather. Unreasonable panic flooded through her as, almost unconsciously, he trailed his hand up one of her arms, pausing when he reached the point where leather and flesh met.

Warmth emanated from his fingers. She had to fight the blush rising up her neck. It had been so long since he touched her like that. She wanted to lean into him, to bask in the feel of his skin on hers. Was he remembering the touch of her skin against his? No. It wasn't possible-

"Falon? You alright?" Havric asked, jolting her out of the mesmeric effect of Falon's hand on hers, but Falon didn't stop. His fingertips dipped under the edge of her glove, making to drag it down.

"Don't," she said, her heart pounding in her chest as shame filled her.

She didn't want him to see what had become of her, but why did she care? He wasn't the man she fell in love with. That Falon was gone. The only person she hurt by not remembering that was herself.

Falon blinked, his gaze sharpening as he stared at her. His expression became a snarl and Sarilla's insides twisted. She had been hated before. Knew the feel of it all too well, but it was so much worse from him.

He gripped her wrists, forcing her down and securing her to the bedpost with the rope before storming from the room, muttering something under his breath as he left, slamming the door behind him.

"I tried to warn you," Havric said, chuckling to himself. "I suppose you've a name. Even kings name their pets, don't they?"

What did it matter what anyone called her? It wouldn't help her get free any quicker. She didn't answer him and they sat in silence until Cedral returned a while later, throwing a brace of rabbits onto the table and slumping on a chair beside Havric.

"You caught those?" Havric asked, picking one up and admiring the kill.

Cedral snorted.

"I've as much chance making that shot as you have at beating me at cards. Falon caught them." He glanced around the room, his gaze seeking out Sarilla. "Why is the Beastie beside the bed? I'm not sleeping there if she's next to it."

"You could always sleep on the floor and give me the bed," Sarilla said. "It's very comfortable."

"Only the best for you," Cedral said, sneering and returning to watch Havric as he prepared the food.

When the rabbits were cooked, Havric took a plate out to Falon before returning to attend to his dinner.

"You hungry, Beastie?" Cedral asked, taking a large bite from a leg and peeling cooked flesh from bone with his teeth.

"Is he staying out there all day?" Sarilla asked Havric, choosing to ignore Cedral.

"Can you blame him?" Cedral asked, glancing at her pointedly before returning his attention to his food.

"He's keeping watch," Havric said. "Though he'd be safer inside. Who knows what's out there."

"We know for sure what's in here," Cedral muttered. "I think Falon's got the right of it."

His chair scraped against the floor as he stood, and the door soon slammed shut after him. Havric frowned as he watched him go, but he didn't say anything.

"I didn't ask to be born like this, you know," she said, not sure why she was trying to defend herself. It didn't matter what she had done before, only whatever she chose to do in the future.

Havric ate in silence, not looking her way. When he finished, he grabbed his plate and scraped it clean as Sarilla's insides ate at her, her mouth watering from hunger. The last thing she had eaten was the stew the previous day and that had only been a few morsels before she had been chased out the cottage.

She hugged her legs to her chest and rested her head on her knees, but it did nothing to ease her griping stomach. The smell was the worst of it. She could shut her eyes to the sight of the food, but not even holding her breath could adequately stop the rich scent.

Sighing, she rolled onto her back and glared at the underside of the bed. It was worn and buckling, a sure sign that more than a few memories had been made on it over the years. Judging from the fact that the cabin had been empty when they arrived and suffering from many years of neglect, it was likely that whoever had used to sleep on the bed was long dead, their memories surrendered to oblivion like they had never happened.

People took so little care of that which they should treasure most. Yet how angry they were when what they would willingly sacrifice to death was taken from them by a memoria.

No matter what else they were, at least memori weren't so feckless. They treasured what they spent a lifetime collecting. They passed on curated versions of their lives to serve as lessons for those to come, understanding that you had more value as another log on the fire than a spark that dies in the night.

"I've some salted meat in one of the packs," Havric said, pulling her from her thoughts. "It won't be tasty, but it'll fill a hole."

He rooted through a bag by the door and produced something that looked closer to a strip of bark than food. It likely tasted no better too, but his kindness took her by surprise. Did he truly care about her being hungry or was he only trying to keep her alive? For what, she didn't know for certain, but she already had several guesses.

He gestured for her to take the food from him and she was about to reach for it when a thought struck her.

"Thank you, but it won't do me any good."

"Oh? Why's that?"

Curiosity hung in the air as he watched her, suspicion written in the narrowing of his eyes.

"Well… I'm a memoria," she said as if it were the most obvious thing in the world. "What do you think we eat?"

Silence rang out for a moment, then Havric threw his head back and barked, the laugh bursting from him. It continued and heat rose in Sarilla's cheeks. She hadn't thought her lie that bad.

"You can't really think me that stupid? You've better luck trying that trick with Cedral. I'm not letting you anywhere near my memories."

He shook his head, still laughing to himself as he returned to the table, taking the salted meat with him.

"What do you think we eat. Ha! Has that trick ever worked?" he asked, watching her from across the room.

"I wasn't asking to feed off your memories," she snapped, her irritation as much goaded by her plan not having worked as by his mocking.

"Oh? A different flavour then? You would prefer I call in Cedral or Falon so you can sample them before making your choice?"

"No. I… I was hoping you'd give me the rabbit's head. It's useless to you, but it still has memories inside it. I could use them…"

She shrugged, keeping her gaze fixed on Havric's boots, afraid her lying eyes would betray her. When he moved, she held her breath, not daring to release it lest she scared him off, but he stopped before her, the rabbit head dangling in his hand by its ears, its blood dripping onto the floorboards. She forced herself not to look away as Havric threw it beside her.

"Thank you," she muttered, trying not to gag as he turned from her.

Daylight poured into the cabin as she pretended to draw whatever nonsense Havric believed she could from a dead animal's head. When she was done with the ruse, she curled back into a ball, waiting for him to finally stop moving about the cabin and get some sleep. He finally settled on the chair on the other side of the cabin, his arms folded across his chest and his chin tucked down. When his breathing evened into a deep, regular rumble, she grabbed the rabbit's head, dragging its incisors across the rope binding her wrists.

It took longer than she had expected for the rope to give way. Unbinding her hands, she crept across the room, easing the cabin door open and peering outside. Falon and Cedral leaned against a nearby tree. Their attention wasn't on the door, but they would see her if she tried to escape. She muttered a curse under her breath. Perhaps they would fall asleep in a bit. They would need to rest at some point.

Electing to bide her time for a bit, she kept the door open a crack and peered out, her legs cramping as she listened with too much interest to their conversation. Not that it was much of one. Cedral did more than his share of the talking, mostly railing against memori or bemoaning Sarilla's presence in the cabin. Falon seemed too lost in his thoughts to pay him much attention, though. She recognised the expression. It was the one she had often seen him wearing when she had used to catch him watching her.

"Isn't it better if we kill her?" Cedral said, his gaze fixed on Falon. "We'd be doing the world a favour-"

"Harm her and it won't matter what's between us. I'll tie you to a post and leave you for the soldiers to find."

Shock tore through Sarilla and she gripped the door frame, the wood digging into her gloves. For half a heartbeat, she allowed herself to believe the dream that he cared about her, but it wasn't possible. That Falon was dead and there was no bringing him back.

"I don't like it here," Cedral said after a moment, glancing around the trees and shuddering.

"When are you ever comfortable outside a tavern or whorehouse?"

Hurt flashed across Cedral's face, but it soon vanished.

Sarilla was beginning to get the distinct impression Cedral wasn't capable of holding a grudge. He just didn't seem able to care about anything long enough for that.

He laughed, his expression transforming into the carefree one he bore in most of the memories she had of him. Carefree and reckless. Pain in the backside. Yes. It was definitely him.

"You used to be comfortable in them too," Cedral said, resting his hand on Falon's knee, their fingers grazing. "I seem to remember a time you didn't want to leave them."

Sarilla tensed, willing Falon to move his hand away, but he didn't. Cedral wound their fingers together, his green eyes searching as Falon's jaw clenched. Resolution flashed across Cedral's face and he leaned in, pulling Falon closer until their lips touched.

A gasp slipped from Sarilla as Falon's eyes closed and a look of longing suffused his face. She tried to turn from the sight, needing to not see that which would only hurt her, but she couldn't tear herself away. Instead, she watched their kiss deepen, committing the painful sight to memory. The lust building between them. The hand Cedral raised to the back of Falon's head. The bastard by birth and the bastard by nature. No wonder they had fallen for each other.

Falon's brow creased and he pulled away, turning from Cedral. "No," he said, staring at the ground under his knees. "Not until you tell me what happened on the road to Dranta."

Cedral searched Falon's face, his breath coming in shallow pants, his mind too lost to lust to marshal thought together.

"You're not still on about that, are you?"

"You left, Ced. I need to know why. What did you do that's so bad that you can't tell me?"

There was a resignation in Falon's voice, like it wasn't the first time he had asked the question.

"Why does it matter to you so much? You've lost months' worth of memories. Why do you care so much about this one?"

"Because that may be the only blank I can ever fill in!" Falon clenched his fists. "I'm terrified I'll never get the rest back and here you sit, deliberately withholding from me the help that's in your power to give. How am I supposed to love you when you're just as bad as that Gods damned memoria in there?"

Venom stabbed through her, searing her veins as she listened to him speak about her with such contempt. It didn't matter how much time had passed or that he wasn't the man she had fallen in love with. The man sat beside Cedral had never loved her. He loved Cedral. Had always loved Cedral. She was the third in a pair. The unwanted hanger-on who still clung pathetically to her memories and the hope they taunted her with.

"You might want to get away from the door," Havric said, making her jump.

He hadn't moved from the chair. His head was still tucked down like he was sleeping, but he nodded towards the window, gesturing outside. Following his gaze, she watched Cedral making his way towards the cabin. Had he seen her watching?

Cursing, she stumbled backwards, barely making it out of the way before the door slammed open. Cedral glowered at her, his face darkening as the door swung shut behind him. How could Falon have ever welcomed such a mean and spiteful creature into his bed?

"There are places you would have to pay to watch a show like that," he sneered.

"Then I'd be asking for my money back," she said, more

than happy for an excuse to direct some of her anger his way. "Do all your attempts end so well or is he just outside your grabby reach?"

Cedral's lips twisted in a bitter mockery of a smile. "Just because Falon wants you alive, doesn't mean I have to endure the sight of you."

He closed the distance between them as she tried to back away, but it did little good. He crowded her against the wall and grabbed her wrists, using them to drag her back over to the bed where he tied her back up with the severed rope. Once done, he forced a bit of cloth between her teeth and tied it behind her head.

"That's so you're too muzzled to bite anymore," he said, throwing the blanket over her and positioning the small hole just above her mouth before binding the blanket tight about her, trapping her bound wrists against her chest.

"Much better."

He patted her head before striding from the room, slamming the door shut behind him.

CHAPTER EIGHT

"You might as well stop that," Havric said from close to her navel as she tried to kick her way free from the blanket. "Injuring me isn't going to secure your release any sooner."

"I can walk."

"In the direction we want you to?" he asked, laughing to himself. "We don't have time to waste chasing after you."

"If you don't let me go, then I'll bring the blackvine down on you."

The lie tumbled easily from her mouth. It wasn't the first she had tried, but it was maybe the most believable.

"She can't do that, can she?" Cedral asked from somewhere off to her right, worry displacing his usually carefree manner.

"Easily and gleefully, so let me down before you see how far I'll go when you push me!"

For a long moment, she just hung there, uncertain if her threat had any effect, then Havric sighed and said, "You're too heavy to carry to Dranta, anyway."

He dropped her to the ground and untied the blanket from around her. As soon as it was loose enough, Sarilla shook herself free from the rest of the dank confines, happier to be out of it than she cared to admit. If the blanket had been a cage, then it was almost as bad as any Renford put her in.

"Dranta?" she asked, blinking as she adjusted to the evening light filtering through the forest. "Why are you going to the capital?"

"None of your business," Cedral answered cheerily, even though he was sneering at her.

"Fine. Then why are you dragging me to Dranta and making it my problem? That's my business isn't it?"

"Nope."

"Look, I need to get to Arvendon-"

"To reunite with your precious king?" Cedral shook his head, not attempting to hide his disgust. "Not happening. He's already got the city. He doesn't need your help terrorising those he has trapped ins-"

"Renford's in Arvendon?"

Sarilla reeled as cold rose in her chest. He couldn't have sacked the city already. How long had she been unconscious in the old woman's cottage for? She looked to the others for confirmation, but Falon only frowned, meeting her gaze for a brief moment before looking away again.

"You didn't know?" Havric asked, watching her carefully. "I... We thought that was why you were heading there."

"To re-join him like the good little pet you are," Cedral muttered, but Sarilla barely heard him.

Renford was already in the city. What did that mean for Lya? Perhaps their father had managed to get her out before the soldiers arrived? At the very least, he could keep

LAST MEMORIA

her hidden, but how long would he manage that for in a city occupied by half of Valrora's army? She had to get to them. She had to help them get out the city, but how was she supposed to do that when she was being dragged the other way?

"Come on," Havric said, taking the end of the rope and leading her along like a horse.

Cedral struck out at the branches encroaching his path and Sarilla winced at the unnecessary pain he caused the trees.

"Your mother must be so proud," she muttered. "You were always so petulant. Impetuous. Arrogant. Younger son. Always a disappointment. Never as good as Veran. His rotting corpse is a better son than you ever were-"

"Shut your mouth!" Cedral grabbed her throat, lifting her off the ground.

"Careful, Ceddie," she said, gasping out the nickname. "You've forgotten whose skin you're touching."

His eyes widened and he dropped her, backing away and running his hands through his hair as it flopped over his face.

"How did you…?"

"She'll have seen it in memories she's stolen," Falon said, his tone hard and filled with accusation.

"Whose?" Cedral asked, his fingers flexing as if he would wrap them around her neck again.

Cedral playing in his father's study, his mother calling him away so his father could discuss treason with his conspirators. Letting the image fade, she stared at Cedral, revelling in the hatred staring back at her.

"Your father's."

Cedral lunged for her. She leapt backwards, continuing to distance herself from him even as Falon grabbed him by the arms and held him back, curses spewing out of him.

71

"How do you have those memories?" Falon asked, his gaze fixed on her. "I thought your mother was the one the king used for stealing memories."

"She… She is. Was. Renford only recently started using my brother and me."

"Then I guess it's fortunate we ran into you by the lake after all," Cedral sniped.

"You care that much that I have them?" she asked, studying him as he strained to break free from Falon.

"Of course I care! You filthy-"

"Do you even remember the last time you saw him?"

Cedral stilled, his expression darkening as Falon watched him warily.

"I do," she said, delighting in the hurt that flashed across his face. "And I remember his disappointment at not seeing you one last time before leaving for Dranta. He assumed you were either too far in your cups or too busy with another man to say goodbye-"

"Shut your mouth before I run you through!"

Falon's grip tightened on Cedral. He held him against his chest, trying to get Cedral to calm down, but Sarilla didn't want him to.

"Go ahead," she mocked. "We both know you don't have the stomach for anything that doesn't involve drowning in alcohol. Your father would be so proud."

"Maybe not, but he will be when I get his memories back," Cedral snapped as he glared at her. "Oh, I hope you resist. I'll take great enjoyment out of forcing his memories from you-"

"Is that why you're going to Dranta?"

Her words rang through the trees as she glanced at each of her captors in turn, searching for an answer in their faces.

"You're hoping to save him, aren't you? But…" She

stared at him, the anger inside her abating as she realised that he didn't know. "Your father's dead. Renford never lets treason go unpunished."

Nobody moved. The wind rustled the leaves about them, filling the silence.

"I wouldn't believe anything a memoria says," Cedral said after a moment, his gaze burning into her before he turned his back on them and stormed away.

"He's dead, Cedral," she called after him, making him pause. "But a part of him is still safe inside me-"

"You want me to believe that, don't you? You want me to think that so I don't kill you for what you did to him, but it won't work."

He pulled out a dagger, moving past Falon and Havric before they could stop him. He pressed it to her chest and she forced her breathing to calm.

"I could give them to you."

All eyes turned to her as she stepped closer to Cedral, her skin dipping around the sharp tip of his dagger, but not breaking. "Those I have, at any rate. The only question is, do you want that? You could finally know the truth about how he felt about you, but I doubt you've courage enough to-"

Cedral sliced her cheek and she flinched in pain. Warmth oozed down her skin and she touched the cut, her glove coming away red.

"I should make you as ugly on the outside as you are on the inside," Cedral said before storming away.

Falon shot her a withering look before heading after him, ploughing through the trees as Havric dragged her along behind him.

It was a long time before they caught up. Longer still before anyone spoke and close to dawn by the time they stopped to make camp. Sarilla's wrists were chaffed, but she didn't complain. She hardly knew what to bemoan first, her aching legs or her empty stomach. Perhaps the way Cursen's ire had been fixed on her since birth?

"I'm going to fetch more firewood," Cedral said, slumping his pack down and not looking at any of them.

"Take care where you walk," Havric said as he sat down to start a fire. "The closer we get to Dranta, the greater the risk we'll stumble across a grave."

"And whose genius idea was it for us not to take the road? No-one would recognise us."

"You might not be as infamous as you think you are," Havric retorted. "But she certainly is."

"Sorry to inconvenience you," Sarilla muttered as Cedral transferred his glower her way.

"Guess that's another plus in the column for not keeping her around then," he said before disappearing into the trees, lashing out at the branches as he passed.

"I meant what I told him," she said, staring after him. "I could give him the memories. They're his if he wants them."

Falon's gaze weighed on her from across the camp, but he said nothing and returned his attention to plucking the feathers from the bird he caught earlier.

"At what cost?" Havric asked, dragging her gaze from the trees Cedral had disappeared between.

"What do you mean?"

He grunted, tending to his kindling fire and repositioning a couple of logs before meeting her gaze.

"The cost you'll demand in exchange for giving him the memories. What is it you want? Freedom? To help yourself to his memories in exchange for his father's?"

She shrugged. "I... I just think he should have them."

Havric frowned. "You're serious?"

He shook his head disbelievingly, but Sarilla wasn't

watching him anymore. She jumped as something dark slithered over the fallen leaves on the other side of the fire, her thoughts flying to the blackvine. Panic filled her until she spotted the scales.

It was a snake. Only a snake.

Nervous laughter bubbled in her throat and silver flashed through the air, gleaming in the firelight as the blade sliced through the snake. It writhed, struggling to adjust to its newly decapitated state as Sarilla stared at it, unable to process how quickly its life had been stolen.

"Why did you do that?" she asked, lifting her gaze and glaring at Falon. "It wasn't hurting us."

"It could have," he said, wiping his sword clean before sheathing the blade.

"That tree might fall on us while we sleep. Should we chop it down now, just in case? Why not cut the whole forest down for that matter?"

"What are you talking about? It was a snake. A poisonous one too."

"Just because something can harm, doesn't mean it will!"

"I'd rather not risk my life to find out," he said, turning from her and returning to the bird carcass.

Sarilla scowled at the snake's corpse. It continued to twitch, the feeble movements growing weaker with each passing moment.

"Why do you care?" Havric asked, making her jump. When she glanced up, she found him studying her, his brows furrowed. "Why do its intentions matter?"

"Because everything is evil. Why should only those better at hiding their crimes survive?"

"That's a rather cynical view."

"It would be your view too if you had the memories I have."

Falon snorted but didn't look up from his ministrations, plucking the feathers from the bird, he skewered it and hoisted it above the fire. "It would probably be other people's view too if you hadn't stolen their memories."

"You really think people are good?" She stared at him in disbelief, unable to believe his gall. "People lie. They deceive and they take advantage. If you don't know that about them yet then you don't know them well enough."

"I know me," Havric observed. "I might not be perfect, but I can at least claim to be good."

She studied him, not bothering to temper her scorn. Either he was lying or he had deluded himself.

"Everyone lies. Everyone cheats. Everyone steals. I've seen it. Some are just better at hiding it than others."

Hostility radiated from Falon as Havric grew pensive, but neither of them spoke again for a long time. Cedral eventually returned to the camp carrying a token log under his arm, as if to excuse his prolonged absence. Whenever Sarilla glanced his way, she was met by narrowed eyes glaring back at her, so she soon stopped looking.

Once the bird was cooked, Havric hacked it into four and passed a quarter each to Falon and Cedral. Glancing her way, he strode over to where Falon sat and picked something small off the ground.

"Hope you're hungry," he said, tossing the bird's head at her.

It landed next to her with a thump and she dodged out the way of the blood splatters.

"That should be enough to satisfy you, right?"

"Very funny," Sarilla said as her stomach growled.

"What was it you said earlier? Everyone lies?"

"So? I bet you lie all the time."

"Just for that, you can starve for another day."

"So much for your being a good person."

She stared at the plate by the fire. The greasy skin reflected the firelight, doubling her stomach's rumbling. As Cedral and Falon tucked into their dinner, Havric continued to watch her. He sighed and handed her the remaining portion. She snatched it from him, half expecting him to take it back at any moment.

"Thank you," she mumbled. "So you don't want me to starve?"

"I lied," he said, grinning at her with a kindness that meant she couldn't help but smile back.

She ate slowly despite her hunger, her stomach strangely full after only a few mouthfuls, no doubt an effect of near starvation. The others had long ago cleared their plates by the time she finished. Havric put the fire out and cleaned up while Cedral lay down on his bedroll, not offering to help. Falon volunteered for the first watch. He settled against a tree, staring out into the forest, his gaze distant. As she watched him, she caught Cedral studying her and glanced away, unable to hide her blush.

She lay down to sleep and discovered that not even exhaustion could lull her under. She rolled onto her side, trying to ignore the twigs and rocks digging into her. Havric laughed as she grumbled into the blanket.

"Stop complaining. I've slept on worse."

Somehow, his statement didn't surprise her.

"You're not high born like those two," she observed, causing Havric to raise an eyebrow and glance up from his pack.

"Is it that obvious or have you stolen memories of me too?"

"No. Not that I can recall, anyway."

"How reassuring."

"You're different from them. That's all."

He looked like he was about to ask her how, but Falon

interrupted before he could.

"What makes you think I'm high born?" he asked, making her flinch at her slip.

She glanced over at him, forcing herself to hold his gaze. Ardent. Earnest. Lying. Rolling onto her back, she stared up at the canopy again, trying to displace the image of his face in her mind.

"Everyone knows of Falon the bastard."

She shut her eyes, begging for sleep to come, though it was a long time before it did.

It was still dark when she awoke to the soft scuffling of the others disassembling their make-shift camp. Havric gestured for her to get up. The soles of her feet protested as she did. They set off and it wasn't long before the pain became too much.

"Want me to carry you, Beastie? I promise not to drop you."

She scowled at Cedral as he laughed, but that only made his grin widen.

"I'd rather a horse, but I can see why you might be confused," she said. "The likeness is uncanny."

Havric's shoulders shook with suppressed laughter. "Shame we don't have any horses," he said.

"I'm sure we could find one somewhere. They're always tied up and left unguarded-"

"We're not stealing any horses. Do you have no moral compass at all?" Havric asked as he handed the rope binding her wrists over to Falon. "I'm going to hunt out breakfast. Keep going straight and I'll catch up with you."

Sarilla slowed down as Havric nodded and took leave of them, but Falon gave the rope a sharp tug.

"Move," he said, his voice as far from the one that had whispered words of love in her ear as could be.

"Do you have to do that? You've already stolen my

freedom. You have to go for my dignity too?"

"You don't deserve either," he said, continuing to lead the way through the Deadwood. "You forfeited your rights the first time you stole someone's memories."

It hadn't been her choice back then. She wanted to defend herself, but what was the point? All he would ever see was a monster.

Soft whispering reached her ears and she faltered, dread trickling down her spine as Falon grunted, the rope pulling taut and halting his progress. She ignored his complaint, searching the darkness and straining to hear the eerie muttering again.

The forest was all but silent. Gone were the hoots and humming of insects. Their absence made her skin prickle.

"What are you-"

"Shh! Didn't you hear it?"

"A hysterical memoria?" Cedral asked, glaring at her. "Yes, I did."

Metal rang through the air as Falon unsheathed his sword. "I heard it too."

"Blackvine. Quick. Untie me!"

"What? No-"

"You don't understand. We have to run and you need to untie me."

"I'm not-"

His eyes widened as he stared past her. She didn't need to turn to know what he saw.

Not waiting to see if Falon and Cedral followed, she ran, their footsteps soon pounding after hers. They overtook her and it was suddenly her turn to chase after them, desperately picking her path through the overgrown roots and trying not to trip up. The rope pulled at her wrists as Falon refused to let go of it, dragging her behind him even though her pace hampered his.

Writhing tendrils reached for them, lashing between the trees. A particularly thick vine crashed to the ground ahead, tearing through leaves and branches before landing with a thump and separating them from Cedral. Falon swore, slamming to a halt and using the rope to swing Sarilla into him to stop her from falling headfirst into the blackvine.

"Untie me!"

"Did you bring it down on us?" he roared as Cedral continued running through the trees.

Ignoring her request, Falon brandished his blade at the darkness. Cursing under her breath, Sarilla raised her hands, biting the glove tip with her teeth and wrenching it off her hand, ignoring the scrape of leather against her already sore wrists. She was so focused on getting the glove off that she didn't notice the tendril shooting over their heads until Falon dropped them both to the ground. They landed in a sprawled mess in the dirt.

Ignoring his surprised protests, she rolled atop him.

"What are you-?"

"I'm sorry," she murmured, planting her hand on the grass beside his head.

She had no idea if it would work or not, but it was their only hope. Her skin touched cold grass and she threw her mind into the nexus, stealing the memories from the plants around them. She took everything, emptying them until it was like nothing had ever grown there, all the while praying it would be enough to deceive the blackvine.

CHAPTER NINE

Her hands filled with memory after memory. They swarmed her, making it hard to pay attention to anything else other than the feel of Falon's weight crushing the grass from above. The warmth of his body. The pound of their footsteps as they had run there.

Blackvine writhed through the air above them, its whispers a deafening cacophony as her hand pulsed with newly stolen memories, the blackness climbing higher up her arms.

She was barely even aware of Falon as he pulled her closer to him, protecting her as the blackvine lashed out above them, always seeking. He was still holding her tight even as the whispers about them faded, leaving only an uneasy quiet behind.

The blackvine had passed them by? Relief surged through her as she dragged in a shaky breath, unable to believe it had worked.

"What did you just do?" Falon asked, staring up at her.

She heard his question, but her mind was too disorientated by the memories she had just stolen to focus on the sight of him. Forcing herself to focus, she sank into the feel of him against her. Warmth heated her chest and thighs from where he held her to him and she wanted to wrap her arms around him, to cling to the pretence that she had her Falon back and never let go of it.

Too lost in the delusion to know what she did, she lifted her gaze to his, expecting to see the same look on his face as had used to be there, but it wasn't. His expression was shuttered as he studied her, the love-sick memoria clinging to him even though she should have known better.

Her breath rasped and she tried to calm it, needing to get her foolish emotions back under control, but she couldn't. He was too close. Far too close.

The feel of his body beneath her. The press of his warmth. He grabbed her arm and she stilled as he lifted it, studying the still-pulsing marks on her hand. He trailed his fingers in the air over the marks, close enough to graze her skin, as if entranced by the sight of her guilt.

She snatched her arm away and pushed off him, needing to create as much space between them as she could. Curse her treacherous body for wishing she stayed atop him and for everything else it longed for her to do to him. That way only led to more pain.

Her pulse thundered in her throat and she looked anywhere but at him as she scrambled away as far as she could, the rope still binding her to him. His gaze prickled the hairs on her neck, but she couldn't look him in the eye, too afraid of what she might find within. Hatred or something even worse?

"I could have fought it," he said, sheathing his sword.

"Steel doesn't work against the blackvine."

"Then what does?"

"Nothing." She scooped her glove from the ground and jammed her hand back inside, eager to return to her pretend life where the marks didn't exist.

"Then how did you stop it?"

"I didn't."

She scowled at her glove as she struggled to get it on with the rope still binding her wrists. Her marks continued to move, mocking her and drawing her gaze back to the evidence of her crimes. Her stomach churned at the sight and she began to shake, her desperation to get the glove back on making the task all the harder.

"Why did you run from it?"

She didn't answer. She had to get her glove back on. The marks... there were too many. He couldn't see her like this.

"Hey," he grabbed her arm, forcing her to still.

Tilting her head up, he dragged her gaze to meet his and she stilled.

"Why were you running from it?" he asked again, his eyes searching hers. "You're a memoria. Surely if anyone is safe from the blackvine, it's you."

"I wasn't running from it," she said, unable to stop herself from breaking his gaze. "I was running with you. Or did you forget that I was attached to the other end of the rope?"

His mouth twisted into a bitter smile. "Lying comes so easily to you, doesn't it?" He shook his head disbelievingly. "Try again. Why were you running? The blackvine's a memoria creation. Aren't you immune to its touch?"

"I don't know. I don't want to risk it."

"You're afraid of it? Why?"

Returning her attention to her glove, she fumbled for an answer. Searching for anything but the truth, but all she found were lies.

Pain rippled through her as she turned to storm away, only managing to go two steps before the rope pulled taut and jerked her back towards him. She stumbled, almost falling into Falon, but when she threw out her hands to stop the fall, he sidestepped them, grabbing her by her arm instead. She flinched at his touch and pulled away, but his grip tightened as he nodded in the opposite direction.

"We came from that way," he said.

"Says the man with the terrible sense of direction. Falon the bastard, the boy who got so lost he was born in the wrong family."

Falon raised an eyebrow at the expression and she cursed herself for muttering it since he had been the one to tell it to her. Was it a saying so common that anyone might have heard it? From the look on his face, she doubted it.

She studied him, watching his reaction as his expression turned to one of scorn, but it couldn't mask the hurt hiding behind it. How many times must he have heard the insult before?

Scowling down at her still ungloved hand, he said, "I can see why you hide them. Those marks are as ugly as you are."

"As black as my heart," she said, quoting a memory she would have disposed of months ago if she wasn't such a masochist. She was a charred carcass. Scorched and barren to anything but pain. To pretend anything else was to lie to the world as well as to herself. "But at least I know who my parents are. You're just an illegitimate bastard your father couldn't be bothered enough to get rid of."

Insulting him made her feel better. It helped to hurt him as he was hurting her.

Anger flashed behind his eyes and she knew she had hit true. She wasn't the only one ashamed of her birth. It was part of why she had fallen for him in the first place.

"And whose memories did you steal to gain that

insight?" he asked, his dagger flashing in the starlight as he unsheathed it. Holding it up, he trailed it over her hand, grazing the tip along the pulsing marks spreading across her uncovered forearms. "They're in the marks, aren't they? That's where you store the memories."

He dragged the blade tip to one of the branches on her thumb and pressed lightly.

"What's this one, I wonder?" he asked, spite filling his voice.

Not taking her eyes from him, she shifted the memories on her hand, moving the more precious ones further up and out of sight to the underside of her arm. The marks rippled as she rearranged them. Falon flinched. Grabbing her gloved hand, he untied the knot quickly and forced the other glove back on her before rebinding her wrists. Pulling the rope taut, he dragged her through the forest after him.

"You'll never find them by getting us lost," Sarilla said after they had walked for a long time without coming across either Havric or Cedral.

She thought he would argue, but instead, he sighed and said, "Maybe." Running his free hand through his hair, he cast his gaze about, searching through the unfamiliar trees, worry furrowing his forehead. "Didn't realise my sense of direction was infamous though."

"Better to be known for that than for being a stubborn idiot."

"Or a... Hey! What are you doing?"

Sitting, she pried her glove off again with her teeth. It scraped across the tender skin about her wrists, but she ignored the pain, whispering, "I'm sorry," as she touched the smooth strands of grass beside her.

The connection to the nexus filled her mind in a rush and she spread her awareness out cautiously, worried she would happen upon the blackvine by accident. The nexus must be how the blackvine was getting around Valrora, which meant it didn't just have access to the memories it stole from those who stumbled across its path, it also could form itself from the memories of the plants from across the continent if need be. It frightened her just to contemplate how many memories the blackvine must already contain. Plants, animals, people. It drained them from every living thing it met, its appetite insatiable.

"What are you doing? If you call the blackvine back-"

"I didn't call it in the first place. I just don't fancy wandering the forest aimlessly for the rest of the night when I can search the forest's memories for Cedral and Havric."

"Trees don't have memories."

"No?" she asked as casting her mind out for the sensation of recently trodden grass. "Then how was the blackvine following us? Did you see eyes? Ears? Maybe a nose? How do you... Wait, I've found one of them."

"You have? Where?"

"Not far."

"Who is it? Ced or Havric?"

"Either. Neither. Could be a wandering vagabond for all I can tell. All I know for sure is there's someone's walking that way."

She stood, using the length of rope to haul herself up before leading the way between the trees. It wasn't long until the faint crunching of leaves reached her ears. Falon halted beside her, his hand hovering over his sword hilt, but he relaxed when Havric emerged from the darkness.

"I was beginning to think I'd be wandering the forest all night looking for you," Havric said, slinging his gear to the ground. "Cedral didn't let you take point on directions, did he? You can't keep a line on a straight road." His smile died as neither Sarilla nor Falon laughed. "What's wrong?"

"Blackvine."

"What? Did she summon it?"

Ignoring the accusation, she sat beside his quiver, murmuring another apology before touching her fingers to the grass once more.

"Is she summoning it again?"

"I… I don't think so. I think she's searching for Ced."

"How?"

"Don't ask."

"I've found him," Sarilla said. "Someone's stumbling around over there."

"What? You can't be serious. Falon-"

"Watch her," Falon said, throwing the rope to Havric. "I'll-"

"Oh no you don't. With your sense of direction, you'll end up in Arvendon. I'll go."

Havric threw the rope back to Falon then disappeared into the trees, barely a leaf crunching in his wake. Falon stared after him, frowning with unease as he turned to face her.

"Why do you apologise?"

"What?"

"Each time you… you know. You say you're sorry. Why do you do that?"

Because she felt guilty. He wouldn't believe her if she told him that, though. All he thought of her as was as a creature capable only of destruction. He would accuse her of lying and dismiss her accordingly.

"I don't like taking their memories," she said, rolling strands of grass gently between her fingertips. "They don't deserve that."

"But people do?"

"I haven't stolen from anyone since I left Dranta. I

wouldn't have stolen from anyone while I was there either if I was given the choice."

"You expect me to believe that?"

"Believe what you want. You always do."

Her chest ached, but she couldn't make that pain stop. Instead, she focused on trying to get her glove back on, needing to hide the evidence once more, but the rope was too tight. The more she struggled, the more painfully it bit into her. Giving up on that approach, she wriggled her wrists, scraping the wounds red raw in her desperation to get the rope off her and get her glove back on again.

"Hey! Wait. Stop that!"

Her wrist seared as she dragged the rope over the bump of her thumb and across her knuckles. Shaking the other hand free, she quickly re-donned her glove, relief flooding her as the marks disappeared from view.

"I'll just tie you up again," Falon said, watching her carefully, his brow furrowed.

"I don't care if you do." She picked up the rope and pulled it through her fingers, touching the knot that had been tied about her wrists. A cage might be confining, but at least it kept the monsters in.

"Why are you so intent on keeping your hands hidden? Without your cloak on, anyone with eyes can tell what you are. Your hair's a bit of a giveaway."

"I don't do it for them," she said, touching her hair as it hung down about her face. Her headscarf must have come loose in the lake too, but in all the commotion, she had failed to notice it was missing.

Falon studied her for a moment, then shook his head, his forehead creasing. "Why do I believe you?" he asked.

"I don't know. Everybody lies."

A smile tugged the corner of his mouth as he held his hand out for the rope and stowed it in his pack after she passed it to him.

"If you try to run, I'll put it straight back on you. You're not fast enough to get away."

Twigs crunched, signalling Havric's return. He emerged through the trees, Cedral following close behind, his perpetual scowl fixed on his face once more, his eyes and cheeks disappointingly unmarred by the black tears of the blackvine's victims.

Guilt flared through Sarilla at the thought. She shouldn't wish that fate on anyone. Not even an ass as big as Cedral, and especially not just because he held a place in Falon's heart that she never could.

"Still here, Beastie?" he asked with even more venom than she was used to. "I was hoping it had caught you."

"Funny. I was thinking the same thing about you."

Cedral made to say something, but his gaze landed on her unbound hands and his eyes narrowed.

"Why isn't she tied up?"

"She saved me from the blackvine," Falon said, his eyes fixed on her. "She could have let it get me, but she didn't."

"Don't be an idiot. She probably called it to us in the first place. For all we know, she's the one who's been bringing the blackvine down on Valrora all these years, picking us off one by one so her cousins in Oresa have no obstacles left to their reclaiming these lands."

"Is that what you think is happening?" All three of their gazes locked on her and she stared between them. "You think the blackvine's a memori vanguard?"

"Isn't it?" Havric asked as he shifted his pack on his shoulder. "Wipe us out and clear the way so they can reclaim their ancestral home."

"All the memori care about are memories. They don't give a damn about a city they were driven from over a hundred years ago."

"How would you know?" Falon asked. "You've never met them. You were born in the palace. As was your mother too."

"If your mother had been sired by any but the old king, she would have been murdered in the belly," Cedral said, causing an uneasy silence to fall upon their group.

He wasn't wrong.

"Are you saying the blackvine isn't their revenge?" Havric asked, seeming uncertain about whether to believe her.

"I'm saying they don't care where they live. You're the ones who put so much stock in buildings and structure for recording your history. Memori don't rely on such imperfect means-"

"Imperfect?" Cedral scoffed. "You actually think what you do is better?"

"I think you're a narrow-minded git too stupid to see that nothing's black or white. I might not like what I was made to do, but I can still see the advantages of what I am."

"Shut her up. I would have stayed in Arvendon with my mother if I wanted to be preached at. Give me the rope."

He held out his hand to Falon expectantly.

"Ced-"

"Just give me the damned rope. She's a Gods cursed memori. You of all people should know the consequences of letting one loose."

Shaking his head, Falon sighed, handing the rope to Cedral, deliberately not meeting her gaze as he did. He couldn't feel sorry for her, could he? It wasn't possible. She was the embodiment of all that was wrong with the world in his eyes.

Cedral wasted no time binding her wrists again, muttering, "Mongrel," as he yanked the rope tight.

"You're comparing me to a dog?"

"And insult the dog?"

"Enough," Havric said, shaking his head wearily. "The pair of you. Do we have to listen to you bickering the entire way?"

"Not if you tie him to a tree and leave him behind for the blackvine," Sarilla said, smirking at Cedral.

"Sarilla…"

Her stomach flipped at the sound of her name. She spun about to face Falon, her eyes wide as she searched his face. She hadn't told any of them her name. Did he remember her? It wasn't possible.

"How do you know my name?"

His gaze narrowed and he frowned. "I'm not the only one whose reputation precedes them," he said after a moment. "Since you're too young to be your mother and too old to be your sister-"

"And too female to be your brother," Havric added, smiling wryly.

Relief flooded through her, the panic ebbing out in a rush and leaving her weak in its absence. She turned from them, needing a moment to control the riot of emotions within her, taking a few steps and dragging in a deep breath. She needed to put as much distance between her and them as was possible, but something rumbled beneath her and the ground gave out in a sudden heave.

CHAPTER TEN

She plummeted down, a tunnel of darkness consuming her as soil and twigs tumbled with her in a hailstorm of dirt.

Almost as soon as she started falling, she was wrenched to a sudden stop by her wrists in a painful lurch. The rope bit into her hands as she dangled, her arms raised above her head, her body swinging in the silvery light pouring in through the Sarilla-shaped hole above.

Whoever held the other end of the rope grunted, pulling it taut as they strained against her weight, their grip all there was between her and a painful death.

A tunnel. She was in one of the old memori tunnels under Dranta. Had they already made it so close to the capital?

"Are you alright?" Havric called from above, his voice echoing and distorting in the darkness.

Panic consumed her as she scrambled, swinging and fighting to find purchase with her feet, the rope scraping as it rode up her hands. No, she was very much not alright.

A frightened squeak broke from her as she dared a

glance into the darkness below. She couldn't see how far the fall was. If the rope gave-

Her body lurched and she shrieked, but instead of tumbling down, she was jerked upwards. It happened again. And again. Each time making her heart pound as she expected to find herself failing, believing the rope to have broken.

Hands grabbed her and pulled her up the rest of the way. She could have wept with relief as she was hauled onto the relative safety of the forest floor.

She let out a whimper as she rolled away from the hole, her face pressed to the ground as she breathed in the fresh scent of the grass. She wanted to move as far from the cavern beneath her as she could, but she didn't dare budge lest the ground gave way again.

"Glad you were tied up now?" Cedral asked from where he stood a few steps back, too far away to have been part of the rescue.

Falon and Havric breathed heavily and Falon flexed his hands, wincing at the red rope burn on his palms. They had saved her. They didn't even like her, but they had still put their own lives at risk to save her.

Trying to hide her confusion, she said the only thing that would come to her mind. "That… That was a grave."

"A parting gift from your people," Cedral added, falling silent as Falon shot him another scowl.

Her people.

Memori weren't people. And they certainly weren't hers.

She shared more kin with her father's people in Frioca than she did with the memori. By the same logic, she was as much Valrorian as memori, but nobody had ever seemed to care about that.

Graves. Blackvine. There was no way she was making it

out of the Deadwood alive.

"Now are you done risking our lives, or can we go and find a God's cursed road before any of us break our necks?"

Sarilla expected the others to argue with her, but Falon and Havric just shared a glance before Falon nodded. "Fine. But we'll stay to the edge of the forest."

They set off, each treading carefully in a line one after the other. Falon and Havric shared the responsibility of taking point, even though Cedral suggested more than once that they should make Sarilla do it.

It felt like a lifetime until they finally happened upon a road. Longer still before the road led them anywhere of note. Sarilla almost wept at the sight of a town when she spotted it further down of the road. If her captors were half so travel weary as she was then she hoped they would be eager to take advantage of the small respite of an inn. She was so tired of sleeping on rocks and twigs that even a stone floor would be a luxury.

She strode towards the town with a renewed vigour, happy to let Cedral shave her bald as a disguise if it meant a break from the forest.

The rope pulled taut. She stumbled, spinning to glare at Falon.

"We're not stopping," he said before she could protest.

"One night, please, that's all I ask for. A bath and a bed. I'm begging. I stink-"

"I've noticed," Cedral said, but it was without his usual bitter snark. Apparently, she wasn't the only one whose weariness of trudging through the forest was beginning to show.

"Please, Falon. I'm cold. I'm exhausted. My feet are almost worn to the bone." Something brushed her arm and she glanced down to find Havric draping the blanket over her shoulder. His concern threw her and it was all she could do to murmur her thanks before resuming her argument. "I won't go any further like this. Prisoner's prerogative."

Havric chuckled. "There's no such thing."

"There is if you insist on dragging me halfway across the country. A distance I've already made once this month. Please, I've been surrounded by trees for so long that they're all I see when I shut my eyes."

"I hate agreeing with Beastie, but I'm not thrilled about spending another night in the rain." Cedral moved towards the town. "We can get a room for one night. It's not like we can't afford it. We'll hide her under that blanket and bring her up to the room before anyone thinks to ask…"

He stilled as he stared at the town. The others shared a glance, watching him warily, their hands reaching for their weapons.

"What is it?" Falon asked, worry creasing his brow as he took a step towards the town. "Soldiers?"

"No." Cedral stepped in front of Falon, trying to block his way. "It's nothing. I just… I realised you're right. It's still light out. We should keep going. We can stay at the next town if we need to-"

"What's wrong with this one?" Sarilla asked as alarm tightened his features.

Perhaps it was a consequence of having pillaged so many memories. A wisdom collected from a thousand falsehoods, but she knew a lie when she heard one. And for a man who loved to gamble, he had a terrible face for bluffing.

She glanced through the trees, searching for what could have scared him. The sign for the Claw and Paw tavern swayed in the breeze. Townsfolk walked the streets, hailing to each other as they passed between the buildings. There was nothing unusual about the place. Nothing to set alarm bells ringing.

"You've been here before," she said, knowing it to be true without needing to see the surprise flash across his face as he glanced at Falon before looking away again.

Havric snorted, breaking the silence. "Cedral hasn't been this far from a brothel in ten years."

"He has," Falon said as he stared at the houses at the edge of the town, a frown furrowing his brow. Did he recognise the place too?

"What? When?"

"He travelled with me when I went to Dranta."

"He can't have. He was forever in my family's brothel last winter. You didn't return until well into spring."

"He never made it so far as Dranta." Falon's voice was distant as he stared at Cedral. "This is where it happened, isn't it? Whatever it is you're keeping from me, it took place in that town, didn't it?"

Raindrops splattered Sarilla's cheek, announcing an oncoming deluge, but she barely noticed them, her attention too fixed on the unhappy lovers.

"I…" Cedral said before shaking his head and turning from them.

Falon's gaze locked on Sarilla. She watched his anger transfer to her.

"You see what you leave behind when you steal our memories? This is what your mother did to me. May the Gods help her if she doesn't choose to give me them back."

"What?"

Sarilla stared at him for a moment in disbelief until the shocked laughter bubbled up and out of her. She knew her timing could have been better, but she couldn't contain it.

"This-? This is why you're trying to get to Dranta?" Her

shoulders slumped forward as she shook from the effort of restraining the hysteria. "This is why you've dragged me through the Deadwood?"

"I don't see why you find it funny," Havric said, the frown in his voice clear. "We can use you as leverage to ensure his memories are returned. It's actually an improvement on what our plan was before we stumbled upon you on the lake."

"It would be if my mother wasn't already dead."

"What?"

"She's dead, Falon." Pain seared through her, but she wouldn't cry. If she started, then she didn't think she could stop.

"You're lying."

Everybody lies.

"I'm not. Or are you surprised there were no celebrations marking the occasion?"

"How?" Falon asked, his anger and disbelief warring on his face.

Grabbing the tip of her glove in her teeth, she wrenched it off, ignoring the white-hot burn about her wrists. Holding out her hand, she held the marks up for them to see.

"They're poison," she said, staring at the black as she moved the memories about, making the branches retreat and reform anew across her hands. "The more we take, the more they grow, the more they spread and the less you know yourself. My brother and I only had to start taking them recently, but Renford used my mother for years. He forced her to take so many that even her face was consumed by them in the end. She couldn't even remember who she was. It was a mercy when my father killed her."

Although trees filled her vision, it wasn't a forest Sarilla

97

saw anymore. Her mind was filled by her memories and she half wished she could stay inside them forever. At least her mother was alive there.

"The monster got what she deserved," Cedral said, jolting her back to the present. "She was stealing memories-"

"She had no choice!" She rounded on Cedral, her hair whipping through the air. "If she didn't, then Renford would have made us do it instead. She did what she had to so she could protect us! Her hands were clean before my brother was born."

"When did she die?" Falon asked, his gaze fixed on Sarilla.

When she didn't answer, he grabbed her arm and wrenched the other glove off. She hissed from the pain and protested as he twisted her arms until her palms were flat against each other, making it so her marks were on full display.

"When did she die? Whose memories are these, Sarilla? If you've got mine, then I swear-"

"She died while you were in Dranta, but Rysen was the one who took your memories. Not me."

She forced down a memory as it tried to rise to the surface, knowing all too well which it was and the pain it would cause her. She didn't want to relive the feel of Falon's arms about her as she wept.

She had already lost her mother and Falon. She couldn't lose Rysen or Lya too.

"Take me to Arvendon. Take me to my brother and I'll help you get your memories back."

Falon scowled at her, mistrust brimming in his eyes. "How?"

"I can convince Rysen to give you them back. But we'll have to go to Arvendon. Renford took him. I was trying to rescue him when you captured me. Help me save him and I'll convince him to give you your memories back."

Falon's dark brown eyes flashed, hope and suspicion warring within. His jaw clenched and he glanced at the others, a silent question in his eyes.

"You can't actually believe her?" Cedral asked, his mouth twisted with contempt.

"I do," Falon said, handing her gloves back to her. "Come on. We're going back to Arvendon."

CHAPTER ELEVEN

Every step towards Arvendon brought her closer to Rysen. The thought spurred her on through the pain in her feet and the ache in her legs.

She was so bruised from sleeping on the ground that her skin was almost as mottled as the canopy above and she was beginning to wonder if the Gods had cursed her to wander the Deadwood forever. She was so sick of seeing trees everywhere she looked and she was as tired of walking in constant fear of the ground giving way as she was bored with the glowers Cedral sent her direction, but she still kept on going.

She trudged on until her legs shook and her steps faltered. They collapsed beneath her and she tumbled, reaching out as she fell. Hands grabbed her arms and hauled her upright. Falon held her wrists before her and a red-swathed blade hilt flashed in the evening light, severing the rope binding her hands.

The pieces fell away and she gingerly removed one of the gloves, revealing the weeping broken skin beneath. She wanted to put the glove back on, but the wound needed to breathe. Forcing her hands to obey her, she removed the other glove, holding her hands down and out of her line of sight.

Falon studied her, watching the threat he had just let loose. Wariness hung behind his eyes, but there was something else there too. It lingered like curiosity, yet had the weight of admiration. The tips of her ears reddened and she glanced away, embarrassed by her reaction.

"We've been treating you a bit rough, haven't we?" he asked, inspecting her ruined wrists. "It's just… it's easy to forget you're just a girl when you're carrying a pair of weapons as dangerous as any sword."

She smiled bitterly, staring at the black marks. "Except you can wipe the blood off yours. My hands will never be clean again."

"You assume my guilt is easily forgotten."

"That which you remember," she observed, earning a baleful look from Falon as he lifted his gaze to meet hers, staring at her from under a raised eyebrow.

"Why do you keep the memories you steal?" he asked. "Can't you get rid of the memories once you have them?"

"I can."

"If all you take is the evidence of peoples' crimes, proof of when they were the worst of themselves, then why keep them?"

Meeting his gaze, she studied the way the inner corners of his eyes scrunched up. She could tell him that she couldn't bring herself to destroy all that was left of those she had stolen from, but that wasn't the main reason.

"I keep them because they remind me how corrupt the world is. I suppose it makes me feel better to know that I'm not alone in that."

Falon stared at the marks on her arm, drinking them in.

"What was it like when you woke up without your

memories?" Sarilla asked, unable to stop her curiosity.

Was it masochism that drove it? A self-destructive tendency that would push her into an early grave? A fascination with the misery she inflicted on others or all three?

Falon's expression shuttered, mistrust darkening his gaze.

"You should get some rest," he said, not answering her question. "We won't be staying here long."

She was so exhausted she hadn't even noticed the others setting up camp about them. Dragging a blanket from one of the packs, she wrapped it around her aching limbs, her body too tired to care about the uneven floor beneath her as she slumped down.

Sleep already beckoned as Falon's voice dragged her back to the domain of the waking.

"It's like being in someone else's body. Nothing feels right. Nails, hair. They aren't the same length you remember them being. You can't understand why you have bruises you've no memory of getting. Why you can't recognise the clothes you're wearing or the people around you. It was like my mind tore itself apart trying to understand why my memories felt too faded to be recent and I realised I might have lost years. That I might never know what they contained. Who I could have loved. The crimes I might have committed. What I must have done to bring such a fate upon myself."

He fell silent, his gaze distant as Sarilla and the others watched him intently, hardly daring to breathe. After a long moment, he asked, "Do you think you can still be guilty if you no longer remember your crime?"

His gaze lifted and met hers. She wanted to look away. She wished she had, unable to stand the sight of the hurt and confusion within. The confirmation of the pain she caused her victims.

"I asked Renford that once," she said.

A betrayal for a betrayal. That's what he always used to say. They betrayed his laws, so he betrayed his vow to the Gods to protect them. It made a twisted sort of sense when you thought about it.

Cedral twiddled his dagger as he spun it absentmindedly, the tip digging a hole into the dirt.

Sarilla stared at the red hilt circling around and again, catching the firelight in brilliant flashes. "Shame to dull it on an enemy as docile as the ground," she murmured, but then the memory of the grave surged to the forefront of her mind and she bit back a laugh. Perhaps it wasn't so docile after all.

"Don't worry, it's still as sharp as my wit and as painful as my overly large cock," Cedral said. He picked the dagger up, examining it like he was searching for a beauty he couldn't see. "You think it's fine?"

"Very."

"Falon designed it for me. You planning on stealing it, Beastie?"

Ignoring his barb, she rolled onto her side and let sleep pull her under, grateful for the escape it offered.

***

Early evening light dappled through the trees as they reached Arvendon.

"What are the chances Forta will favour us with another boat?" Sarilla asked as she peered around the lake's edge.

"Which ended so well for you last time, Beastie."

"Why do we need a boat?" Havric asked, pausing as he made his way around the lake's edge.

"To get to the tunnel you used to escape from Arvendon. It's under the rock face, right? Your boat was coming from that direction-"

"It is and we were, but we aren't." Havric ducked a low-lying branch, resuming his progress around the lake. "Soldiers followed us to that tunnel. Either they've now found out how to get into it or they'll have boarded it up. There's no way they'll have left it unguarded." He shook his head. "Ma's going to murder me for that. It was our best route in and out of the city."

Sarilla frowned, trying to make sense of his meaning. Laying it aside, she asked, "Then how are we getting in? The front gate? Forgive me for doubting Forta will be so giving."

"What's wrong with the front gate?"

"For a memoria and two sons of traitorous nobles?"

"Should I be insulted you've no crimes to lay at my door?" Havric asked.

"What do you mean, two traitors' sons?"

Falon's question caught her off guard. She stared at him in bemusement. Didn't he know?

"You and Cedral," she said, thinking it the most obvious thing in the world since at least one of their father's had already been executed for their crimes.

"My father isn't a traitor," Falon said, scowling at her. "Why would you think he is?"

She stared back at him, too stunned to do more than blink. She had assumed he knew. Was he telling the truth? Did he truly not know what his father had done? Sarilla had provided Renford with the evidence herself. She was the one who had seen the treachery in the memories she had been ordered to search.

If Renford was in Arvendon, then he wouldn't have left the treason to go unpunished. Now she thought about it, it was probably the reason Renford had sent his army to Arvendon in the first place.

No. Falon must know the truth. Surely he would have

asked why he was even in Dranta? He would have wanted to know what was important enough to put him in the path of Renford and his memoria.

"Renford knows, Falon. He knows."

Falon searched her eyes, then cursed, glancing at the city. "Let's go," he said, setting off at a brisker pace than before.

"How are you at climbing?" Havric asked as he followed her.

"Climbing?" She glanced at the city wall. "You're not serious?"

"If you can't go under it…"

"Then use a door and go through it. Don't attempt to scale it and fall to your death."

"It's not as sheer as it looks."

"And the rocks below? Are they made of feathers?"

"No, but if you fall, you won't be worrying about them for long." He flashed her a grin and pointed along the city wall. "There's a staircase built into the rocks. It leads to my family's tavern. We used it for years for smuggling in alcohol, but half the steps have crumbled away so we don't use it much these days."

"You're a smuggler?"

He was light on his feet, to be sure. Near silent in a forest. But Havric didn't seem like the illicit type.

Everybody lies, cheats and steals.

"It's a family business," he said, shrugging as if it was of little consequence. "One that will be mine when my mother finally hands over the reins."

She couldn't help but laugh at the long-suffering grumble behind his words.

"She sounds formidable."

"Only person I've met with fewer morals than you. If I wasn't determined to avoid her while we're back in the city,

I might introduce you."

"You don't want to see her?"

"After revealing the location of her prized tunnel? Truthfully, I was hoping Falon's quest would keep us away from Arvendon for a bit longer. At least long enough for one of my sisters to do something stupid and make me look like the good child again. Now, they're idiots, but not even they couldn't manage that in five days."

Smiling despite herself, Sarilla followed Havric and the others about the lake. It was full dark by the time they reached the rocks. Havric led the way and Cedral followed while Falon brought up the rear behind Sarilla. They climbed the mossy stones, moving cautiously to avoid falling into the lake, stepping exactly where Havric walked. Sarilla prayed Cedral didn't make a mistake and doom them both.

She practically hugged the wall, leaning against it and trying to ignore the way it scraped her skin, but better that than tumble into the water. Just the memory of her last night-time swim stole the breath from her lungs.

Havric stopped and reached out through the darkness at one point, causing Cedral to stop suddenly and for Sarilla to slam into his back, causing him to grunt and mutter something she couldn't hear, but was sure it had to have been insulting.

Havric started to climb and Cedral scrambled up after him, sticking closer than a shadow as Sarilla reached out, feeling at the wall. She couldn't find the staircase. The rocks were surely too worn.

"You alright?" Falon asked, his voice a whisper in the darkness behind her.

"Yes, perfectly fine. I'm travelling with lunatics who seem to think these dents are steps."

"You'll be fine. Just start climbing."

"I think I'll wait here. You go up. I'll follow you in daylight."

"The guards will see you in daylight."

"Fine. Then I'll wait here and you can throw a rope down for me."

"We don't have one long enough."

"Then... I..." She turned, staring at him through the darkness and knowing he wouldn't be able to see her. It was too dark for any but memoria eyes to make out much at all.

"Don't worry. I'll catch you if you fall."

Did he mean it?

"Go. You'll be fine."

She turned and gripped the small ledge before starting to climb. She had to feel out the next step, each ledge seeming more unstable than the last.

The protrusion beneath her foot wobbled and she shifted her weight, scurrying to the next. She turned to whisper a warning to Falon as a crack tore through the air behind her, as did the noise that escaped him as he fell.

CHAPTER TWELVE

She didn't stop to think. She grabbed for Falon, throwing her weight against the rock wall to stop them both from falling and clinging onto him. He heaved himself back up, panting as he leaned against the stones, his legs dangling over the edge as he stared at what might have been his fate. Turning, he looked at her through the darkness.

His hand still gripped hers as she searched his face, his rough stubble gleaming golden in the starlight. She didn't know this man. This wasn't the man she had fallen in love with, but his touch still soothed a part of her she had thought dead and buried.

Didn't he realise she still wasn't wearing her gloves? A thrill shot through her. Warmth spread from his fingers and she resisted the urge to squeeze him back, his thumb absentmindedly caressed her palm.

She was a fool. She knew how this would end, but her heartbeat still quickened in her chest, clinging to the hope that it could ever be the same between them as it once had been.

Then Falon's hand stilled, his eyes opening and his gaze piercing her to the stone wall. She could almost hear his thoughts. Let go before she steals your memories. Get away while you still know to fear the monster who could steal those you still have left.

"Falon?" Cedral hissed from above. "You alright?"

"Fine. We're coming up now."

His grip on her hand tightened and another familiar thrill jolted through her as he murmured thank you, oblivious to the effect his words had on her.

Pulling her hand back, she grabbed the cold step above, his heat leeching from her and seeping into the rock. She focused on the sensation, willing it to douse the feelings growing inside her like weeds as she hauled herself up, joining Cedral and Havric where they lay atop the dilapidated rooftop, peering over the city.

Where the capital had grown outwards over the years, Arvendon had grown up. Buildings piled atop each other, each connected by rope bridges that criss-crossed the canyon-like streets, branching from doorways and linking houses with the main walkways. People crossed the footbridges, wheeling barrels and talking amongst themselves as others passed above and below them. Clothes dried on ropes stretched across the streets, wafting in the breeze as it whipped through the city, swaying the footbridges.

"How's it coming, Hav?" Falon asked as he joined them and cast a wary eye over the windows looking down on them. "We're not exactly hidden up here."

Havric grunted where he hunched over the centre of the rooftop. A creak whined through the air as he heaved a trapdoor open, revealing a pit of darkness. Falon dropped into the hole and Cedral followed soon after.

"I'm ready whenever you feel like it," Havric said to

Sarilla as she hesitated, his voice straining as he held the trapdoor open.

Muttering a prayer to Forta, she lowered herself so her legs dangled over the edge, lingering there for a moment before letting go. Her stomach dropped as she fell, but strong hands grabbed her waist and lowered her the rest of the way into the darkness. They moved her out from under the trapdoor as it slammed shut above them, closing out what little light there had been as Havric landed lightly on the floor beside her.

The forest filled her nose as Falon's breath tickled her neck and she sank into the sensations. Into the warmth and safety of his arms. For a moment, she lost herself in the pretence, remembering things as they had been and longing for them to be that way again even though they never could.

"Where to now?" Cedral's disembodied voice asked through the darkness.

Falon's hand released her waist and trailed upwards until he grazed her chin, the rough pad of his thumb stroking her cheek and turning her breathing ragged. Her heartbeat raced as he dragged his thumb across until it grazed her lips.

"Why do you feel so familiar?" he asked, making her breath catch in her throat.

Light burst into the room as a door scraped open. Falon's heat left her and he was several steps away from her before either of the others could look their way.

Sarilla avoided his gaze as she joined Havric by the door, heat flushing up her neck and burning her cheeks as laughter from outside filled the room.

"What are the chances we'll slip through without being noticed?" Havric asked, staring down the corridor uneasily. He looked as if he was contemplating staying in that room forever.

"I wouldn't bet on it," Cedral said. "Want me to scope it out?"

"My mother would be on you the instant you entered the room. Her profits take a hit every night you choose another establishment's entertainments. She'll have already figured out we all left Arvendon together."

"Then best not to delay the inevitable," Cedral said as he grinned and stepped out into the corridor.

"Wait!"

Three pairs of eyes fixed on Sarilla as she waved at them, hating how their gazes lingered on her marks, but needing to draw their attention to them all the same. Realisation dawned as their gazes moved from her hands to her hair and Falon reached into his pack, pulling out her gloves. He handed them to her as Havric produced an old sheet from the depth of the room. He shook off the worst of the dust before tearing it with his teeth and handing her a strip for her to use to conceal her all too distinctive hair.

When she was done, Havric's gaze flickered over her, surprise filling his eyes.

"What?" she asked.

"Nothing." He glanced at Falon apologetically. "It's just... I can almost forget what you are with your hair bound like that."

His ears reddened and he turned away, making his way down the corridor, Cedral on his heel. Sarilla hurried after them, darting past the doorway the laughter was coming from. She glanced inside as she passed and her gaze locked with that of a venerable woman with familiar dark eyes, who wore all her weight on her hips. Her eyes widened as she stared at the corridor and Sarilla flinched, thinking the woman had realised what she was, but the woman's gaze was directed past Sarilla.

"Oh no you don't-! Havric! Get back here!"

A hand grabbed Sarilla's arm and tugged her along, urging her to run faster. They reached a spiral staircase at the end of the corridor and hurried down it. When they reached the bottom, Havric flung the door open and they raced along the rope bridge. It bounced with every step and Sarilla had to grip the handrail as she chased after the others, all too aware of the sixty-foot drop below should she slip.

Havric led them across one rope bridge after another, the shouts behind them soon growing quiet. He guided them through the maze of streets, up and down spiral staircases where rope bridges merged and along the rickety wooden planks until Sarilla was so lost that the only way she knew would certainly get her out involved a long drop off a rope bridge.

"Where are we going?" she asked between gasps.

"My place," Havric said, turning down a narrow walkway. "It's my sanctuary from my mother. Falon and Ced's homes are too suspicious, but we should be safe at mine. At least for a bit."

He led them to a dingy apartment on a lower level of the city that wasn't much to look at. Inside or out. When he unlocked the door, it whined open, revealing a room that would have sufficed as a large storage cupboard in the palace, but Havric didn't appear ashamed of it.

Cedral swung his pack off and sank onto a battered stool beside a barrel in the centre of the room that Sarilla guessed was supposed to act in the stead of a table. He stared about him, his nose wrinkling in distaste.

"Don't say it," Falon said tiredly as he dropped his bag to the floor and leaned against the far wall, his eyelids fluttering shut as if he were taking a standing nap.

"Say what?" Cedral asked as Havric lit a small lamp and

cast a warm orange glow about the room that did little to improve the place.

"Whatever thoughtless comment is about to come out your mouth."

"Come on. Don't pretend you aren't thinking the same. Gods, Havric, could we get any closer to the pavement without actually being on it right now? We're practically on ground level."

"And there it is," Falon said, sighing.

"At least tell me you've got something to drink in this place? There's nothing a little alcohol won't make seem at least a little better."

"Insightful as always," Havric said, producing a bottle of wine from a crate at the back of the room. Uncorking it, he poured them each a cup and wryly toasted, "To Arvendon and the king's present occupation. May it be as brief as it is unwanted."

"Did you spot the guards stationed on the upper and lower bridges?" Falon asked, holding the cup before him as he stared into its depths. "I didn't have time to count them, but it looked like the king's got them stationed across the city."

"And in the stair towers," Havric said.

"I noticed. Is that why we took the long way round to get here?"

Havric nodded and Sarilla frowned, replaying her memories of their route through the city. She didn't remember seeing any guards, but she wasn't exactly in the best of states for forming memories. She knew she had been pushing herself too hard, but she had been so desperate to reach Arvendon. Now she had got there though, she was so exhausted that she was struggling to stand.

She needed sleep, but she needed to ensure that her

family was safe more.

"Perhaps you should let your Ma know about this place." Cedral sniffed the wine, pulling a face. "She might be able to liven it up a bit. Gift you with a few crates of the good stuff."

"You've the manners of a horse's rear end," Havric said. "I'm sorry my home's not up to your usual standards, but since I have neither your wealth nor your decadence, I suppose that's hardly surprising."

"You could have all the money in the world and you'd still be as bereft of taste as you are now." Cedral grimaced as he downed his wine in a single swig. "Remind me to pack something decent to drink next time we go uselessly gallivanting across the country. I don't like being so sober. It's unsettling." He held out his empty cup to Havric. "I'll need a fair bit more if I'm to spend the night here though."

"Good luck with that. That was the only bottle," Havric said, tipping it upside down.

"What? Your family owns a tavern. How do you only have one bottle of the stuff?"

He kicked the barrel beside him, searching for something else to drink, but it rang hollowly. Cursing under his breath, Cedral rose from his stool and began searching the room, hauling crates aside and creating chaos in Havric's previously orderly, if plain, room. Havric squeezed his eyes shut as if to block out the sight of the carnage.

"I suppose we should discuss plans while he destroys my home."

"Ced!" Falon's voice cracked through the room, making Cedral pause. "Sit down before Havric kicks you out. You'll be out on the bridges then because there's no way the guards aren't watching your house."

Cedral scowled as he sat, but not before pinching

Sarilla's cup of wine as he passed and finishing it off. She didn't care though. Memori didn't have a high tolerance. One glass and she wouldn't remember anything until the next day.

"I suppose our first step must be to figure out where my brother is. Arvendon has a prison under the city, right? Will Renford be keeping my brother there?"

"The one under my father's residence?" Falon asked, swilling the contents of his cup about without drinking from it. "The one that's dug into the rock and is as heavily guarded as the sun by the clouds on a rainy day?"

"It can't be that bad."

"They'll be fifty soldiers at least. More now, likely. The king's got an entire army to keep occupied while he's here. He'll have plenty to set to guarding those he took prisoner while taking the city."

"Great. I don't suppose your family have any secret entrances?" she asked Havric.

"No. Or if they do, they left my great uncle Sydas down there to rot out of malice."

"There is a secret entrance of sorts," Falon said to his cup.

"If it involves fewer guards, then I say we use it," Cedral said, eyeing Havric's cup of wine. "Fifty to four is worse odds than Havric's got of-"

"Nobody guards it," Falon interrupted, casting a weary gaze at Cedral. "But I don't know where the entrance is. My father only mentioned it once. It's a secret only the ruler of Arvendon should know, so he never shared any details with me. He's still waiting on that legitimate son he's been hoping for all these years."

"Great," Cedral muttered. "So at least we know that if your father is locked up down there, which he probably is, and if we somehow make it down to him, we'll at least have an easy time of getting back out." He grabbed Havric's cup, quickly transferring the contents into his stomach even though Havric made no move to stop him. "This is madness."

"Ced-"

"No. I'm done. I was willing to go with you to Dranta. I owed you that much since I bailed on you the first time, but I'm quitting while I'm still alive here. Are you really so desperate to get your memories back that you'll risk losing the rest of them too?"

"You don't understand. You don't know what it's like."

"Don't I? I can't remember half my nights! Does it look like that bothers me?"

"Not as much as it should," Sarilla muttered under her breath.

Cedral threw a glare her way, but she didn't think he had heard her words, even if her tone had been enough.

"Have you considered that after all this, those memories might just be months of you scratching your arse? Sure, maybe you've lost a couple of good fucks, but-"

"If I've lost nothing of importance, then why won't you tell me what happened back in that town? Did I catch you fucking the first whore you could find? It wouldn't be the first time."

When Cedral didn't answer, Falon cursed and pushed off the wall. He strode towards the door. "I'm going to find out what's happened here since we left. If you're going to go, be gone by the time I'm back."

The door creaked shut behind him. As Sarilla made to follow him, Havric waved for her to stay put.

"I'll go. You should stay hidden. We don't need to add to the number of people we're breaking out of the prison."

Would he rescue her? Cedral would happily leave her to rot.

As the door closed again, Cedral barked a laugh. "If they think I'm staying with you, then they're bigger idiots than I realised. I'm going to find a proper drink. Don't wait up."

He left without another word, and Sarilla tried not to wish too hard that it was for good.

Left in a half-destroyed apartment with only memories for company, it was a moment before the realisation struck that she was alone. After all her attempts to get away, it couldn't now be so easy, could it? She could run. It would be so simple to disappear in the city, to lose herself in its maze-like streets, but if she did, what chance did she have of getting her brother back?

She had stolen memories of Arvendon, but her knowledge of the city was patchy at best. Mainly she knew her way about the finer houses, the ones Renford's nobles plotted his downfall from inside of. Strange as it seemed, at least with Falon she had a chance of getting her brother back.

Curling up on the bed in the far corner of the room, she was out before she could remember her head hitting the pillow. She awoke as Cedral stormed through the door, his face set in a scowl as he kicked over a stool then slumped down on another. Ignoring him, Sarilla yawned, her eyes drifting shut again.

"Nowhere's serving. Most the taverns are closed on the king's orders. The only damned place open is Havric's, but that's just because they've other ways to drown your sorrows."

"I'm surprised you didn't dive straight in," she mumbled into the pillow.

"Havric's mother pestering me the whole time might have killed the mood a bit."

Turning her back on him, she rolled over and nestled against the pillow, already half asleep again. If he said something else, she didn't hear him, instead waking with a start to a crash that shook the room. Jolting up, she took in Falon and Havric's reappearance, along with the table crate that had been knocked over like the stool.

Falon's shoulders drooped as he stumbled backwards, only stopping when he fell against the wall. He sank to the floor, resting his arms and head on his knees as he curled up in a ball, the others watching him with concern.

"What is it?" she asked Havric. "Did you find his father?"

"He's hanging off the first walkway. King Renford's already had him executed."

There was silence for a moment before Cedral swore.

"That's it then. No way am I dying for the sake of rescuing a memoria. I'm sorry about your memories, Falon, but they're as good as gone. No way can we get in and out of that prison alive. Unless Beastie here can steal the memories we need from your father's corpse, then we might as well give up now."

Sarilla shook her head, too tired to do more than despair of Cedral.

"You can't, can you?" Havric asked, frowning as he glanced her way.

"What?" Was he thinking about the rabbit's head?

She was about to burst into laughter at the thought, but then Falon raised his head from his arms and the hope in his stare pierced through her.

"Can you do it?"

"I... I don't know. I've never tried."

Cedral snorted and shook his head in disgust.

"Look at that. Even Beastie has her limits."

"You're not helping," Havric said before returning his attention to Sarilla. "So it might be possible? You might be able to find the location of the tunnel in his memories?"

"What? You can't be serious. Let the poor man rest in peace. He doesn't need her rifling through his memories-"

"He's already dead," Havric snapped. "What more does he need them for?"

As they bickered, Falon stared at her Sarilla, his gaze boring into her, his grief written on his face. Whether it was for his father or his memories, she couldn't tell. His relationship with his sire had always been strained, filled with a desperation on Falon's part to prove himself as worthy, an attempt that was only ever met with coldness.

Of all the things she had admired about Falon, she had loved him for that the most. In all her life, he was the only one she had met who shared her determination to prove themselves as better than the world thought them to be.

"Is it possible?" Falon asked, drawing her from her thoughts.

Could she do it? Technically, perhaps. And the knowledge of the tunnel would certainly help in rescuing Rysen. But the real question wasn't whether it was possible to take the memories of the dead, but whether Sarilla could bring herself to do it.

It would mean breaking her vow to herself. The Lord of Arvendon might be dead, but she would still be stealing another's memories. Though, as Havric had so bluntly put it, what use did the dead have of memories?

Treacherous excitement stole through her at the thought of taking them. She tried to force it down, knowing the heady rush for what it was, but it surged through her blood in an intoxicating wave, consuming her mind and body like the prospect of sight to a blind man.

"Maybe. It will depend on how long he's been dead for. Memories fade when they aren't maintained. Once the body stops taking care of them..." She shrugged, uncertain of how to describe the process.

"So you'll try it?"

Desperation rang in Falon's voice and she glanced down, tracing the pattern on her glove with her fingers. Would she?

Dead was dead, after all. It wouldn't technically count as breaking her vow, certainly no more than stealing from plants had.

"I'll try."

"Then we should go sooner rather than later," Havric said. "I don't know how long he's been dead for, but he's not getting any fresher."

"Welcome to the dead father's club, Fal," Cedral said with a snort. "Fair warning. It's as fun as a knife in your gut."

Havric scowled and pushed Cedral out the door. Falon followed behind as Havric lingered by the door, waiting for Sarilla.

"You really do hate what you are, don't you?" he asked, shaking his head as if he still couldn't quite believe her capable of think of herself as monstrous.

"Wouldn't you?"

He stared at her and although it wasn't trust staring back, it was the closest to it she had known in a long time.

"If it helps, I won't think any less of you if you do this."

"Perhaps you won't, but I will," she said as she left the room and followed Havric down the rope bridge.

He led them into a part of the city she recognised, where the buildings were even taller than those that had already towered over them from the sides of the walkways. He guided them to the higher levels. They tried to keep their movements casual as they passed beneath the soldiers stationed throughout the city. Sarilla was too occupied keeping her gaze fixed on the rope bridge to pay much attention to them, though. Her fear of falling hitched up a notch with every level they climbed, the stretch of empty expanse beneath them increasing each time.

"Ompft," she said, colliding with Falon when he stopped just in front of her.

The rope bridge shook beneath her and she gripped the handrails, her eyes squeezed shut as she waited for the shaking to stop. When the bridge stopped swaying enough for the fluttering in her stomach to cease, she forced her eyes open, looking around to see what had caused Falon to halt.

Bodies hung from the rope bridges, criss-crossing the streets like garments hanging on a clothesline. They danced a dead man's jig as people strode along the bridges they dangled from, causing the marionettes below to jolt and sway. There were hundreds of them. Soldiers strung up like wind chimes, their armour weighing them down and clanging the music of the dead. Their uniforms proclaimed them to be men of Arvendon. The deep purple of their garb matched the bruised discolouring where the rope had squeezed the life from them. Had Renford put them all to death?

Cedral stared wide-eyed at the bodies as Sarilla leaned over the handrail. More corpses swayed hypnotically below. She glanced up and followed Falon's gaze. It was fixed on the body of an elderly man, his bulging eyes staring sightlessly at the lower levels, his face was swollen, his neck bruised where the rope dug into his flesh. Even disfigured though, Sarilla still recognised him. She was so engrossed by the sight that it was a moment before she realised what Havric and Falon had failed to mention earlier.

"How exactly am I supposed to reach him?" she asked.

The body swung from the side bridge, well out of arm's length from the one they stood on. There was nothing below him except the cobbled street, and that was a long way down. Leaning over the edge as far as she dared, she searched for a way across to the corpse, but there was none. Could they get to the bridge above and haul the body up somehow?

"Are you ready?" Cedral asked behind her.

Ready? As she turned to ask just what he thought she was ready for, a pair of hands wrapped around her hips and threw her from the bridge.

CHAPTER THIRTEEN

Her strangled scream cut short as she crashed into the Lord of Arvendon. His corpse swung from the impact and she had no other option than to cling to him. She breathed through her mouth, trying not to think about what she was hugging for her life. The rotting stench was stronger now her nose was pressed against decaying flesh. It invaded her nostrils, making it impossible to pretend she wasn't clinging to a dead man. Every muscle screamed for her to let go as she retched, swallowing down the bitter bile.

"What in the Gods' names were you thinking?" Falon whisper-shouted from the bridge behind her.

"Just speeding this whole thing up. She needed to get across-"

"Not like that I didn't!"

Her fingers slipped as she twisted to glare at Cedral. Her heart lurched and she tightened her grip with her legs, the rope above creaking as she swayed in the breeze, slowly rotating about.

"She's there now. She might as well get on with it."

She wanted to yell at Cedral, but she didn't dare move

again enough to try. Get back to the bridge and scold Cedral afterwards. That was the order. She would have all the time in the world for making him pay for having thrown her once she made it back to the rope bridge.

Rysen. She was doing this for Rysen.

Gripping the Lord of Arvendon's body tighter with her legs, she let go with her hands and tugged off a glove, stuffing it into her waistband and hovering her fingers over his purple jaw.

"I'm sorry," she said as her fingertips touched cold skin.

Her stomach churned as she opened her mind up to the dead man's memories, the decay surging into her.

His memories were incomplete, like a painting kept too close to a flame, bubbled and burnt in parts and deteriorated to the point of being senseless. The futility of her search hit her in a rush. Whatever knowledge the man possessed while alive, it was gone now. She released her grip and pulled her mind back, only too happy to draw it out of the sludge.

How was she supposed to get to Rysen back now?

"We're too late," she said over her shoulder. "They've decayed too much already."

Falon swore. He ran his hand through his hair, leaning forward against the railing, his knuckles clenched as white as Sarilla's skin. He stared at his father and Sarilla felt like she was intruding on his privacy, on his moment of goodbye to the man he tried so hard to please but had never been good enough for. The man whose death was just another failure on Falon's part.

Havric murmured something comforting as Cedral placed his hand on Falon's shoulder, looking as if he wished to do more, but he held himself back.

A strong gust of wind swayed the body beneath her and her stomach lurched. She clung tighter, frantically searching for a way back to the rope bridge. Could she pull herself up to the walkway above? She didn't think so.

"How am I supposed to get back?"

"You'll have to jump," Cedral said, leaning over the handrail and holding a hand out to her. "Don't worry, I'll catch you. Trust me."

He winked and Sarilla glared back. "Forgive me for not believing you."

"Swing towards us," Havric said, scowling at Cedral and pushing him aside. "Let go when you get close enough and I'll haul you the rest of the way."

He hadn't asked her to trust him. He didn't need to. The statement hung unsaid in the air as he held his hand out to her. She met his gaze and pleaded, silently begging him not to drop her as the angry whine of the rope above decided the matter.

She shifted her weight, pendulum rocking the Lord of Arvendon through the air. The distance to the bridge closed a little more with each swing, the rope's whining growing louder and louder until she threw herself into the air, launching across the void. She lost height fast and panic filled her as she fell, blindly reaching out. Her hand met with something solid and warm and she gripped it tight, clinging to her lifeline as her body continued through the air, hurtling past the planks. Her arm almost wrenched from its socket as Havric's grip pulled her up short.

For a moment she just hung there, suspended beneath the bridge, dangling with the corpses, then hands grabbed her arm and pulled her up. She lay on the planks, clinging to them as she dragged in her breath, her cheek resting against the rough grain. She was alive. She was safe. Relatively.

Clutching the handrail, she dragged herself to her feet, glaring at Cedral as she rose. How dare he throw her? He could have killed her. Knowing him, he was probably angry she hadn't fallen to her death. As she was about to give her fury free rein, her gaze caught on something pure white behind him, making her forget the tirade she had been about to unleash upon him.

Hair billowed in a breeze-rippled cloud, the pale body swinging from the rope bridge across the street. She was less than half the size of the other bodies. Although her head tipped forwards, concealing her face, Sarilla would have recognised the black roots anywhere.

"Lya?"

Sarilla's voice cracked as she stumbled forwards, transfixed on the sight of her lifeless sister. It couldn't be.

Hands caught her as she reached the handrail, clinging to her, dragging her back and stopping her from falling from the bridge.

"Let me go! Lya! Lya!"

She needed to get to her sister. It didn't matter that Lya dangled out of reach. It didn't matter that her sister must have been dead for days. She had to get to her.

Hands turned her about, wrenching her from the sight of her sister swinging in the breeze. They tried to make her look away, but she wouldn't let them. She had to-

Her gaze landed on the larger body dangling next to Lya and her heart broke in her chest. Rysen's handsome face was so distorted he was almost unrecognisable. With his hair shorn as it was, she might have been able to convince herself that it wasn't him, but there was no denying the black marks winding up his hands, searing his guilt into his flesh. Someone had bound his wrists before him, displaying his crimes for the world to judge him by.

"Rysen! No! Rysen! Let me go- Let me go!" The hands held her fast. They wouldn't budge. Wouldn't let her get to her family. "Rysen!"

She choked on her sobs, struggling against the arms holding her back, no matter how much she fought. The grip tightened as anguish wracked her body, her sobs wrenching through her. A hand clamped over her mouth, quieting her grief. No. She had to get to them. She had to save them. She kicked, trying to elbow free, needing to reach Lya and Rysen. She had to protect them.

"Sarilla! Stop!"

Falon's breath warmed her ear as he gripped her to him, holding her back as he squeezed her tight, as if he could protect her from the world that had already beaten her.

"I know you're hurting, but you can't do anything now."

"I have to get to them!"

"You can't save them. Sarilla, listen to me. You can't save them."

"No. I need... I need to-"

"We have to go. Now. Before any soldiers come to investigate the commotion."

"I can't leave them!"

They couldn't be dead. Renford wouldn't have executed them. He might not have ever cared about them, but he wouldn't do that to her. Another body hung beside Lya and Sarilla forced herself to look, already knowing who the tanned, Friocan features belonged to, but she couldn't bring herself to feel any sorrow at the sight of her father's corpse. She was too drowned in the pain of Lya and Rysen's deaths to feel any ripples for her father's.

Tears poured down her face, her body convulsing as shudders wracked through her. Falon clutched her, his touch robbing her of the numbness she craved. Better not to feel anything than to be consumed by the pain. Better yet to tumble off the bridge and plummet into the welcoming embrace of oblivion.

Clanging armour echoed down the street, distorting off

the stone buildings, but she barely registered the sound. The bridge shook from the approaching soldiers, but she didn't care. Lya and Rysen were dead. What was the point in fighting anymore?

"Take her."

Falon's grip shifted, his touch disappearing. Good. Oblivion couldn't clear away the pain so long as he was still holding on to her.

"Get her somewhere safe." Strong hands gripped her and Falon's breath warmed her face as he forced her to meet his gaze. "Sarilla. Sarilla, listen to me. You have to go before the soldiers realise what you are. Havric will get you somewhere safe while Ced and I distract them."

"I'm not risking my neck-"

Falon glared at Cedral, silencing him as someone called, "What's going on over there?"

Nodding to Havric, Falon motioned for him to take Sarilla before he spun about, blocking them from view. Havric pulled her backwards, dragging her from the soldiers and her family.

It didn't matter. She could still see them. She had already made the memories.

Lya's hair billowing in the breeze. Rysen's lifeless eyes staring sightlessly.

Havric dragged her across bridge after bridge, leading her down spiralling staircases and between rows of layered houses. They flitted past without registering in her mind, but she didn't care. Nothing mattered. Not anymore.

She barely noticed the voices as he led her into his family's brothel. Laughter assaulted her ears as she struggled to process it, staring about the room, unable to comprehend the red cushions lining the walls and the plush curtains draping from the ceiling. Some were already drawn and granted the semblance of privacy to the occupants within, but the privacy was belied by the grunts and moans coming from behind the velvety fabric.

"Soldiers were blocking the way back to mine," Havric said, his voice distant. "Falon will know to find us here when he realises we're not-"

"Havric!"

The bellow rang through the room, silencing the laughter as a large woman barrelled past Sarilla, knocking her aside as she pulled Havric into a hug.

"Ma-"

"You will tell me everything, my boy, or so help me I'll put you in charge of the whores for a month. I'm sure you remember how demanding they can be."

"Ma, leave off." Havric wrenched free and swatted her hands away. "We need somewhere safe to stay for a time. And something strong to drink wouldn't go amiss."

"You disappear without even a note and this is all the explanation you give? I spent three days walking around staring at corpses just to make sure you weren't one of them. Oh no, my dear son, you owe me-"

"Not now, Ma. You can yell tomorrow, just not now. Tonight, pretend I'm not your son and get us the strongest bottle of whatever you have."

"You'd be in Cursen's ire if I did. The king's banned the sale of alcohol. 'While the city's in a state of unrest.'"

"I don't care. Either bring us something or I'll go back there and get it myself."

He met his mother's gaze in a silent battle of wills and she clucked, knocking the underside of his chin with her knuckles before bustling to the bar.

Havric dragged Sarilla to an empty table near the back of the room and urged her down onto the cushions. A moment later, his mother slammed a heavy bottle on the table. Cups clinked as she slapped them down too.

"When you feel like giving the woman who birthed and raised you an explanation, you'll find me behind the bar. Though you should know, what little patience I had was used up two days ago, so I wouldn't push it too much longer, son of mine."

As she left, her overburdened hips swayed as she wobbled across the room. Havric watched her go as if she were a fire raging and already too late to stop.

"She's going to save the king the job of hanging me," he muttered, uncorking the bottle with his teeth. Seeming to realise what he said, he glanced at Sarilla apologetically. "Sorry. I didn't mean it like that."

He poured them a cup each and she downed the first, pouring herself a second. She didn't want to remember anything. At least the alcohol would bring her oblivion. She tipped the contents down her throat, the taste finally registering with her dulled senses. Bitter and foul, but no less than she deserved.

She had reached Arvendon too late. It was her fault they were dead. She should have fought harder.

Had death cleansed them of their sins? They hadn't looked like monsters as they had been hanging there. They had looked just like the soldiers surrounding them, all swinging in the breeze together.

She stared at the contents of her cup. The dark-brown liquid shimmered merrily in the lamplight, mocking her as it distorted her reflection until her face looked noose mottled too.

If they were monsters, then so was she.

"Everyone always used to say that I looked like her. Lya looked like her too, but Rysen took after our father. Except her hair. We all had her hair."

"You mean your mother?"

"Lya and I... We were cursed to be like her both inside

and out. The Gods marked us at birth."

"What do you mean? Sarilla?"

A loud bang across the room snapped her attention from her drink as she glanced up to find Havric's mother cleaning a mug with a rag, her motions jerky. Wisps of her white hair peeked out from under her cap and Havric grimaced as she slammed the mug down on the counter, staring at her son as if daring him to keep defying her.

"You should go to her. Make the most of her..." Before she's gone too.

Concern filled Havric's eyes as he studied her. Sighing, he pushed himself up from the table, rapping his knuckles against the wood.

"Stay here. Falon and Cedral will arrive soon. I'll be just downstairs. I don't feel like receiving a scolding in front of the patrons."

Sarilla didn't notice him leave, she was too busy watching Lya and Rysen's bodies swaying in the breeze. Warmth trickled down her cheeks, but soon even that sensation failed to register.

How long before the alcohol set in? She didn't want to remember anything. How much would she have to drink to make her forget they were dead?

"I told you not to try to leave me."

Renford's voice dragged Sarilla from her thoughts and she stared into his dark brown eyes. Oblivion couldn't come soon enough.

CHAPTER FOURTEEN

Renford closed the curtain to their section, the metal hooks holding the fabric up clinking as he concealed them from the rest of the tavern.

Metal scraped, the sound a familiar one. How many soldiers did Renford have standing just out of sight?

Fear shivered through her. She knew who waited on the other side of the divide without needing to see them, just as she didn't need to feel the rope around her neck to know they wished her strung up beside her siblings.

Renford's guards always hated her. Their distrustful stares had always followed her about the palace, watching, waiting for an excuse to run her through. Tranten would be there, waiting nearby among the rest of Renford's guards. No doubt unsmiling as always. His lingering gaze had always made her feel unclean.

"You should have listened to my warning," Renford said as he sat across the table from her. "They would still be alive if you had."

Did he want to watch her swing too? She squeezed her eyes shut, but it did nothing to stop the onslaught of memories of Rysen and Lya his words invoked.

"Are you changed so much that you're now proud of your shame?"

Renford's voice bit across the table and she flinched as if his words were a whip. He stared at her hands where they rested on the table. One was still ungloved, the black vines almost indistinguishable from the pattern of her gloves. She must have forgotten to put it back on.

She should put it back on. Renford would be pleased if she did. He liked to pretend she wasn't a monster.

His shoulders relaxed as she tugged the glove on, but she felt no relief. He rested his palms on the table, his fingers twitching as if itching to take her hands in his as he stared across the table at her.

"I'm sorry their deaths pain you," he said at last. "You know I couldn't allow them to live. I have my duty. I must protect my people. If you're honest with yourself, you know you'll see that what I did was right. Your brother-"

"Don't. Please, Renford. Don't."

"I never wanted to bring you distress. I would have kept them safe if you let me. You know that, don't you?"

Safe. If they had stayed in the palace, they would have been safe. Monsters, but safe.

"This is your fault, Sarilla. You knew what would happen when you left."

"I didn't go willingly," she said, the need to placate him pouring out of her on instinct. "Rysen-"

"Don't lie to me. I saw you in the Deadwood. You could have come back. You know I hate it when you lie to me."

Hot tears spilt down her cheeks. She couldn't stop them. She tried wiping them away, but they kept flowing.

Renford's gaze tracked her gloved hand as she swiped at them, a wariness there that had never used to be so strong.

"You can't hide from what you are," he said, his voice low. "You're an abomination, one that's only here because I was too weak to do what was needed. I should have had the strength to dispose of the memoria threat before your mother ever had you."

"So you killed them?"

Her voice broke and she reached for the alcohol again, not caring about the way Renford watched her as she poured the liquid down her throat.

"You left me no choice when you left. I had to protect my people. You're a danger to them."

Lya and Rysen danced before her eyes, the ropes about their necks creaking and groaning as the wind rushed through the streets. Pain shot through her and she fought the memory down. Another rose in its place. Rysen. His hand clenched about the neck of the wagon driver as he pilfered from the man's mind.

Renford was right. They were a danger to his people.

She tried to force the memories away, needing to escape the pain, but every word Renford spoke dragged her back. He clutched her hands in his, drawing them to him and holding them to his chest as he stroked her gloved fingers with the pad of his thumb. Lifting his gaze to meet hers, he raised her hands to his lips and kissed them, his dark brown eyes glinting gold in the candlelight.

He had killed them. He had ordered them put to death. He was guilty of murdering them, but unlike her hands, his didn't carry the marks of his crimes, tallying them for all to see.

Monster. Just like Rysen and Lya.

Renford wasn't. He was their saviour.

"I could have protected you from this if you had only stayed in the palace."

But she had tried to. She had begged Rysen, even gone so far as to inform Renford that her father had returned illegally from his exile. She would have done far worse to keep her family safe and Rysen knew it, that was why he had never been able to trust her since. He would never be able to trust her again now.

She had tried to resist the allure of freedom. She had kept fighting, but once Rysen had managed to get her out the palace, she couldn't fight anymore. Redemption was too tantalising to resist and a cage confines as much as it protects. Freedom was her chance to not be what Renford forced her to be.

What Rysen and Lya had died as.

"Sarilla?"

She dragged her gaze up to meet his, struggling to recall what he asked her. Her memories were usually clear as the sky on a summer's day, but they were now riddled with holes. Whole segments of time passed by without her noticing. Good. The alcohol was setting in. Oblivion was coming for her.

"That was you, wasn't it? On the road when the blackvine attacked? Were you trying to get back to me?"

Lie. Lie, Sarilla. Everybody lies so tell him what he wants to hear.

She forced her eyes shut to stop the tears, but still they tumbled down her cheeks. She flinched as Renford reached up and smoothed them away, his fingers soft against her skin. Unable to stop herself, she leaned into his touch. It didn't matter that he hated her. He loved her too. Renford was the only one left who loved her.

She hated how much she needed him. The half-uncle who was more of a father than hers ever had been. Ever could be now.

He was her moral compass. Her persecutor and

defender all rolled into one. He condemned her in one breath and ordered her to be what he hated in the next.

"I couldn't let them go. I'm sorry, but they sealed their fates when they left my protection. Valrora is dangerous enough without memoria loosed upon it."

"And me?"

Her voice cracked. It sounded wrong. Unnatural. Monstrous. Had she really just spoken?

Pain rippled across Renford's face as he stared at her, his expressions as honest as always. He couldn't even bring his face to lie to her.

"What would you have me do?" he asked, lowering her hand to the table, still clasping it in his own.

"I can't free you. I can't lose you on my people again. I already have enough guilt on my shoulders from the havoc your brother wrought while he was free, so I cannot let you go, but nor will I repeat the mistake I made when I let your mother live all those years ago. My father's mistake when he let your grandmother live."

Renford's father. Her grandfather. The long-dead king she had never met, but who had caused her so much suffering by bringing her grandmother to the palace in the first place.

"You're the near spit of her, just as your mother was. I see that, yet still I can't stop myself from making the same mistakes my father did. His weakness flows through me."

He stroked her glove, his gaze boring through the dirty leather. It was a far cry from the beautiful gift he had presented her with.

He released her and she pulled her hand back, lowering it beneath the table. He trailed his fingers along the tabletop, drumming a light rhythm, like the creaking of a strained rope.

"Your marks have spread since Dranta."

She clenched her hands under the table, hating herself for still caring what he thought of her. Renford had killed her family. She shouldn't care about anything he thought ever again.

"I always thought my father's failing was letting that monster into his bed, but I was wrong. There are more ways to drive a person insane than by stealing their memories. History will remember me as the second fool king driven to madness by his memoria."

His words triggered memories to surge up and she welcomed them since they forced out the images of Rysen and Lya. They had belonged to her mother, just a fraction of those she had pushed the memories into Sarilla before she died, passing on her burden before it was lost forever.

King Lucien Denvard looked much like Renford did now as he made his way into Sarilla's grandmother's bedchamber, except far more haggard, his body withering a little more with each visit to his pet memoria's bed.

Another memory rose to replace the last, this one of mother and daughter being dragged before the throne. Boy Renford sat atop it, vowing revenge for his father, who had died when too many of his memories had been stolen from him, leaving him too dazed and confused to avoid falling to his death on the palace steps.

Renford had ordered Sarilla's grandmother to be executed, but he had spared his half-sister, staying his hand in an act of mercy that had doomed thousands.

It wasn't love. Not then. That came later. Though he fought against it, determined not to succumb to the same weakness as his father, he couldn't help but care for her. Still, the lesson of his father taught him enough to keep his distance. Though he allowed himself to use her ability for his own ends, he never permitted himself to touch her.

More memories flickered through Sarilla's vision, each

showing how Renford's disgust had grown over the years in response to the extent of the marks consuming his half-sister's body. Perhaps that was why his affections had been so easily transferred to his niece instead, to a woman who looked like the one he loved, but who didn't yet bear any evidence of her crimes.

Opening the curtain, Renford gestured to his guards.

"Bind her hands and get her out of here."

One of the men grabbed Sarilla's gloved wrists and wrenched her up, forcing them behind her back. She grimaced, pain shooting through her still-healing wrists as he secured heavy chains about them.

Lya and Rysen had worn similar chains. They must have weighed them down as the rope tightened about their necks.

No. Don't think about that. Focus on the darkness. It swarmed her mind in alcohol-fuelled waves and she welcomed it-

"Sir?"

The familiar voice dragged her back, forcing the darkness away. Falon, Havric and Cedral stood in the doorway, their backs to the night, each of them dressed like they were part of the king's army. What were they doing? They shouldn't be there. Were they trying to dance the dead man's jig too?

"There's an uprising on the lower levels, Your Majesty," Falon said as she stared at him. "You should seek refuge while it's quashed. We'll ensure your prisoner is escorted to the dungeons."

"Another one?" Renford sighed. "Very well. Tranten, take half your men and go with them. I will wait here while you bring back more guards. Be sure to ensure she reaches the cells."

Falon and Havric exchanged a quick glance before

studying the guard assigned to them. Had they hoped they could trick Renford into giving her up?

Renford waved them away, and Falon grabbed Sarilla's arm. He led her out of the tavern as Havric and Cedral hurried along the rope bridge ahead, six guards encircling their group. Falon gripped the hilt of his blade, readying himself to-

"Hold a moment, Falon," Renford called from behind them, his voice filled with amusement as Falon's grip tightened on Sarilla's arm.

By some unspoken command, the guards around them turned, their weapons drawn and levelled at Sarilla, Falon, Havric and Cedral.

"Did you think you could just take her from me?" Renford asked, his cruel laugh stabbing through the air. "That I wouldn't recognise Arvendon's bastard? Oh Falon... Of course you don't remember our meeting. Sarilla made quite sure of that, didn't you, my pet?"

Falon's grip tensed on her arm, but she couldn't turn about to face him.

Everybody lies.

He hated her. She was a monster. She had always been one. She would always be one and he would hate her now for sure.

"How strange," Renford said, laughing to himself. "Half a year and half a country away, yet here we are again. The king, the memoria and the traitor. And with you once again trying to steal my memoria from me. How little things change. Just think, it was your memories that brought me to Arvendon in the first place. What irony indeed."

"Sarilla? What's he talking about?" Falon asked without looking at her.

She couldn't look at him. The betrayal in his voice hurt

too much already. She couldn't stand to see it written across his face too.

"Is that why you came here, my dear? You ran straight into the arms of your lover, hoping to rekindle what you emptied his mind of? I once promised I wouldn't kill you, Falon." Renford stepped between his guards, closing the distance between them of a bold man who didn't fear the rats he had managed to trap. "I'll abide by my vow since I am a just king, no matter what my subjects say of me, but I cannot give you a clean slate like last time. Sarilla took your memories, but apparently your betrayal runs too deeply rooted for that method to work. Instead, I will give you a chance of redemption. You can either rot in my dungeons or you can join me. I require a Lord of Arvendon who can quell the unrest. The allegiance of the son is just what I need. Serve me and you'll get what you've always wanted."

"And what of my memories?" Falon asked, his voice cold and filled with hate. Just the way it should be. She was too monstrous for his love.

"You'll have to earn those. Redeem your family's name first. Prove your loyalties and I will consider ordering your memories returned to you."

Renford's lips curled in a cruel, mocking twist Sarilla knew Falon couldn't understand. His word was his vow, it always had been, which was why he always chose his words too carefully. Falon would never get his memories back. Renford had hated him from the moment he discovered that Sarilla was in love with him. The promise she had extracted concerning his sparing Falon's life had been a reluctant one, but her wording had been so careful. Too careful. He couldn't break it now.

"Will you follow me? I'll spare the lives of your friends too if you do."

Falon's fingers flexed and Sarilla wished he would reach for his sword. He could end it there. Drive the knife the rest of the way home into her chest, but he nodded instead.

"Then your first duty is to take my memoria to the dungeons. I leave for Oresa in four days and will know what to do with her by then. Tranten, lead the way."

As the guards started moving about them, Falon dragged her down the footbridge by her chain. She stumbled on the uneven planks. Although he flinched each time she tripped, he refused to help her.

Houses. Footbridges. Soldiers, both alive and dead. Bodies. She passed them all as he led her into the bellows of the city. None of it registered.

The soldiers outside the barracks stilled as they approached. They stared as she was led past them and made the sign of the Gods in fear. She might have laughed at their reactions if she had been able to hold on to the thought for long enough.

She truly was a monster of their nightmares. Bound and broken. A beast content to curl up and die in whatever pit they led her into.

A cell door wailed open and Falon marched her inside. He tethered her chains to the back wall and locked the door on his way out. Cedral and Havric watched her from the other side of the bars. Renford too, his face half-hidden in shadows.

"I'm going to rid the world of memori, Sarilla," he said. "In so doing, you can trust that I will set you free from all of this."

He left. As did they all. Only Havric lingered by the bars. He watched her, confusion and hurt warring in his eyes. Then he left too, and oblivion finally dragged her under.

CHAPTER FIFTEEN

Her father's dangling body swam through her mind and she fixated on the sight. Better to focus on him than on any of the other horrors that kept invading her vision. It was the best way to distract herself from the image of the others.

His neck mottled with purple and blue lines like Rysen's had been.

No. Don't think about Rysen.

His face had been so pale, but Rysen always used to be so tanned.

No. Don't think about that.

Focus on the venom in Falon's eyes. His sneer. Remember that. Better that than Lya's slight figure. She was a child. Not a true monster. No child could be that.

Memories festered inside Sarilla, corrupting her mind, forcing her to watch them play out in gory detail.

Water dripped just out of sight and she tried to fixate on it. To empty her mind and focus on the sound.

Drip. Lya's tangled hair wafting in the breeze, so mockingly alive.

Drip. Falon's face as he lied to her.

Drip. Her mother's eyes, maddened by the corruption staining her skin.

Drip. Rysen. Where was his laughter now?

Drip. Drip. Drip.

No!

She had to drown the sound out. She thought she screamed. She needed to stop from hearing the unstoppable drips!

Her throat ached. From her screaming? Had she screamed? Or did it ache because she hadn't drunk anything in…

How long? Did it matter?

No. Why would it matter? Nothing mattered anymore. They were dead.

Lya's white hair had snagged, snarling in the rope's knot. It looked painful. Had she screamed? Had they laughed? Had they made Rysen watch? Had they mocked him as he struggled to get free, even to the last? Unwilling to give up, even at the end.

Who had they killed first? Together, perhaps? Or was that too much to hope for?

Her father would have been last. Renford would have seen to that. He hated the man who had found love in her mother's arms more than he ever could her children.

Good. Her father got what he deserved for siring memoria half-breeds.

Her chains strung her arms out behind her painfully. The odd angle prevented her from sleeping. Oblivion too had abandoned her, it seemed.

She deserved this. This was penitence for her crimes. For not being able to save them.

She had failed them. She should have fought harder. Should have been better. Done better.

Her manacles chaffed. They bit into her already damaged skin, tearing open the scabs only just forming on her wrists.

Good. That was good. Focus on the pain.

Metal against flesh. Which gives first?

Rub. Rub. Rub. Crack and weep.

Flesh. Flesh gave first. She could feel the pus drying. It stuck to the metal, ripping the wounds open again every time she moved.

Pain. Penitence was pain.

Her guards heckled through the bars, taunting her, but they never stepped inside. Were they afraid? She was a monster. They were right to stay away.

They should let her die. Thirst. Hunger. Slowly rotting away. It hardly mattered which. At least she would die, eventually. One way or another.

She couldn't move. Warm liquid trickled down her leg. It pooled in her boots.

Shame. Suffering. Penitence. Was this atonement?

She kicked off her boots. She couldn't remember why.

The Gods would judge her fairly. They would see that she was a monster. They all were. That was why they had been killed.

She would be condemned. They would all be condemned.

Water trickled down the wall and mixed with her urine on the floor. It was dark enough that she could have pretended it was only water down there if she cared enough to try.

Cold. Wet. Rotting.

Rotting. She was rotting with them. The family that sins together, rots together.

Numb. That's what she wanted to be.

Her feet were numb. Were they still there, or had they

rotted away entirely? They were a message from the Gods. She couldn't outrun her fate.

No. Still there. White, wrinkled wretches, but still there. They resembled snake skins, but where was the snake now? You should always be wary of the snake. It could bite you at any time. Best to kill it before it had the chance.

The guards should add that to the litany of taunts they assailed her with as they baited her like a mangy dog. Idiots. She was no dog. Her crimes proved it.

They hounded her with taunts about her family. Her failure. She should have swung with them.

This was right too, though. This was better.

This way, she didn't have to watch them slowly rotting beside her. All dangling in a row.

She was glad of anything that meant she didn't have to see them again. They dogged her as it was. How much worse would it be to see them in death too as she swung beside them?

She hated the sight of them. Hated Rysen's hands, how they were covered in the evidence of his crimes. Even Lya's fingertips betrayed her guilt.

Her family deserved this. No. They deserved worse. They escaped lightly for their crimes. Their father most of all since he had brought this upon them.

They should have been made to suffer for what they had done. What she had done. What they were.

Renford had been merciful. They deserved to die.

The realisation chased away hope. Hope never amounted to anything, anyway.

The world would be better off without her. Living only inflicted pain on others.

One emotion stayed with her as the others fled. One rooted too deeply to be cut out by knives or ground down by stone. It snaked through her in coils of writhing blackness, filling the emptiness left behind when all hope had died, suffusing her body and mind so love and hope could never return.

She accepted the darkness. That was what it had always been waiting for her to do.

Rysen and Lya had been filled with the same darkness, so death would have come for them sooner or later. Monsters weren't pets. The Gods couldn't let them live. They needed to be destroyed and their deaths were a promise. A promise that the Gods wouldn't suffer her to live for much longer either. They would set her free soon.

Soon.

Footsteps.

Not the guards. She recognised those sounds. They feared her. Feared to get close.

Her saviour? Had he come to set her free?

He would free her, then he would free her people. He had promised her. He said he would come for her in four days. He was many things, but never a liar. Never that. Not like her. His word was his law and he had promised her.

Four days. Four days paying for her crimes. Four days of suffering. He had promised her and he had come to deliver.

Footsteps. Yes, different from the guards. Lighter. Unburdened by heavy armour that clanked with their every step. This new pair marched with determination. Not with fear.

He would set her free. Was she ready? Did it matter? The Gods never let their victims decide if they were ready. Death came when death came and hers was here now.

Had Lya been ready?

Had Rysen?

Had her mother?

Had her father?

No. She wasn't ready, but death was here for her anyway, come to set her free.

No.

Falon stood before her cell. His sword was drawn. Yes. Good. Not Renford then, but Falon. He had come to slay the monster. That was better.

She was ready now.

What was the point of living when all it brought was death?

Do you hate her yet? I know you don't, but you should. She has seduced you with her desperation to disprove herself the monster the world thinks her.

Perhaps you even pity her. The snake that hatched among the goose eggs. You think it's the Gods' fault for cursing her so, for dealing her a hand she could never win.

Like the darkness that wrapped around what counted for her heart, she has wormed her way inside you. Without even touching you, she has made you forget what she is capable of.

Where you should feel contempt, you feel compassion. Her struggles have blinded you to her true nature, but I advise that you look beyond her crimes. See to the hatred within. That's where you will find the darkness.

I was blind to what she was once too. For that, I have lived with my guilt ever since.

She is the beast who broke a thousand minds. The pillager of thoughts and feelings from innocent and guilty alike. The snake that filed down her fangs and curbed her appetite for goose flesh, all so she might bide her time among the meek.

But incarceration isn't the path to redemption, and a snake untested by temptation cannot be forgiven. What value has a lifetime's resistance if there was never the opportunity to fail?

No, redemption is a lifelong plight. I should know. It is filled with stumbles and failures. It haunts you until the end of your days and all you can do is pray for resilience enough to endure it.

I have striven for years for redemption, both from my failures in life and those of my birth. A bastard must always earn forgiveness for the sins of the father, so if anyone knows the burden of redemption, it is I, not her.

As I stood there in the dungeon, staring at the filthy beast chained before me, I saw only the memoria I thought she was. One with eyes so black they hid the true darkness within. But despite everything I knew that she had done, some part of me still wanted to save her. To rescue the girl who struggled for redemption and sought forgiveness for the crime of her birth.

Even knowing what she did to me, how she had destroyed my family, used and manipulated me, stolen from and lied to me, even then, I still couldn't hate her. Like you, I pitied the snake that was relieved to be caged and contained. The memoria who hated the darkness within. I thought there must be some good buried deep inside her since I had loved her once.

How wrong I was.

Perhaps you will decide that she earned her redemption, but I think not. Just remember, monsters are made as frequently as they are born, so perhaps you will not look so favourably on me either by the time this tale is through.

CHAPTER SIXTEEN

As I stared back at her through the bars, I wondered how I ever could have forgotten the sight of those eyes. They absorbed the darkness as it permeated the dungeon, making them appear all the blacker for it.

What else had she taken from me? What other memories had she made me forget?

The stench from inside her cell crawled across my skin. Good. Memoria should live in their filth. She was too adept at disguising her true nature, and I was glad of any reminder of what she was. I had fallen for her act twice now, but never again.

Her hair stuck to her face, darkened by days' worth of dirt. The muck hid the memori in her, making her pretence of being a victim that much more believable. With the marks on her hands concealed behind her back, it was all too easy to believe her to be the guilt-ridden girl she pretended she was, but I couldn't be tricked again.

To think that I had once felt sorry for her. This destroyer of identity and certainty. I had watched her bear a kingdom's hatred, believing that she strove for redemption like I did, seeking forgiveness for the crime of her birth. In my eagerness, I had lost sight of the monster, ignoring the evidence of the corruption within her.

No, that was wrong. She wasn't corrupt. She needed at least a grain of goodness inside her in the first place for that. She was born a creature of pillage and plunder. Even without my memories, I was a fool indeed for forgetting that.

Gall churned my stomach like someone had taken a hot poker to my gut and left me to fester. She had known who I was the entire time. Likely knew me better than I did myself. Who I cared about. What I hoped for. I was an open book to her.

I would have searched the world for my memories if I had to. That was how all-consuming the emptiness inside me was. She had known that, yet still she taunted me, flaunting her blackened hands. For that alone, I would make her pay.

Ced had known not to trust her, so why had I been so eager to believe her lies? Was it some lingering effect of whatever had once been between us? No. I couldn't believe that. Didn't want to believe it.

She opened her mouth to speak, but only a rasp escaped her. Gone was all the sweetness from her liar's tongue. Good. It was easier to know her half-truths for the lies they were without it.

She cleared her throat, wetting her pale, cracked lips before trying again. She looked so frail, as if the act of speaking would steal all the strength still in her, but thinking that was to forget the deceit that lurked within.

"Is it time?" she asked as she swayed, the wall and the chains all that held her upright.

Time for her to return my memories to me? It was long past time for that.

"Why did you do it?"

She shut her eyes, unable to hold my stare. I flinched, needing for her to open them again. She looked too normal like that, too little like the monster she was. I had to see her eyes again so I wouldn't forget.

I could force them open, peel back her eyelids until she had to meet my gaze. I could make her look at me and demand an explanation for why she had done this.

I shoved the key into the lock and wrenched the door open. Water dripped from above. It trickled down the back of my neck as I stepped into the cell, my boots splashing in the puddles and announcing my approach. Still, she kept her eyes shut. Metal clanked as I untethered her manacles, yet she didn't look at me. It was only as I hauled her up by her restraints that her eyelids cracked open.

Finally.

Black. Black like her heart. Black like my stolen memories that were stored somewhere in her hands.

If not for the guards watching us, I would have wrapped the manacles about her neck and choked her until she returned my memories to me. Could I force them out of her? I wanted them back, but did I dare risk losing the rest in the process? Who knew what she would take from me if I gave her half a chance.

"Time to go," I said instead, gesturing towards the cell door, but she stayed where she was. "You can move or I can drag you."

I expected her to resist. To fight back as she always had before, but there was nothing, not even a spark of resistance as she took a stumbling step forward, her legs giving out beneath her as she splashed to the floor.

I didn't catch her. Instead, I fought back the instinct to help. She deserved none of my pity.

She pushed herself unsteadily back up and made her

way out of the cell. I followed behind, trying to ignore each time she tripped, faltering like a newborn foal. I wouldn't help her. She was dangerous. I had to remember that.

The guards flanked us as I hurried her on. They had become rather adept at following me over the last few days, barely leaving my side as I made my way about Arvendon, trying to repair what damage I could to the city my father had built from nothing. His body no longer hung from the rope-bridge outside, so in that at least I had made progress.

We climbed the arduous steps to what had, until recently, been his home. It was the king's now. At least until he continued his campaign east. His soldiers patrolled the corridors. His advisers occupied the rooms, filling them with their maps and their reports. Everywhere you looked, you couldn't escape the evidence of the forthcoming invasion. Nor the scars of what had already been destroyed. All the paintings of my family had been used for kindling, the walls stripped as bare as my mind had been without the memories she took from me.

The king said it was so I might start afresh as the new Lord of Arvendon. That's what I was, after all, but the title rang hollow, even though I had yet to dare speak it aloud. For so many years, I had longed for it, hoped to stand in my father's stead when that day came. Now it was mine I realised why he had never legitimised me, even though he had no other children to speak of. I was born a bastard, and a bastard was all I would ever be. A true son wouldn't have fled in the night. I should have stayed by my father's side, instead I had gone in search of my memories and now he was dead.

The ascent out of the dungeons was laborious since she looked like she might collapse at any moment, but we eventually made it. The guards outside the throne-room doors parted to let us pass. The king was deep in

155

discussions with his advisers as they outlined their plans for the army's imminent departure for Oresa.

The sooner they left, the better. Arvendon was already a shadow of itself. Every day the army lingered in our walls was another day closer to starvation. Most of the stores were already empty, and it didn't look like the king would leave much behind when he departed. Perhaps it was a good thing half the city's populace was dangling from a rope-bridge. There were no crops left to harvest and hanging was a faster death.

An expectant hush fell over the ballroom as the king spotted us. He motioned for his advisers to be silent and waved us forward. My skin crawled at how his gaze never left her as we approached.

Everyone in the room watched us. Their hostility threw me. I had caused a great many reactions over the years, but never that. It was a moment before I realised it wasn't my arrival that had triggered it, but hers.

My stepmother always hated me, the evidence of her inability to conceive, but not even she had looked upon me as the crisis, catalyst and downfall all rolled into one. Was that the expression on my face each time I looked at the memori who had stolen my memories from me?

Only King Renford looked upon his pet with an emotion other than contempt. Apparently, I wasn't alone in my struggles. There was another who found it difficult to remember what she was.

Noses wrinkled as we approached the king. Whether from her smell or her presence, it was hard to tell. Both were foul, yet only one made me want to gag.

Some nobles I passed were familiar to me, but not many. None of those who had been close to my father were in the ballroom. They were still dangling on the rope-bridges outside.

Her bare feet squelched on the tiles as she stumbled through the room, water seeping down her sodden body. She was still so wet that when she stopped before the king that a puddle began to form on the floor. Her chains jangled as she shivered. She had to be half-frozen.

I forced away the pity trying to build inside me. I had to remember what she was.

"My good people of Arvendon," the king said, never taking his gaze from her. "Might I present my memoria to you all."

Everyone stared at her, their accusation piercing dagger-like through the air.

"Will you string me up beside them?" she asked, her voice rasping through the room.

It took me a moment to understand her meaning. Kill her? Is that what she thought was going to happen? Oh no. She wasn't dying with my memories still inside her. She wouldn't get to escape until I had what I was due.

The king watched her, his expression inscrutable. Unease filled me as I studied him, this man who knew about parts of my life that I didn't even know myself. Of all those months I had no recollection of. If not everything, he at least knew something of my time in Dranta. What sort of advantage did that give him? I recalled nothing of my time in the capital. I didn't even remember my father ordering me there to kill the king, though I remembered his disappointment upon my failed return well enough.

"String you up?" the king asked. "Is that what you want? If it's death you seek, there's a quicker way about it."

He nodded at the guard beside him, the one with a cruel scar twisting his mouth. The man withdrew his sword and the steel rang as it cleared the scabbard.

My hand gripped the hilt of my bastard blade before I knew what I was doing.

"No-one goes near her," I said, my voice echoing off the walls of the ballroom as I stared down the guard, moving to stand before her.

"You would draw your weapon in my presence?" the king asked, his voice so calm that it caused the hairs on my neck to prickle. "Is this the loyalty I'm to expect from my new Lord of Arvendon?"

Loyalty. There wasn't a single person in the ballroom who expected me to give the king that after what he had done to my father. He was toying with me in giving me my father's title, and everyone knew it.

"She doesn't die until I get my memories back," I said, Ced's voice ringing through my head, telling me that I had revealed my hand too early. Too publicly. Now they all knew my motivation, but concealment had never been my forte. Unlike his. Unlike hers.

The king leaned forward in his seat as he studied me. "Look at you, barking at any threat, supposed or otherwise. But you forget your place, dog. I shall do exactly what I wish with her." His eyes flashed with challenge and I forced down the urge to fight back as he asked, "You would protect her after everything she has done? After everything she's taken from you?"

"I'll do what I have to for as long as she has my memories."

The king's mouth curved in a sharp sneer, his gaze passing between me and his pet. "Is that why? Not out of love then?"

I flinched. Not love. Never that. Surely I was never so taken in by her?

The king's weighty stare turned from me to his pet.

"And what of you? Where are your loyalties now? My father's blood runs in you, at least as much as does the blood of the creature that destroyed him. If I offered you a chance of redemption for what you are, would you take it?"

A small frown formed on her brow as confusion filled her eyes.

"I'm not afraid to die."

"Who said anything about your dying? What I wish for is your help. Help me destroy the memori in Oresa and you'll have your redemption."

Did he mean it? He had said as much before, but I still couldn't believe it. It was what my father had wanted the king to do all along. If he had done it sooner, then my father wouldn't have sent me to Dranta to assassinate the king in the first place. In which case, my memories would never have been stolen and my father would still be alive.

I stared at her, waiting for her answer. The memori needed to be destroyed. She was just one and yet look how much devastation she had wrought.

She swayed, her body seeming all the frailer in the brightly lit ballroom and with everyone's gaze fixed on her.

She nodded, but I didn't know whether to feel relief or not.

"Then we leave within the hour," the king said, turning back to me, a smile on his face that filled me with unease. "See to it that she's made ready for the journey."

"Me?"

"If you insist on being her guard dog, then you can be her maid too. Tranten."

The king waved forwards the man with the mutilated face as I held back my treasonous comments. "Take two men and go with them," he said. "I don't want them getting lost."

Only too happy to be out of the king's presence, I retraced the wet footprints across the ballroom floor, Tranten and the other guards following behind us. The

159

manor was bustling as I led her away, shouting out orders
to a servant as she passed. The girl bowed, racing off to
attend to me as we continued upstairs. Arvendon's bastard
was afforded that much respect, at least.

I took my charge to the only place I could think of
where I might find suitable attire for her in the short time
we had before the army was due to set off. My stepmother
would be cursing me were she still alive for taking a
memoria to her rooms. The thought improved my mood
somewhat.

When we arrived, I dragged my charge to the tub behind
the divider. She didn't protest as I cut away her soiled
clothes with my dagger, dumping the ruined garments on
the ground. I left her hands bound and gloved behind her
back, not wanting to see the marks again, even though they
would remind me of what she was. The sight of my
memories would only rile me up, and I was already angry
enough with her. I kept my eyes averted as she swayed
weakly before me, still somehow remaining standing
despite how frail she was from her stay in the dungeon.

A servant teetered into the room, her arms straining
from the steaming bucket of water she carried. She slowed
as she stared at the naked memoria in the tub, the bucket
shaking and beginning to splash as I grabbed it from her,
sending her to fetch another. As she scurried from the
room, I upended the contents over my charge's head and
she shook from the force of it. She looked ready to topple
over, so I urged her to sit in the murky pool at her feet.

Another servant arrived and others followed after, each
carrying another bucket. One also brought a tray holding a
loaf of bread and a tumbler of water. She set it down on a
stool quickly before hurrying back out the door.

I poured a cup and tried to hand it to the memoria in
my care, but she refused to take it, her black eyes fixed on

mine, her expression unreadable. I placed the cup against her lips, but she only stared back at me, the water trickling from her closed lips and mixing with the filthy liquid in the tub. The cup was almost empty when she parted her mouth. She choked, her frail body wracking from the exertion. When she regained control, I tipped a little more water down her throat, flinching at the sound of Ced's voice as he mocked the king's guards where they waited outside the chamber.

I stood quickly, backing away from her, biting back a curse as I tried to distance myself from the tub before my friends entered the room. I didn't want them to see me at Sarilla's mercy again.

CHAPTER SEVENTEEN

Ced barely spared her a glance before throwing himself onto the bed. The mattress bounced, creaking unhappily under his weight as his dagger swung awkwardly at his side. Why he still carried it, I didn't know, he barely used it for scraping the dirt from under his fingernails.

"She's still alive then?"

"Cedral." Havric scowled as he shut the door, but Ced just shrugged, crossing his boots on what had once been the finest sheets my father could buy his demanding bride.

I smiled. Ced would have done the same if my stepmother was still alive, that was just how he was and he made no apologies for his actions. It was both the greatest and worst part of him. What had drawn me to him and what had driven me away.

"I was just saying-"

"I don't want to hear it," Havric said. "I've already listened to you going on about her for longer than anyone sane would have."

Ignoring Havric, Ced turned my way and asked, "Why are you up here, anyway? Trying to make her look nice for the executioner?" He grinned at Sarilla, his top lip curling mockingly as she hugged her arms tighter about her legs. "Your family's been looking real pretty since a crow pecked their eyes out."

I started to say something to get him to stop attacking her, but I caught myself just in time. Why was I still trying to protect her? She deserved the worst Ced could sling her way and more.

"The king isn't executing her," I said instead, moving through the room in search of anything Sarilla might use to dry herself.

"He already knows that," Havric said wearily. "We were watching from the back of the ballroom."

"Apparently being the Lord of Lanlethe still merits some modicum of respect," Ced muttered. "Why has he got you looking after her? Is he hoping you'll get angry enough to see her off for him?"

It wasn't the most unlikely notion Ced had ever come up with. The king was far from being above tormenting those under his rule, and he didn't seem capable of killing her himself. Maybe he was hoping I would do it for him.

"She wouldn't have made it far in the state she was in," I said, the excuse ringing hollow even in my ears.

"So? Why are you doing it? Beastie here isn't your concern."

"She is as long as she has my memories."

"Falon-"

"No. I don't want to hear it. I need her alive. A rotting corpse is no use to anyone. Besides, I'm not letting her out of my sight until I get my memories back, so you can either help me or return to whatever tavern you just dragged yourself out of."

Havric snorted as Ced looked as if he was about to try to defend himself. Before he could argue Havric said, "I suppose that means you're joining the army in their march east?"

"Wherever she goes, I go."

"They're almost ready to leave. I'll fetch your pack and meet you down by the gates when I'm ready too."

"You don't have to come."

"If the alternative is staying here and receiving another ear lashing by ma, then I really do. Come on, Cedral. Unless you're staying in Arvendon?"

"Falon?" Ced asked, raising his hesitant gaze to meet mine.

"I don't care what you do," I said, slinging a towel over my shoulder and turning my back on him. He followed Havric out and I sighed when they were gone. How had Ced and I gone from once being so comfortable in each other's presence to this?

Sarilla shivered and I glanced over at her, reluctant to get close to her again. Letting her freeze to death in the tub would hardly help me get my memories back though, so I made my way over to her.

She swayed as I helped her stand, upending the last bucket over her to clean away the remaining muck. She shook from the force of the water, her hair shimmering silver in the dim light as she fought to remain upright. I focused on the black roots, fighting to keep my gaze from lowering to the watery sheen on her skin. There was nowhere good those thoughts would lead me.

Using the towel, I covered her up before trying to get her to climb out the tub. She almost fell in the attempt and I was forced to lift her out, moving carefully so I didn't touch her any more than I had to. I was wary now I knew the sear of her bite. She weighed less than she had only a few days ago. Worryingly less. Her bones practically protruded through the towel.

Why did I care? Had she spared any concern for me when she starved me of my memories?

I carried her to the bed, trying to focus on anything other than the almost naked woman in my arms and the arousal between my legs. I told myself it was just a bodily reaction, completely unconnected to reason – just like how my groin kept overruling my head wherever Ced was concerned. Apparently, I was attracted to the deceptive type.

In need of a distraction from her, I made my way over to my stepmother's wardrobe and rooted inside, hunting for clothes that would fit Sarilla. Havric was far better suited to that sort of task than I was. Having grown up with four sisters and a houseful of whores, he had more than a few stories about the art of feminine dressing.

As I rifled through the wardrobe, I was reminded of just how excessive my stepmother's tastes had been. Silks. Crushed velvets. Several fabrics I didn't know how to describe, all were folded within, most barely worn and wholly unsuitable for the task of accompanying an army to war. Eventually, I found a riding outfit I hoped would fit Sarilla well enough for the journey. It looked new, but that was unsurprising since I couldn't remember seeing my stepmother within ten feet of a horse, let alone atop one. Only those who travelled or dwelt on Arvendon's lower levels rode horses, and my stepmother had likely never been below the fifth elevation in her life.

The leather was supple and simply designed, no doubt another reason for its disuse. I held it out to Sarilla, but she didn't take it from me, instead motioning to where her arms were still manacled behind her back.

"You'll have to unlock them eventually unless you intend that I wear a towel for the journey."

"It would be no worse than you deserve," I muttered,

grabbing her hands and stabbing the key into the lock.

It clicked open and the manacles fell to the floor with a clunk as Sarilla stretched, groaning as her body emitted several loud cracks, her muscles righting themselves. The towel slipped a little and I looked away hastily as she pulled it back up.

I muttered a curse to the Gods for whatever game they were playing. Black eyes. Just keep focusing on that and don't let yourself forget again.

She reached for her gloves and pried them off, never taking her eyes off me as she dropped them to the floor. I tensed, unable to look away from the marks branching across her hands and arms. Which of them were mine? What part of the stain on her flesh was the evidence of what she had stolen from me? It was so much worse to see them now, knowing that they contained the missing part of me.

She made her stumbling way back to the tub and swished her hands in the water. Although she cleaned off days' worth of grime, she needn't have bothered since her hands were no less black for it. As she dried herself, I turned my back on her, searching in the cabinets for a new pair of gloves since the last had begun to reek. Even if I trusted her to not use her ability, which I didn't, there was still no way the king would let her travel with her hands uncovered. The sight alone would incite fear among the soldiers.

There were two satisfactory pairs of gloves in the cabinet. Both were sturdy enough for the march east, but one was elbow length and the other cut off just above the wrists. It was too short to completely hide her marks, reminding us all of what she was. I knew which pair I should pick, but when she finished dressing, I gave her the elbow-length ones instead, cursing myself for the fool I was as I made my way over to the tray the servant had brought.

At the rate the army was eating through Arvendon's supplies, a loaf was practically a feast. I tried to hand her it, but she refused to take it.

"You need to eat," I said. "Unless it's death you're after, in which case, return my memories and I'll be more than happy to help."

I expected her to snap back at me. To lash out with a retort as she always had done before, but she just sat on the bed, curling into a ball as she lay down, her eyes staring at nothing.

I don't know how long I watched her for before one of the guards knocked on the door, signalling that it was almost time to go. Returning to the cabinet, I pulled out everything suitable that she might require on the journey. The options were slim, but they would have to do.

I packed the food in with the clothes in case she changed her mind later, or in case I grew frustrated enough with her disinterest in living to force the bread down her throat.

"You hate me," she said, her voice a quiet rasp that made me flinch.

Turning back around, I searched her face for any sign of guilt. An apologetic crinkle in her frown. A sorry twist to her lips. Any proof that she was more than just the product of her memori blood.

"What should I be feeling after you stole my memories? After you got my father and half of Arvendon strung up? After you could have given me my memories back at any point-"

"I couldn't."

Her words were so faint that I almost missed them. I waited for her to elaborate, but she didn't.

"That's it?" I asked. "That's all the explanation I'm to get?"

She couldn't even bring herself to bother to lie to me.

Disgust poured from me and I barely registered closing the distance between us, nor the way my hand clenched about the hilt of my bastard blade as I did. She didn't flinch, not even as I pressed the edge of the sword against her throat.

"Why couldn't you?" I asked, the rage inside me so strong that my hand shook.

"I… I can't tell you-"

"Then give them back to me! Do it and I'll grant you the death you're clearly so eager for."

Black eyes stared up at me and I wondered at the resolution filling them despite everything. She wasn't sorry. Whatever her reasons for taking my memories, it was clear she still stood by what she had done.

"Why did you do it?" I asked, letting all the pain and anger of the last few months pour out through my voice. "What did I do to deserve such a punishment?"

She didn't answer me. Eventually, I gave up waiting. Lowering my sword and cursing her to the Gods and back, I turned about, grabbing the pack from where I had dropped it before making my way towards the door to signal for the guards to come in.

"I took them because it was the only way to save your life."

Her whisper rang through the room and I turned back around. She held my gaze, her eyes blazing with a rage and pain I couldn't understand, then she pushed past me, making her unsteady way towards the door.

"Wait…" I said, scooping the manacles up from the floor.

She stopped as they clinked, her whole body shaking as

she turned back around, her black eyes pleading.

"Don't. Falon, please don't chain me up again. I'll give you my word that I won't-"

"It wouldn't matter if you did. Your word means no more than the water in that tub."

She tensed, but she didn't fight me as I locked the manacles in place, binding her gloved hands before her.

"So this is to always be my fate?" she asked, staring at the metal dragging her arms down and slumping her shoulders forward.

As it seemed it was to always be mine to be her captor.

We left the room and the king's guards fell in about us, their gazes passing hostilely over Sarilla as they kept a wary distance from her. We made our way through the manor to the grand foyer, which teemed with people as advisers and soldiers bustled back and forth, making last-minute travel arrangements and sending the servants scurrying about. Only one set of eyes drew our way in the chaos though, and a shiver passed through me as King Renford's pale blue gaze raked over Sarilla, approval flashing deep within and setting me on edge.

He waved us forward, his guards tensing as they noticed who had caught his attention.

"I've ordered a wagon be readied to transport her, it's waiting outside the city gates," the king said, speaking to me even though he didn't spare so much as a glance my way. I couldn't fault his forethought though, since Sarilla looked like she wouldn't last long atop a horse. "My guards will escort you there. I would hate for my pet and her love-sick guard dog to wander off by accident."

I took Sarilla by the manacles and led her away, the guards falling in step again, not bothering to hide their contempt for either of us. The city gates teemed with soldiers when we arrived, but the wagon was easy enough to locate. I stowed the bag I had packed for Sarilla and she climbed unsteadily up, her bound wrists making her ascent awkward. She had just managed it when Ced and Havric found us. They led four horses and I marvelled at Havric's resourcefulness. I had known he would make a good travelling companion before we had left Arvendon, but I hadn't known the full extent of it.

"Figured you would be as keen as we are to avoid another week of trekking through the forest on foot," he said, handing me one of the reins.

"I told you we wouldn't need a fourth horse though," Ced muttered as he glared at the back of the wagon.

"Except that you meant that we should drag her behind one of ours."

"You would have suggested it too if it wasn't my money you were spending."

Ced slung his pack into the wagon and it landed heavily beside Sarilla. He laughed as she flinched to avoid being hit by it.

"I forgot to congratulate you, Beastie," he said, grinning in that snide way of his that I always hated. "You're the newest member of the dead fathers club. Havric's going to start feeling left out."

"Shut up, Cedral," Havric said, catching my gaze before pulling a face that made it clear he was approaching the end of his patience as far as Ced was concerned.

"Of course, you've a dead brother and sister too," Ced continued, ignoring the warning. "Does everyone you know die, Beastie, or just the ones you care about?"

"Why don't you go sit up front and try not to piss anyone off for a bit?" Havric asked, trying to move Ced away.

Ced ignored him, his attention still fixed on Sarilla.

"Gods but you're a cold one. Did you even mourn your

family-?"

"That's enough." I shot Ced a glare, hating my needing to step in and defend her, but I couldn't stop myself. "At least she was born a monster. What's your excuse?"

His gaze fixed on me, unease flickering across his face. "Look. I don't have to be here-"

"Why are you here? I didn't ask you to come. All I asked you to do was tell me what happened that day you left me to go to Dranta alone."

Ced turned from me, a blush rising up his cheeks.

"What did he do?" I asked, rounding on Sarilla. "If you won't give me my memories back, the least you can do is tell me what I've lost."

"It's not my place-"

"Don't give me that tripe. You have no right to keep my memories from me!"

"He's trying to redeem himself. If I told you what happened, then you wouldn't be able to forgive him. Everyone deserves a chance at redemption."

"Not everyone."

I glared at her for a moment longer before the need to get away became too much.

"Watch her," I said to Havric as I mounted one of the horses and urged it through the crowd. Soldiers leapt out my way, narrowly avoiding being trampled since I barely saw them through my anger-narrowed vision.

It was a long while before I realised that I had managed to slip away before the king's guards could chase after me. Or maybe they had made the choice to stay with the memoria rather than follow the traitor.

How dare she speak of redemption? How dare she keep my memories from me and taunt me with them? She had no right to decide for me whether Ced deserved my forgiveness.

It hurt all the worse because she knew the details of everything she kept me in the dark about. She remembered every secret, every whisper, every touch. Every foolish emotion I had ever felt for her.

I rode east, making far better time than the sedentary march of the army behind me. At the rate they had to travel, it would be five days before we could clear the Deadwood.

I had only travelled that far east once before, when I accompanied my father on a visit to Alfora. We had stayed for a month-long celebration of Lord Sandeth's daughter's marriage, but the reports from Alfora since then had been far less mirthful. Less fortified than Arvendon and Dranta, it had been easy prey for the blackvine.

I might hate the king for what he had done to his people over the years, but I couldn't fault his decision to attack Oresa. I only wished he had called his banners sooner. If he had, my father might never have rebelled. I might never have gone to Dranta, and Sarilla would never have had the chance to steal my memories.

It didn't matter. I would make them both pay for what they had done.

CHAPTER EIGHTEEN

Acrid smoke choked the air as I weaved through the make-shift camp, moving between the tents and campfires as they wound down the road, stretching far beyond the bends that blocked the rest of the army from view. It wasn't tactically sound to stretch the army so thin, but since nobody wanted to venture far into the forest, it was our only option.

It would be a miracle if even half the soldiers made it out of the Deadwood. We were too far from Dranta to fear the graves, but the thought of the blackvine creeping up on us from between the trees was still enough to make frightened babes out of grown men. They seemed to be competing for who could stand the furthest from the treeline and still piss into the forest successfully. After three days on the road, there had already begun to be more than a few constipated faces among the men.

Firelight reflected in silver sheens off Sarilla's hair, guiding me through the camp towards where she and the others had settled down for the night. Someone, likely Havric, had already built up a fire. There would only be a pile of damp sticks if Ced had been placed in charge. Sarilla sat beside Havric as he tended to a pot above the fire, his attention half on the food and half on the soldiers as they flinched every time Sarilla shifted, no less at ease with her presence than they had been at the start of the march.

"Evaleon's army is still several days ride away," I said, dumping the sack of oat rations I had gone to fetch. "The talk is that their forces will join with ours outside Oresa."

"Rather a good-willed gesture from the Queen of Evaleon, don't you think?" Havric asked.

"She's got a better chance of destroying the memori with us now than waiting until the blackvine's made it west enough to pick her people off too."

Havric nodded, his attention still on Sarilla as she stared into the flames, oblivious to the hostility that rippled through the soldiers every time she moved. The guards the king had assigned to us stood nearby, staring out over the trees and the camp, as little at ease with their charge as they had been in Arvendon two days ago.

Running between the camps, a stripling of a soldier careened to a stop by our fire, his eyes bulging as he stared at Sarilla, his mouth opening and closing with no words coming out.

"What is it?" I asked.

His wide eyes flickered to me before returning to Sarilla. "The king wants her."

"That's hardly a secret," Ced muttered, kicking dirt into the fire with his heel and drawing Havric's scowl.

"Wants her for what?" I asked, ignoring him.

"Does it matter?" Tranten said, not waiting for the boy to answer before grabbing Sarilla's manacles and yanking her in the direction of the king's tent.

He weaved between the fires and the soldiers as Havric and I shared a glance.

"One of us should go with them," Havric said, starting to rise.

"Stay. I'll go. We'll have a burnt dinner if you leave either me or Ced in charge."

It was a weak excuse, but I set off after Tranten and Sarilla before he could challenge me, the silvery gleam of the fires reflecting off her hair guiding me.

Was I doomed to always be trailing after her?

I caught up as they reached the king's tent, just in time to see the soldiers nearby stiffen at Sarilla's approach, their hands moving to the hilts of their swords. Tranten swiped aside the tent flap and motioned Sarilla in before letting it drop again in my face. Ignoring the hint, I lifted the heavy fabric and followed them.

A soft-orange glow lit the tent walls, but it was broken by the shadows cast by the heavily armoured figures gathered within. The king's advisers were there, their foreheads furrowed in scowls so deep that you might plant seeds in the grooves. I couldn't see what they stared at and for a moment I thought it was Sarilla's presence that had the room gripped in so tight a vice, but then I noticed the man kneeling before the king.

I knew him. He had visited my father a few times over the years, staying with us in Arvendon. He must have been one of the nobles who travelled with the king's retinue from the capital, but it was clear that whatever privilege he once had was now ended.

He quaked, his hands clenching as he pleaded with the king. When he caught sight of me, he flinched, quickly glancing away again.

Was this the man my father had sent me to meet with in Dranta? The one who was to provide me with an introduction to the king? If he was, then perhaps he knew what had happened to me in Dranta. If I could get him alone, then maybe there was a way to discover what I had forgotten without needing to get my memories back.

"Good. You're here," the king said, gesturing Sarilla forward. "There's no point dallying. Get along with it."

My stomach twisted as I realised why the king had summoned his pet memoria. He certainly wasted no time in returning to his old ways.

Despite his command, though, Sarilla didn't move. Instead, she just stared at the kneeling man, but I doubt she saw him. She didn't even move as Tranten took the key from me and unlocked her manacles.

It was hard to tell in the light of the tent, but I thought she looked even paler than normal. I wanted to believe her as sickened by the prospect of stealing another's memories as she had always claimed to be, but as she had so often reminded me, everybody lies.

If I had killed her when I had the chance, if I hadn't been so obsessed with getting my memories back, the fate now awaiting this man at her hands might have been avoided. Sarilla might hate what she was, but the man standing idly by with a bucket as the fire rages is as much to blame for the ensuing carnage as the one who lit the flame.

Tranten tugged off one of Sarilla's gloves, his scarred lip curling in disgust as he glowered a warning at her, practically daring her to try to touch him.

He exposed the marks spreading up her arms like poison. Had they already started to corrupt her as she claimed they had her mother? It was impossible to know for certain if anything Sarilla said was true, so the best course was to assume every word she spoke was crafted for her own ends.

Sarilla met the king's stare and held it, fighting a silent battle of wills with him until something changed. The spark of resistance in her eyes died, resignation wiping all expression from her face as she reached for the man.

I waited to hear her say she was sorry, but her lips stayed shut as her fingers uncurled, hovering for a moment by his neck as he trembled, their gazes locked. Then she closed the distance and a frightened sob escaped him as Sarilla's eyes drifted close.

I didn't know what he had done, didn't know what crime had brought him to the king's attention. Whatever it was, he didn't deserve his fate. Nobody did. Sarilla wasn't just destroying the illusion of privacy, she was stealing his very identity and killing the man he had been. In that moment, it wouldn't have mattered to me if he had murdered a hundred people. Bile still rose in my stomach at the thought of what was happening to him. What had happened to me.

All this time, I had let myself believe she told the truth when she said she hated what she was, but she hadn't even tried to resist.

I ducked back out of the tent, eager to get away as I gulped down desperate mouthfuls of the fresh night air, trying to ignore the frightened whimpers behind me. The thin fabric did little to muffle the sound.

Had I acted the same? Had I let my terror show as my identity slipped from me, memory by memory.

Had Sarilla hesitated? Had she murmured her apology before touching my cheek?

When she emerged with Tranten a short time later, she kept her head down, refusing to meet my gaze as she made her way back through the camp, her wrists already gloved and rebound. It didn't matter. I no longer needed to see the marks to know her for what she was.

Tranten threw me the key before urging Sarilla along the road, weaving between the soldiers. I followed behind, sparing a glance at the tent and my fellow memory-stripped traitor within, before turning my back on him and whatever insights he might once have given me into my past.

When we reached our campfire, Sarilla sat back down in the same spot as before, her gaze fixed on the flames as Havric stirred the bubbling pot. He shot me a questioning gaze, but I didn't answer him, instead sitting in the gap Tranten seemed determined to keep between himself and Sarilla, watching her as she picked up a slightly charred stick from where it dangled out the fire at an odd angle. She prodded the logs, attacking them until bright orange pieces broke away and fell into the embers, seeming oblivious to the flames licking up the stick and reaching for her hands, almost to the point of caressing her gloves. She stared into the heart of the blaze, her eyes drinking in the firelight as Havric pried the stick from her and tossed it into the flames.

"I can't say I'm an expert on how flammable memori are, but I'm not particularly keen to find out."

Sarilla didn't protest, instead she just continued to stare into the flames, the orange light dancing in her eyes and bringing a life to them that had been absent before.

It was like she was dead inside. Had she been that way in Dranta? What for either of the Gods could have made me ever look at her with anything but disgust? She was entrancing, to be sure, with her dark lashes and captivating eyes. But flames were captivating too, yet I wasn't foolish enough to get too close to them. To touch the fire was to be burned. How then had I forgotten common sense enough to get scolded?

I was jolted out of my thoughts as Sarilla strained against the manacles. It took me a moment to recognise what she was doing.

Pain flickered across her face as she tugged off her gloves, her desperation making her hasty. She grimaced in pain, fumbling with the fabric and cursing her frustration as she struggled to slip her gloves off her hands. She looked close to weeping with relief as she eased her hands free. That was when Tranten and the other guards noticed what she had been doing.

Tranten leapt back, wrenching his sword free and yelling at her to put her glove back on, but Sarilla's gaze was fixed so intently on the fire that I doubted she heard him. Instead, she just held her hand up to the blistering heat, as if she would reach out to touch the flames for real this time.

I leapt forward, landing in a crouch before her and snatching her hand back from the fire. Her palms were already hot enough to blister and her fingers burnt mine.

"What are you doing?" I asked, staring into her eyes as they danced with firelight and tears.

"It's too much," she said, her hoarse whisper rough on the night air. "They're too much. I had to stop them."

"What are you talking about? What have you done? Sarilla, your hands…"

I stared at her palms uncomprehendingly, at her marks as they faded before my eyes.

"Ced was right," she said, the marks bubbling like an oil canvas kindling a fire. "I couldn't mourn them. Not like I should have."

"There's very little Ced's ever right about," I muttered, pulling a jar of salve out of Havric's pack and rubbing the cream on her inflamed palm.

The skin was red raw. Had she been trying to cause permanent damage?

I stilled as I realised whose hand I massaged. Panic flared in me, but I was too afraid to let go lest I reminded her of my presence.

"It hurts," she said as a tear rolled down her cheek, dripping to the ground. "Gods... it hurts."

"That tends to happen when you stick your hand in a fire," I murmured.

"Monsters aren't made to be mourned," she said, a second tear tumbling down. "They don't deserve it, but I... I needed to know that I could still feel."

Her gaze flickered to Ced as he stared back from across the fire, watching her with the same confusion as the rest of us.

Beneath my fingers, the bubbling blackness shifted, the lines reforming as the darkness spread, redistributing and filling the gaps that had formed.

"Sarilla... Your hands... What have you done?"

"I burned them away. I had to. I had to clear my head so I could mourn them, but Gods it hurts. It's too much. The pain is too much. I can't... I can't-"

"The memories," I said, realisation flooding through me on a cold wave that brought a shiver to my bones. "Which?"

I forced her to meet my gaze as I searched her eyes, fear clenching my hands around her injured ones, but she didn't flinch.

"Which memories did you destroy?"

She wouldn't have. Not mine. She knew what they meant to me. She couldn't have done that, could she? If she had ever loved me as much as the king said she did, then surely she wouldn't have destroyed my memories?

Her laugh echoed around the camp in a disquieting ripple as terror tightened my chest.

"I don't know." She hiccoughed, then laughed even harder. "Don't you see? They're gone. I can't remember them anymore."

CHAPTER NINETEEN

Elation drained from her face as she stared back at me, the lifeless expression I hated so much returning to her until she was back to being a creation the Gods had forgotten to finish making, neglecting to add the final touches that made us alive.

How was it possible that this creature had ever been capable of love?

"Would you even believe me if I said your memories were fine?" she asked at last.

"You know I wouldn't," I said, fighting the urge to pull my hands back from her. "Prove you still have them. Better yet, give them back and rid yourself of them if they're such a burden to you."

She stared at me, but no answer came from her. Fury built inside me and I only just managed to hold myself back from shaking her.

"Why won't you-!"

"I remember you walking up the white stone palace steps in Dranta," she said, her voice so quiet that I had to strain to hear her even though she was only a breath away.

"Your suspicion as you walked the corridors. Every thought that crossed your mind the first time you saw me."

Heat burned through me as defiance flared behind Sarilla's eyes. Was she enjoying my embarrassment? So she was alive in there after all.

"That doesn't prove anything. Tell me something else. Something you could only know from my memories."

"I remember the name of the woman you lodged with while you were in the capital."

"At least one of us does. Something else. Something I can verify."

"You'll just have to trust me."

"That's not good enough! I need proof-"

"I don't care what you need, Falon!" She pushed me away, walking around the fire in the direction of the wagon. "I'm going to bed."

I wanted to chase after her. To shake her until I could force some semblance of decency inside her, but instead I turned about to find something to kick. As my gaze landed on the sack of oats, Ced cried out behind me. I spun about to find Sarilla's blackened hands wrapped around his neck, their darkness pulsing like black blood coursing through her veins as she clung to him, her eyes shut.

I lunged at her, needing to stop her from doing to Ced what she had done to me, but before I could drag her off him, she released his neck, stumbling backwards into Tranten as she blinked, her gaze sharpening more with every second that passed.

Tranten shoved her to the ground, forcing her roughly into the dirt and holding her down by his boot as the other soldiers crowded around, accusation and fear pouring from them as they stared between Sarilla and Ced, morbid curiosity filling their gazes.

"What did you do?" I yelled, grabbing for Ced as he

slumped over.

Dark lines pulsed across his neck, bleeding into his skin as black tears leaked from his eyes, sludging down his cheeks. Was this what the noble in the tent had looked like after she took his memories? What I had looked like after she had stolen mine from me?

I had allowed her to get loose. I had given her the opportunity to do this to him, once again forgetting what she was.

"Cedral?" Havric gripped Ced's shoulders, shaking him gently.

"Is he alive?" I asked.

Havric nodded, but the confirmation did nothing to reassure me.

"What do you take from him?" I yelled, rounding on Sarilla again as the soldiers shifted, looking ready to attack her. If I wasn't so selfish then I would have let them, but no, I had to have my memories back. I had to keep her alive and put others at risk. I had to give her the chance to do to Ced what she had done to me.

"Ced?" I asked, kneeling beside him. "Cedral, wake up."

He groaned, rolling to the side, his eyes still shut and leaking that strange black substance. Pressing his hand to his forehead, he grimaced, looking up at me.

"Are you alright?" I asked, helping him sit. "What did she take? Do you know who I am? Do you remember who you are?"

Real tears tumbled down after the black, rolling over the dark tracks as if they weren't there. Ced scrubbed at them with the back of his hand, wiping away the real ones but leaving the black untouched. Reaching up, I hesitantly brushed my fingers over the marks. Although I felt nothing, vague images flashed through my mind, fading before I could be certain what I had seen.

"Ced-"

"Relax. She didn't take anything."

"Cursen's piss she didn't," I muttered. "Your face is telling a different story. Your eyes are leaking black."

"If they are, then it's because she gave me memories, not because she's taken them," he said, avoiding my gaze as he looked at Sarilla.

"How would you know what she has or hasn't taken- Wait? Did you say she's given you memories? Whose?"

"Some of hers. Some of my father's and…" He glanced up at me, the black in his eyes not quite hiding his guilt as the marks lining his neck faded. "And some of yours."

"What do you mean mine?"

Ced refused to meet my gaze, so I rounded on Sarilla. "What did you give him?"

"Everyone deserves a chance at redemption," she said, shifting uncomfortably under Tranten's boot. "Now he has it."

"What are you talking about? They're my memories-"

"And now it's his choice whether he tells you about them."

My mouth dropped open as I stared at her, so overwhelmed by how faulty her logic was that I couldn't properly process her meaning

"You had no right! Those are my memories-"

"She only gave me the ones I'm in."

"Shut up, Ced! It doesn't matter how many she gave you. Even one is too many, don't you see that?"

"I just meant-"

"Take them back," I ordered, glaring at Sarilla. "Take them back and put them in me."

She stared at me, defiance filling her face as she repeated, "Everyone deserves a chance at redemption."

"Why did the memories do that to him?" Havric asked,

breaking the silence that followed Sarilla's statement. He was studying Ced calmly, as if testing the taste of a new ale. He wouldn't be so unfazed if it were his memories being passed around, his thoughts and emotions being shared for others to pry into.

"Your memories aren't completely compatible with those of a memoria," Sarilla said, grimacing as Tranten flexed his leg, his boot pressing harder on her back. "The black forms when we take yours inside us. When I pushed them back into him, the lachryma was shed as his body adapted the memories into a more compatible state."

"What's that supposed to mean?" I asked, my anger still pouring from me unchecked.

"That you don't have the space to absorb new memories like we do. At least not in any detail."

"So... he's filtering out what he can't retain?" Havric asked as he studied Ced's face with interest.

"Filtering?" A chill coursed through me. "You mean he's purging my memories?"

"Not yours," Sarilla said, watching the last of the black fade from Ced's cheeks. "Those are compatible already. He's purging mine."

What? I could understand her giving away the memories she had stolen from others. Why would she show them any more respect than she spared the people she took them from? But to give away her own...

"An exchange," Ced said into the silence. He met Sarilla's gaze and something I didn't understand passed between them. "I get to remember a bit more about my father. She gets to forget the sight of her family swaying in the breeze."

He pushed himself up, making his way over to her, holding his hand out and gesturing for Tranten to move aside so he could help her. He didn't even flinch as she raised her ungloved hand to take his.

"I'm sorry," he said. "The sight of them like that-"

"Please, Cedral. I gave you those memories so I could forget. Don't remind me now."

She gave him a small smile before continuing her way towards the cart. She climbed in, then lowered the fabric, shutting the world out.

"She's not the heartless monster I thought she was," Ced said, sitting down beside the fire and staring into the flames, looking as if he didn't really see them.

"You sure of that?" I asked. "She had no right to give you my memories. They aren't something that should be passed about like that!"

Ced didn't answer. From the far-off expression on his face, I wasn't even certain he had heard me.

Angry enough to do something I knew I would regret, I grabbed my sleeping roll and lay it out on the other side of the wagon, turning my back on Ced and whatever had once been between us. If the thought of letting Sarilla anywhere near my mind didn't revolt me, I might have asked her to purge my memories of him altogether.

How could he condone what she had done? Whatever it was he feared me finding out must have been bad indeed if he favoured this outcome.

I tossed and turned for half the night, unable to mute the rage boiling inside me for long enough to drift off. That was why I was still wide awake when the shouting burst from the trees an hour or so before dawn. I shot up as the soldiers about me roused themselves from sleep, searching out the source of the commotion as more cries rang between the trees, coming from the front end of the train, this time closer than before.

"Blackvine," Sarilla said from where she perched on the edge of the wagon, watching the trees with a strange stillness as the soldiers about us surged into action, forming a defensive line and readying their pikes. Others unsheathed their swords, their nerves already showing from the way their weapons quaked.

"They don't stand a chance," Sarilla said, causing the nearby soldiers to flinch, their gazes fixed in the direction of the screaming.

"You don't know that," I said.

"I do. As do you if you're honest with yourself."

"Then do something about it!" I yelled. "Help them like you did before when you stopped it from finding us."

"I'd die just trying to take a thousandth of the memories needed to hide this many people," she said, jumping down from the wagon. "We can't stay here and expect to survive it. Stay or go, Falon. What's it going to be?"

Her gaze bored into me, asking her real question. Live or lose our memories, then die after a couple of days stumbling blindly through the Deadwood.

I met Havric and Ced's gazes. Neither looked happy at the prospect of abandoning the soldiers and running, but was there any sense in us dying with them?

At a nod from me, Havric reached into the wagon and pulled out our packs. He tossed Ced and I ours before grabbing his own and mounting up.

"Come on," I said, untethering a horse and helping Sarilla climb up. It was tricky with her wrists still manacled together, but she eventually made it up.

"What are you doing?" Tranten yelled, fighting to reach us through the soldiers as they scrambled into formation. The other guards were already nowhere to be seen.

"Go!" I yelled, slapping the horse under Sarilla and urging it on as Tranten launched himself at us.

I dodged backwards and leapt for another horse, barely having time to grab its reins before the frightened animal darted for the trees, already on edge from the blackvine's proximity.

Ced and Havric's horses cleared a path through the soldiers and I soon caught up, hastening mine through the camp and into the undergrowth, glad to disappear into the forest even though the soldiers' screams chased our flight.

We were just past the treeline when Ced shouted something behind me. I spun in my saddle to see what had caught his attention, fear clenching my gut at the sight of the blackvine reaching for us through the darkness.

CHAPTER TWENTY

Ced shouted as his horse stumbled, the thick tendrils of the blackvine wrapping around its fetters. The horse dropped as I turned my own about, already racing for Ced as he flew through the air, his mount crashing to the ground. He landed with a thud a few yards from the horse as the blackvine swarmed the creature, its eyes wide and filled black.

"Ced, move! Now!"

Vines reached for him, snaking along the ground, reaching past the mound his horse was buried in. They groped blindly, latching onto everything and anything in their path as Ced rolled onto his side, groaning but making no attempt to rise.

My pulse pounded in my throat, drowning the blackvine's whispering in my ears as I leapt from my horse, already swinging my sword. I severed one of the vines reaching for Ced, but my blade met with no resistance and it felt like I hacked at smoke. The limp, mutilated tip still writhed as it hit the ground, the worm-like stub recoiling and rearing back before surging at me with a determination that hadn't been there before.

"To your left, Falon!" Havric shouted as I cut the reformed vine again.

More reached through the darkness, coming for me and Ced with none of the blind groping from before. They shot from almost every direction, near invisible in the night as Havric's horse thundered to a stop behind me. He jumped down as I sliced through three vines with one strike, my blade useless against the endless onslaught. For each one I hacked, yet two more launched at us, their cleaved carcasses disintegrating before they hit the ground.

My horse let out a panicked shriek as coiling bands wrapped around its neck, consuming it as Havric grabbed Ced and heaved him up onto his horse, the only one the blackvine had yet to claim. I still kept hacking, fighting to hold back the dark tide long enough to give Havric time to get Ced to safety, but there were too many vines.

"Go!" I called, narrowly avoiding another as it reached for me. "Get him out of here!"

Havric mounted up behind Ced as he swayed atop the horse, still dazed from the fall.

"Falon-"

"Just go!"

Friend, confidant, lover. Once Ced had been all three. Whatever he had done, whatever ways he had wronged me, it couldn't change that. He had been there for me when others weren't, willingly suffering his father's disappointment to keep company with a bastard when no-one else would.

Havric's horse darted away as if the Gods themselves chased after it, leaving me alone with the surging tide of blackvine. I followed, slicing at the tendrils reaching for me as I ran, not daring to look back yet already knowing what I would see. My feet crunched fallen leaves as the vines reached after me, filling my ears with strange whispers that grew louder each second.

I wouldn't be able to escape it. It was catching up too fast.

"Run, Falon!" Ced called.

He clung to Havric as the horse darted between the trees as fast as it could through the thick undergrowth. My gaze locked with his and I tried to convey everything I needed to say to him in that look. Forgiveness, love and everything in between. With the blackvine bearing down on us, it no longer mattered what he had been keeping from me, only that I had wasted so much time believing that it did. I wanted to tell him I was sorry. That I had let my pride and a memoria's deceit come between us. That I was a stubborn fool, too blind to see what I had done to us by clinging so tightly to the past.

Havric's horse reared back, almost throwing Ced off, but he managed to hold on, unable to see what had frightened the horse as I could. A stray vine reached through the darkness and my stomach plummeted. The sight spurred me on faster than I had ever run before, but they were too far away.

The blackvine wove through the air, finding Ced's ankle before my sword could sever it. Ced's scream tore through the night as the darkness hissed, recoiling as my blade cut through it, the tip dissolving as it fell to the ground, releasing Ced's foot too late. Far too late.

The horse lurched away again as Havric regained control. They bounded between the trees, leaves tossing into the air with every crash of the horse's hooves. I raced after them again, the blackvine still reaching for me as it surged in my wake.

There was still a chance Ced was alright. The blackvine had only touched him for an instant, perhaps it hadn't been long enough or maybe there was something Sarilla could do. He would be alright. He had to be. He was only there because of me, because he had wanted to help me get my memories back, even though he knew that my doing so meant my finding out what had happened between us.

Leaves crashed to my left, and the heavy beating of hooves reached me. I strained my neck, searching the trees and the darkness for the source. Shock coursed through me at the sight of Sarilla's brilliant white hair streaming like a flag in the breeze behind her. It rippled with each jolt of her horse as she rode for me, her wrists still bound before her.

She wouldn't have time to slow down so I could mount up behind her. If she tried, then the blackvine would be on her in an instant.

"Jump, Falon!" she called, reaching out with her manacled hands as she drew level with me.

I didn't hesitate. I leapt into the air, praying I timed it right even though a swift death trampled under hoof was preferable to being consumed by the blackvine. I collided with the horse mid-air, my face striking its hide as I clung to its flank with everything I had as Sarilla guided us around the trees, dodging the branches whipping at us. It was all I could do not to fall off, my clenched hands screaming in pain as my stomach ached with every jolt of Sarilla's knee.

The whispers of the blackvine faded behind us as I reeled at our having escaped and Sarilla's having come back for me. She had risked her life to save mine. Why? After everything I had done, after everything I had said, she had still risked her life to save me. Was it possible she still cared as the king said she did?

The horse lurched and my grip slipped. Straining, I raised my foot into the stirrup, using it for leverage as I hauled myself up behind Sarilla.

The saddle was too small for us both and I had to pull her against me. I tried hard not to think about the way her body pressed against mine, the feel of her familiar in ways I couldn't describe as we jolted between the trees.

Dawn crept through the leaves as we plunged into a small glen, almost riding over Havric and Ced.

Sarilla pulled her horse up with a sharp jerk, only just managing to stop us in time. The sudden command caused our already frightened beast to baulk and I jumped off as it reared up, deciding it was better to get down than to risk being thrown. Grabbing the horse's reins, I dragged its front-half down, soothing the panicked creature as Sarilla clung to it. She slid from the horse, her hands still bound and making the movement awkward. I reached for her as she stumbled, exhausted by the ride.

"Thank you for coming back for me. I... What are you doing?" I asked as she grabbed my cloak, doing her best to dig through my pockets.

"Give me the damn key, Falon!"

"What?"

"I won't spend the rest of my miserable life in manacles just because you haven't sense enough to save yourself, so give me the key before you get yourself killed! Did the Gods forget to give you a survival instinct as well as a sense of direction?"

She had come back for the key, not to save me. She shrieked in frustration when she didn't find what she looked for, so I reached into my waistband pocket and pulled it out. She snatched it from me and struggled with it for a moment, unable to wrangle it into the lock.

"Is that why you saved me?" I asked, studying her face as I took the key from her and inserted it into the hole.

I twisted it and she shook her wrists free from the manacles, rubbing the tender, red skin and wincing in pain.

"You'd like that, wouldn't you? It would make it so much easier for you to hate me if I was a monster who only cared about herself."

"Are you?" I asked, waiting for her to raise her black eyes to meet mine.

Black eyes. Remember what she is.

I couldn't read anything in her expression, so couldn't tell what she was thinking, but I preferred it that way. At least then I could continue believing she was the same heartless memoria she had always been. Hating her would be so much easier that way.

"Falon!" Havric called from the other side of the glen, dragging my attention from her to where Havric knelt over Ced, struggling to keep him still as Ced bucked and writhed.

Ced's scream echoed in my head and I forced myself to face what I had been hoping to be spared, my heart breaking at the sight of the lachryma leaking from Ced's unseeing eyes.

CHAPTER TWENTY-ONE

"Help me hold him down!" Havric called, trying to stop Ced from hurting himself as he lashed out blindly. "He slid off the horse. I couldn't hold him up any longer."

"How bad is he?" I asked, hurrying over to join them. "The blackvine only had him for an instant. He'll be alright, won't he?"

"However brief it was, it looks like it was long enough," Havric said as I peered into Ced's eyes. They were just like they had been when Sarilla pushed her memories into him, only this time, the lachryma didn't fade, nor did his screams.

"You can help him?" I asked Sarilla, unable to tear my gaze from the sight of Ced's black, sightless eyes. "Can't you?"

When she didn't answer, I forced myself to look up, half tempted to shake the answer out of her, but as I glanced her way, I was glad she hadn't spoken, I didn't want to hear her confirm what her eyes had already told me.

"I… I can't touch him. If I try, then the blackvine might spread to me."

"There must be something you can do."

"I… I'm sorry, Falon. There isn't."

Of course she wouldn't try to help him. She hated Ced. She likely wouldn't try to save him even if she knew how.

"We should go," she said, making to climb back atop her horse, "We don't know how far away the blackvine is-"

I scrambled up and grabbed her arm, pulling her back.

"Please," I said. "There must be something. Think, Sarilla, you owe me that much."

"There's nothing-"

"Don't lie to me. Not about this."

I searched her face for proof of the lie. She couldn't be telling the truth, not about this.

"I wish I was, Falon, I'm sorry, but there's nothing I can do. I would save him if I could, but I don't know how."

My fist collided with tree bark and the trunk juddered as pain shot up my arm. Sarilla gasped as leaves tumbled down, showering us with autumn and death.

Turning my back on her, I knelt, squatting beside Havric and whatever it was that remained of Ced. Dark streaks pulsed across the once whites of his eyes. What had been the rich golden-brown of his irises were now so black that they merged with his pupils.

What had they done to him?

I grasped his head in my hands, trying to force him to look at me and praying I would see some sign of recognition from him, but there was nothing. If he even saw me, then he made no acknowledgement of it.

"Ced? If you can hear me, then say something. Please. It's Falon."

I waited, but the only sound was the chirping of the birds in the trees.

"Come on, Ced. I know you're still in there somewhere.

Please, fight this."

"Falon…" Havric placed a hand on my shoulder, his voice set and filled with a resignation I didn't want to hear. "We need to go. The blackvine won't be far behind us. We can't-"

"We're not leaving him!"

My shout rang through the forest, bouncing off the trees and echoing back at us, leaving silence in its wake.

"I know," he murmured. "I didn't mean that. I just… We can't stay here. The blackvine-"

"Then we lift him back onto the horse and take him with us."

"I can't hold him and ride-"

"Then fetch some rope. We'll strap him to the horse if that's what it takes."

"Fine," Havric said, glancing over his shoulder to where his horse chomped at a fern nearby. "Hold him so he doesn't hurt himself while I get it."

We swapped places and I gripped Ced's shoulders, holding him down even as he kicked and lashed indiscriminately at everything in his reach. Havric rooted around in his pack, returning a few moments later to help me scoop Ced up and lift him back onto the horse. The fresh, soapy scent that always clung to him was still somehow detectable despite his having been on the road for days. It was the one that always lingered on him, even after a long night in a tavern or rolling in the sheets.

He kicked me as I heaved him onto the horse's back, but I barely felt the pain. There had to be a way to fix him. Ced was too much full of life to die like this, his body wasting away until it was as ruined as his mind.

"Hurry," Sarilla said, leaning in to help hold Ced still as Havric and I fought to strap him down. "We need to keep going. Who knows how far behind us the blackvine is."

"And where exactly are we going to?" Havric asked, tying the ends of the rope off, then mounting up behind Ced. "I don't know about you, but I was a bit too distracted with getting away to pay much attention to where we were running too."

"We need to get back to the army," Sarilla said, catching me off guard.

She wanted to return to the king? Why did she want to go back to the man who had been holding her prisoner? What had changed that meant she no longer feared to be under his control or hated what he made her do?

"And how do you suppose we get back to them without running into the blackvine," Havric asked. "If any of the army still remains, that is."

Sarilla hesitated, then she sat in the crook of a tree. I realised her intention a moment before she pressed her hand to its trunk, her marks pulsing as she shut her eyes. When she opened them again, she raised her gaze to mine, the corners of her eyes creased and her expression filled with confusion.

"What is it?" I asked. "Is the army no more?"

"Their numbers have somewhat dwindled, but what's left is regrouping."

"So what then?"

"It's the blackvine," she said, grazing her lips with her teeth as her frown deepened. She moved as if to touch the tree trunk again, but stopped, her hand hovering over it.

"Is it close?"

"No. Or at least, I don't think so. I… I thought I would be able to sense it in the nexus, but I can't find it anywhere."

"It must be somewhere," Havric said, watching us from atop his horse. "It can't have disappeared, it was huge. Maybe you just can't sense it?"

"But it has to be there. It's using the nexus to move about the country, so it must be there somewhere, but it's like it's vanished."

She fell silent as Ced moaned, writhing in the sunlight breaking through the canopy above, dappling his face and causing his skin to burn and blister everywhere the light touched.

"Gods… What's happening to him?" I asked, trying to calm him as he bucked in pain, his skin reddening and breaking as the black on his face boiled.

"It's the sunlight. It's burning him."

Sarilla's meaning hit me and I grabbed a blanket out of Havric's pack and threw it over Ced. It settled over him, blocking the sunlight. He stilled, his groans quieting a little and returning to that strange, incomprehensible muttering he was making before.

"What if it has to?" Sarilla asked, frowning as she stared at Ced.

"What are you talking about?"

"The blackvine. What if it has to vanish? The lachryma burns if the light is too bright."

"That's why you wear the gloves," Havric said, his forehead furrowed. "So the memories don't fade."

Sarilla nodded. Spinning to face me, she asked, "How many times have you crossed paths with the blackvine?"

"Twice now. Though it's been attacking Arvendon for years. Why?"

"Were any of those times during the day?"

I shook my head, glancing to Havric, who nodded in agreement.

"Always at night," he murmured. "I didn't think to make the connection…"

"The blackvine must be hiding from the sunlight," Sarilla said, staring at Ced. "Full blooded memori can't be out in daylight either. It damages their memories, that's why they lived in their tunnels beneath Dranta."

"Why they built their city in Oresa underground," I said, earning a nod from Sarilla.

"I knew they were hiding from the sun," she said, "I just didn't realise they couldn't take the memories of sunlight either. The only reason I can must have something to do with my being only half memori. I have more resilience against the effects of the sunlight than they do."

"What of Ced?" I asked. "Does this mean we can burn the blackvine from him?"

Sarilla glanced from Ced to me and back again. "In theory. Though we'd likely cause him a lot of pain if we did. But even if we managed to purge the blackvine from him, it won't bring back the memories they've taken."

"So... you mean that he won't be Ced, even if we manage to get the blackvine out of him?"

Forget what Sarilla did to me. At least she left me with enough to piece together some semblance of who I had been. The blackvine had taken everything from Ced. There was nothing left except what the memoria had turned him into.

She watched me uneasily for a moment, then nodded. "I'm sorry."

"If you're right about all this," Havric said, glancing skywards. "Then we have until nightfall to get somewhere safe. Can we make it back to the army in that time?"

"Even if we could," I said. "We'd be no safer with them than we were last night. We need somewhere more secure."

Gesturing to the tree, I asked Sarilla, "Can you see if there is anywhere safe nearby?"

She touched the tree trunk again. She was silent for a minute, then said, "Nowhere I can find."

"But there must be houses riddling these parts. We're in Venn territory, it's littered with settlements from the eastern foragers."

"If they're here, then they've been long abandoned. They'll be impossible to find this way. The nexus doesn't have a very long memory."

"Then what do we do? Dig a hole and hope the blackvine can't tunnel?"

"It wouldn't work," Sarilla said, her voice distant as she continued to search the nexus, her eyes moving back and forth beneath her closed lids. "There is something... It's like a... a hole? It's a gap in the nexus. I can't sense anything there. Like the one where Arvendon is, only smaller."

"A large building?" I asked.

"Or a rock outcrop."

"Whatever it is, could it keep us safe?"

"Maybe. Without the connection to the nexus, the blackvine has no way of knowing where we are. It wouldn't be able to find us up there, even if it followed us to the base of the rocks."

"But can we make it by nightfall?" Havric asked. "The horses won't be able to travel at speed for long with two of us apiece on their backs."

"I don't know. It's a long way."

"We'd best hurry then," I said as she released the tree trunk and pushed herself up. I grabbed the horse's reins and helped her mount before climbing up behind her again, holding her to me as she led us on through the forest.

CHAPTER TWENTY-TWO

Sarilla led the way through the forest, driving our horse on as though Cursen himself chased after us, yet our progress was painfully slow as the horses struggled to plough their way through the thick foliage.

"Why are you running from the blackvine?" I asked, causing her to stiffen in my arms, dragging her attention from the path she was cutting through the trees.

"You'll think I'm being hypocritical," she said after a moment's hesitation, swiping aside a branch.

It flicked back into place with a vengeance, slicing my arm but I ignored the pain, my gaze fixed on the back of her head as I wished I could know what contrary thoughts raged inside. Were my stolen memories a riot of grey in her world of black and white?

"You're already a walking contradiction. Whatever you say won't change that opinion."

She glanced back to where Havric led his horse after ours, Ced still strapped across its backside like a saddlebag. He muttered the same nonsensical ravings as he had been doing all morning and I tried to tune it out, not wishing to see him in that state.

Gripping the reins tighter, Sarilla sighed, the black marks on her hands rippling water-like across her skin. In all the commotion, she hadn't put her gloves back on. I had considered asking her to, but I didn't want her to know that I was worried about the sunlight damaging my memories, or for her to be reminded of the control she had over me.

"I… I don't want it to invade my mind. No-one should suffer such a violation."

Her confession shocked me so much that I forgot to duck and hit my head on a low-hanging branch. After everything she had done, after all the minds she had intruded, all the lives she had ruined, she feared the same fate she inflicted? The hypocrisy was outstanding considering that the evidence of her crimes stained her hands black.

"You can't be serious? Sarilla…"

"I have as much right to privacy as anyone else."

"You're sure about that? You don't think you've violated that right a few too many times to call upon it now? What of the rights of all those you've stolen from? How many of them are dead because of what you did?"

"I know what fate I deserve for what I've done. My crimes have earned each of the trials the Gods have thrown my way and worse."

"You've got that right."

"But I still can't let the blackvine catch me."

I shifted my grip about her waist and reached forwards, clasping her hands in mine and tracing my thumbs along the black. "Like I said, a walking contradiction."

"And what does that make you?" she asked, her muscles tensing from my touch. "All you've ever wanted is acceptance. For people to finally stop thinking of you as no more than Arvendon's Bastard. Renford offered you that chance. You could have stayed as the new Lord of Arvendon in your father's stead, but here you are, keeping company with a memoria. It's hardly going to help how people see you."

"You don't know anything about what I want," I said, knowing that she knew it for a lie even as I said it. She had my memories for Cursen's sake. "Besides, you know the king well enough to know that his making me Lord of Arvendon will have so many strings attached that I'll accidentally hang myself by the time the year is over.

"Even if that's true, all you're doing is proving to Renford that your loyalty isn't worth his trying to buy."

"You think I care about that? All I want is to get my memories back."

"Your reason doesn't matter. Everyone will think you did it out of love for a memoria and they'll loathe you for it."

"I've been hated before. I'm sure I'll survive," I said, not liking how close to the truth Sarilla had struck. I did care and well she knew it. She was all too aware of my need to prove myself to my father and the rest of Valrora.

"Have you stopped to consider that maybe you're better off without your memories?"

"That's not the point and you know it. It doesn't matter what they contain. They're mine and you have no right to keep them. Do you have any idea what it's like? How unsettling it is to know that someone else understands you better than you do yourself? Anything could have happened in those months and I've no memory of it. What if I... I don't know... Reunited with my mother? Fathered a child? Don't you think I should know about that?"

"Would you want to know if you fathered a bastard?" she asked, ducking another low-hanging branch.

I tensed, the idea twisting my insides unpleasantly as our bodies swayed in time with the jolting of the horse. I couldn't have been that reckless, could I? After having lived with the censure of my birth, I long ago decided it was better to die without an heir than inflict a bastard's fate upon any child of mine. What could have changed in me so much in my time in Dranta that I would have put that scruple aside? Yet was it anymore inconceivable than my having fallen for a memoria? There were several things I had done in those months I never would have thought I could do.

"I didn't, did I?" I asked, feeling as if I lived and died in every breath as I waited for her to answer me.

"No," Sarilla said after what felt like an eternity.

"Thank, Forta," I said, relief flooding through me. "There are enough bastards already in this world."

Sarilla made a small sound that might have been agreement. I stared over her shoulder to the blackness pulsing on her hands as she clutched the reins. I was about to ask her what she thought she knew of the world, then I recalled she had known more than just her memories. After everything the king had made her steal, was it any wonder that she thought ill of people?

"Memories," I said. "That's what the memori are forcing into people through the blackvine. That's what destroys their minds."

Sarilla didn't answer me, instead urging the horse on through a narrow gap between two trees.

"But…" I continued. "The blackvine's huge. How many memories would be needed to create something that large?"

"Enough to make my crimes look like mere misdemeanours in comparison."

Not to your victims, I thought, fighting the urge to

speak the words aloud. Her moral compass was as broken as Ced's mind.

"How many people must it have stolen from to get so big?"

"Countless, but there are not just Valrorian memories in there. The blackvine consumes from everything it touches. Soldiers, the forest, animals. It takes indiscriminately, its appetite ever-growing. It'll soon be too much for even the memori to control."

"Then why unleash it in the first place?" Havric asked, manoeuvring his horse beside ours. "You said they weren't trying to reclaim Valrora, but why else would they have set the blackvine on us? Revenge?"

"I don't know," she said, her voice catching in a way I had heard many times before, yet that was the first time I realised it for the tell it was.

"Another lie?" I asked, causing her to still against me.

She half-turned, meeting my gaze over her shoulder before turning back around and fixing her gaze ahead of her.

"We have to hurry," she said. "If we don't pick up the pace, we've no chance of making it there before nightfall."

Without waiting for a response, she urged the horse on at a furious pace as she wove through the trees, only slowing so she might grab onto a branch and check our direction in the nexus. My backside hurt from having spent all day riding and the horses flagged as the day waned, seeming on the verge of collapsing by the time the light filtering through the trees vanished completely.

Havric and I leapt down to spare them some of their burdens, but from the way their laboured hooves dragged across the ground, it was clear they couldn't go much further. I felt bad that we were likely riding the creatures to their deaths, but there was little I wouldn't do to stop the blackvine from getting me.

"How much further?" I asked, trying to gauge how far away the blackvine was just by judging from the strange stillness about us.

"Too far at this pace," Sarilla said, jumping down from her horse. "We'll have to run the rest. The horses won't make it in this condition."

"Let's hope we will," I said as Sarilla set off between the trees, jumping roots and ferns with ease despite the darkness.

"It's this way, come on!"

"Grab the packs," I said to Havric as I unsheathed my blade. "I'll get Ced."

I sliced through the ropes binding him to the horse and hauled him over my shoulder as Havric jumped down, slinging the packs onto his back. We ran after Sarilla, our boots pounding loudly, but failing to drown out the whispers growing steadily louder.

I followed Havric's outline as he chased after Sarilla. Ced bounced on my back as my feet stumbled on the uneven ground.

"Can you protect us again if it comes to it?" I asked as we caught up with Sarilla.

"Not with Cedral drawing it to us. If we leave him-"

"Not an option."

"Fine, but if we end up like him too-"

"It's up here!" Havric called, pointing at something in the darkness ahead. "The rocks. That must be it!"

I strained to see what he was pointing to, but I couldn't make it out. As I paused, I felt something whip through the air behind me. Shifting Ced's weight, I drew my sword.

"Don't!" Sarilla yelled, pausing as she hauled herself up the rock face. "You can't stop it. Just climb already!"

Realising that she was right, I threw myself at rocks and

scrambled up behind her, Ced's weight dragging me down. It wasn't as tall as those Arvendon was built atop, but I was still exhausted by the time I gained the top.

Panting, I laid Ced down before leaning over the edge and staring at the forest canopy below, watching the tide of whispering vines writhing in a black sea that lashed at the rocks but failed to reach our refuge.

"What do you reckon? Think we're safe?" Havric asked, peering down beside me.

"Ask me again if we've made it to dawn," I said as Sarilla bent over Ced, examining him as he murmured nonsense into the night.

She grabbed his dagger, catching my eye as she stuffed it into her waistband.

"He's not going to need it," she said, shrugging.

I swallowed my anger. It was better directed at me, anyway. I knew what she was. The only mystery was why I was still surprised by her lack of morals.

She moved away from us and sat in a rocky crevice a short distance from the edge of the rocks, her gaze fixed on the vines below as I stayed with Ced, my hand squeezing his as I offered him what comfort I could, unable to tear my gaze away from the black marring his beautiful face. Could he feel my presence? If I told him I was sorry for letting her come between us, would he even hear me?

I wanted to hold him and pretend everything was as it had used to be, back when he made me feel like I had nothing to prove. He had helped me ignore my stepmother's malice and my father's neglect. Even Arvendon's mockery had hurt less, shielded as I had been by the knowledge that Ced had loved me for me.

I reached up, half hoping I could brush away the black from his face and get my Ced back-

"Don't touch the marks."

Sarilla's voice echoed over the rocks and I pulled my hand back.

"Why?" I asked, staring over at where she sat, her head turned away from me.

"He's still connected to the blackvine. I don't know for sure, but if you touch the marks, there's a chance the blackvine will cross into you too."

"Would it leave Ced in the process?"

"Probably not, so I don't advise that you give it a try to figure it out."

Standing, I made my way over to Sarilla. She sat with Ced's dagger gripped in her lap. I had designed that blade for Ced, not for her. He wasn't even dead and already she was a carrion picking at his life.

"We can't keep bringing him with us," she said, interrupting my thoughts. "You have to let him go or the blackvine will keep finding us."

"You don't know that," I said, taking the dagger from her.

"I do. He's calling to them. What do you think he's been muttering all day?"

"He's speaking nonsense."

"He's speaking memorian."

"He can't. Ced wouldn't know how."

"Until yesterday, I had never ridden a horse. Other peoples' memories have a way of teaching you things."

I chose to ignore the implications of what she had just said, instead asking, "Can you understand him? What's he saying?"

"Nothing important. An unchanging litany describing where we are."

"How did you learn to speak memorian?"

Her forehead creased as she stared out into the night.

"You should stop his suffering. It's kinder than leaving him like this."

"You know I won't do that."

"His mind's gone, Falon. Even if you could severe the blackvine's hold on him, there'll be nothing left if you do. Cedral's as good as dead."

"And I should believe you? After all the lies you've told, why should I trust anything you say ever again?"

"You're hardly a model of virtue."

"What's that supposed to mean?"

She opened her mouth, then hesitated. Her jaw clenched as she forced herself to look up and meet my gaze.

"You forget that I have your memories, Falon. You've committed all the crimes you accuse me of and worse-"

"Oh? Stolen other peoples' memories, have I?"

"No. But you've stolen plenty of other things that weren't yours to take-"

"Falon!"

Havric's cry had me drawing my sword, expecting to find the blackvine reaching for us. Instead, my stomach plummeted as I spotted Ced rolling off the edge of the rocky plateau, falling towards where the blackvine waited for him.

I didn't stop to think before leaping after him. Landing atop Ced halfway down the rocks, we crashed together in a tumble of limbs, still falling and drawing closer to the blackvine with every spin. I threw out a hand to stop us from rolling any further. Clinging to him, I fought desperately to hold on even as he writhed, his crazed mutterings louder than before and filled with his need to reach the blackvine.

"Ced! Please, snap out of it! It's me. It's Falon!"

There was no change. I might as well not have spoken

for all the attention he paid me. Sarilla had been right, my Ced was gone. Even if we could get the blackvine out of him, I wouldn't be able to get him back.

Smoky tendrils lashed at the rocks beneath us, drawing closer, Ced's mutterings leading it right to us. I wouldn't be able to get him away before it reached us.

I prayed to whatever God was listening, already knowing I was wasting my breath. Ced was gone, but I couldn't abandon him to the same fate as the rest of the blackvine's victims, his body slowly failing until it reached the same state as his ruined mind.

I searched his face one last time, praying I might see some glimmer of recognition, but there was nothing. Feeling the air about me shift as the blackvine reached for us, I gripped his dagger and pierced it into his chest. His body shuddered beneath me as I searched his face, half-hoping, half-fearing his mind would return in his dying moment, but it didn't. Ced was gone.

Sarilla and Havric shouted to me from above, telling me to move as the blackvine reached for me, but I couldn't.

The blackvine surrounded me, an icy tendril entwining about my wrist and filling my mind with darkness, but I didn't care. Ced was dead.

I wished I was too.

CHAPTER TWENTY-THREE

Whispers roared through my head as the darkness swallowed me. The blackvine filled my mind, consuming parts of me I hadn't known existed, but that I never would be able to forget again.

Thoughts filled my head, most of them not my own as the blackvine writhed through me, invading the darkest recesses of my mind. I wanted to draw it out by my nails, but I wouldn't have been able to grasp it even if I dug my fingers through my skull.

Was this how it had been for Ced? Had he been so buried by the darkness that light was only a fading memory to be snuffed out by the encroaching black? Had he struggled as panic clasped him tight? Or given in and let it claim him?

I wanted to fight, but the further I sank, the less I could remember why. It was so much easier to just let go.

Images swarmed into my head with the darkness, assaulting my vision. I screamed, the memories scouring my mind until all that remained were shreds of who I had been. I couldn't stop it. Not the invasion of the new or the destruction of the old.

People and places flashed through my head as memory after memory crammed into my skull until it felt like it would burst. That's when I felt them in my mind, the voices and the creatures the words came from. The monsters with pale faces and black eyes, who lived in near darkness and shunned the light. I could feel their fear of it, their terror of the damage it would cause to what they treasured. How they rifled through my mind, blotting out all the memories that were so bright that they burned. I reeled as the creatures poured a blackness thick as tar atop my memories, dousing them until the only ones left were dark.

When they were done, the creatures began rummaging through what remained of my past, sorting through my tattered memories with a detached efficiency that left me reeling. Images flitted through my head and I tried to cling to them, gripping each fraying shred as a lifeline to keep from sinking into the sea surging through my mind.

Mine lacked the detail of those featuring the barefooted creatures in long grey robes, their eyes blacker than night. Their memories were so clear that I wasn't certain they were memories at all. My own in comparison were half-forgotten, and my head hurt from just trying to make out what they contained.

Let them go.

I did, and the memories faded away. Some left more easily than others. Those that lingered longest were the occasional memory that was clearer than the rest, so vivid and brimming with emotions so intense that it seared me for one blinding instant, reminding me of who I was. But then the creatures would cast it aside, flinging it into the blackness as they pulled forth another for examination.

Silvery tracts staining my mother's cheeks. Her kiss

goodbye. The way her hands shook as she cradled her infant one last time. I relived the sorrow as she passed me into my father's arms, bidding me goodbye before leaving Arvendon forever, my stepmother's scowling presence looming over the entire scene.

As swift as the memory came, the recollected agony vanished. Gone and forgotten as another replaced it.

My father yelling. His anger misdirected, but still so painful. Shame brimming within me. His disappointment in the only son he would ever sire. Then it was gone too and the shame was no more.

Ced's lips brushing mine. The flare of heat between us then… nothing. Gone. All of it was gone.

Mocking laughter. Guards barring me from entering the ballroom at my stepmother's behest. My hands clenching about cutlery every time we sat down to dinner. Her loathing twisting her a little more each day as I reminded her of her failure. Then she was gone too.

My exasperated leap into a cold lake after a stubborn girl. Ice invading my bones as I dived after her, fuelled by a fear that I wouldn't be able to save this girl I felt a strange draw to, this stranger and familiar rolled into one. Black eyes. Pale skin reflecting the starlight. Her hood sinking to the bottom of the lake.

The memory didn't fade. Another's excitement filled my mind, as they brought forth another memory, dragging it to the forefront. Sarilla's hand clenching me tight, clinging to me outside Arvendon and stopping me from falling to the rocks below, her hand so black in the darkness, her white hair tumbling down as she fought to hold on.

Voices erupted in my mind, their excited frenzy drowning out all thought as they spoke in strange words that somehow made sense to me.

Memoria. A half-breed?

More images filled my head, memories of this girl with dark, cynical eyes that never seemed to smile.

Black eyes. White hair. Black hands.

After all this time...

She's not the curator. She can't be. She's too young.

She may still know where the inherita is. We must bring her here and find out.

See if he has more memories of her. He might be able to help us locate her.

Sarilla. That was her name. The word tumbled into my mind, landing like a pebble in water and breaking the surface of the thick, black sludge coating the rest of my mind. More images of this Sarilla filled my vision, showing me more of this woman. Her self-hatred, her need to prove herself as other than a monster. I clung to the memories, unwilling to forget a single thing about her. She was magnificent.

More tumbled into my mind, but they were different this time, unfamiliar and strange in ways I couldn't describe. A child running through a palace, her white hair streaming behind her like ribbons in the breeze. A young boy racing with her, chasing after, laughter glinting in eyes that were so like hers. Hatred filled me at the sight of them, but the emotion wasn't mine and it left me reeling. Who had the memory belonged to? Who could ever have hated her so much? I had a sudden need to protect her, to defend her from the world's hatred as I caught sight of a man's reflection in the glass. There was something familiar about the scar mutilating his mouth, but...

Another image chased away the last. Sarilla was older now, her hair bound behind her head in an elegant plait. If there were marks on her hands, then they were concealed by a fine pair of gloves as she stood solemnly, her gaze downcast as the man atop the throne gestured her towards the man kneeling on the stones before him. Again, I felt the hatred towards her. The loyalty of the memory's maker towards the king. A willingness to do whatever it took to protect him from the creature with weapons for hands.

"Why are you showing me this?" I asked, the words heavy upon my tongue.

It knows we're here. How is this possible?

Its mind... it's different from the others. Can you sense it?

"What are you doing in my head? I can feel you there. I can hear you!"

What strangeness is this? The others we assimilated had not the room within. Is this damaged? Is that why it can take the blackvine?

Damaged? Was I damaged? I couldn't even remember who I was, so perhaps I must be.

The blackvine's touch always proves too much for their kind. But this one... he is strange. Feel how empty he is.

The memories. Their kind cannot contain them with their own. Their minds have not the capacity, but his has so much potential.

Could that be what keeps him sane? The deficiency of his memories leaves him with room enough to comprehend the rest?

"My memories?"

I had lost them. No. That wasn't right. They had been taken from me.

Help us find her, the voices said, latching onto my thoughts as they released the merest trickle of memories from the blackness coating my mind.

Sarilla's body pressed against mine as we rode through the Deadwood, the smoky scent clinging to her hair and filling my senses as we jolted and swayed atop the horse. Sarilla in my arms in the darkness under the trapdoor, the soft skin of her cheek beneath my fingers as I brushed back her hair.

She was so beautiful. Not in a conventional way, to be

sure. Her features were too severe, her colouring too extreme. But in an exotic way that captured my attention. I loved her and I would die doing what I must to keep her safe, to protect her from the monster the world wanted to turn her into.

We would protect her too.

We would talk to her.

"Why? What do you want with her?"

The inherita-

We would offer her protection. Bring her to Oresa so we might offer her safety.

Memories of a little white-haired girl and her older brother dangling from a rope bridge assailed my mind. It was my memory, but it wasn't mine alone. They were the memories of others there too, others who had seen the bodies swinging, but where mine were filled with sorrow at the sight, the memories that didn't belong to me were consumed with a sick satisfaction at what they saw.

Many would wish that the one you care for endures the same fate. Bring her to us. We can protect her. We can keep her safe. Let us help you save her from them.

"What's the inherita," I asked. "Why do you seek it and what does it have to do with her?"

I felt their hesitation. Their reluctance to share details of the secret they guarded, but I held fast.

We… We wish to learn of what has become of it, a voice said as new images filled my mind. They were disorientating at first, too complete next to my own, more fragile ones. They were made by creatures for whom remembering was an art, not half-breeds like Sarilla. They were true-born creatures of the dark.

Through the eyes of countless memori, I lived in their underground world, hiding from the sunlight and experiencing a life I hadn't known could exist. A flood of fear at a sudden rush of sunlight filling a chamber through a broken screen, memori scrambling for safety in the darkness. A mother sitting with her young child, playing in the water streams trickling through their underground city. The fear of an elderly man offering his memories for curation in the inherita, his dying body failing even as pride surged through him at how some of the memories he tended over the years had been selected to live on forever in the inherita, a record of memories from those now gone.

"I'm saying they don't care where they live. You're the ones who put so much stock in buildings and structure for recording your history. Memori don't rely on such imperfect means."

Sarilla's words filled my head again. Was this inherita what she had meant?

The images shifted through a mosaic of memories I watched a memori child through the eyes of a hundred onlookers as she stood solemnly before an old crone. Both were dressed in robes of blackest night and stood atop a raised plinth in the center of the room. Unadorned pillars held up the chamber's high ceiling as memori gathered about them, watching the event with respectful reverie and attention as they formed their memories of the moment.

The old woman held the young girl's face between her hands. Uneventful though the scene seemed, the watching memori were rapt with attention. Through the memories filling me, I felt their awe at the honour bestowed upon the young girl. The chosen successor to the crone. I knew their pride at witnessing the passage of the inherita to the girl, felt them wonder at the memories passed onto the protege. A living record of every important event in the memori's shared past. A carefully cultivated history, protected and passed down through the years from the crone to the child, containing the wisdom meant to guide the memori and safeguard them wherever their future led.

The memories filling my head changed abruptly. Where before they had been orderly and detailed, the next were a chaotic jumble. A bombardment as the army stormed Oresa, soldiers spreading through the city like the wrath of the Gods, cleaving and slaughtering as they put every man, woman and child to the sword. I watched the purge and how the king and his men happened upon the temple of inherita and the young curator within. He couldn't have known what she was or what she possessed, but through the eyes of another, I watched the king take her with him as he returned to Dranta, leaving the blood-soaked soil of her kin behind.

I saw no more of the king or the girl, though I could guess what had become of them. Instead, the next memories shared with me were of what remained of her people as they fled through their tunnels, attempting to escape the soldiers bearing down on them.

Without the curator to guide the memori, their way of life was all but destroyed. Memori died with no way of adding their lives to the inherita. Although they tried to start afresh, the comfort of knowing that their memories would survive their death was nothing to the grief for the history they had lost.

I watched as, driven by desperation, the new curator had poured her memories into the ground, creating the blackvine as a means of seeking out the inherita stolen from them. Trapped by the sun as they were, the memori couldn't search out the lost curator for themselves, but through the blackvine, they could search the entire continent.

The blackvine's first victims were the soldiers King Lucien left behind in Oresa to safeguard it from the memori's return. Then the blackvine coursed through the

219

tunnels, clearing the city and making it safe for the memori once more, corrupting Valrorian minds and stealing their memories as it searched out the stolen child.

The blackvine wasn't their revenge. It was their restitution.

They set it to scouring the countryside, seeking out what had become of the curator, accumulating memories from any unfortunate Valrorian it met on the way. Through them, the memori learnt of how King Lucien had marched his army back through the Deadwood, but they had never been able to discover her fate. It had been as if she had ceased to exist, but still they searched on, continuing to look because the pain of the inherita's loss hurt too much to give up.

They weren't monsters. Their pain was what we had inflicted on them, bringing the blackvine down upon ourselves. We created it with our hatred when all they wanted was what we had stolen from them.

Our help in exchange for yours, Falon. Help us find our inherita. Help us reclaim what is ours and we will help you keep her safe from the world that would destroy her.

CHAPTER TWENTY-FOUR

Light crept between my eyelids even though I squeezed them shut. The blaze pierced into me, making me miss the darkness.

I turned, needing to shield myself from its onslaught. The memori had the right of it by hiding in their tunnels and shutting out the sunlight.

"He can't be," a man said from above me. "Perhaps it didn't find him?"

I thought I recognised the voice, but I didn't know if he was a friend, foe or passing acquaintance. Although the sight of him might engage my memory, I wasn't ready to face the assault of the sunlight to find out.

"The fool," another voice said. "Why didn't he just leave Cedral be when he rolled off the rock? We would have been able to find him again as soon as the sun was up."

Relief washed through me at the sound of her voice. She was there. She wasn't just a memory.

I had to see her again. Forget the sunlight and the pain it would cause. I needed to be certain she was there.

I pried my eyes open to the spearing of dawn into my skull, wincing but not shutting them again. Instead, I pushed myself up onto my elbows, drinking in the sight of Sarilla and the familiar stranger as they leapt back from me in surprise.

"Falon?" Sarilla asked, holding her hand to her chest as she dragged in a steadying breath, her wide eyes fixed on me.

"You're here," I said, lost in the intense black of her eyes.

The ends of her hair tickled my neck as she leaned towards me and clasped my face in her hands, the crease at the top of her nose crinkling as she stared at me. It was strange to see her through my own eyes again. To stare at her as she was, unaltered by the anger and hatred expressed towards her in other peoples' memories. They didn't see how the slight raise of her eyebrows was apprehension, not mockery. How her lips were twisted from wariness, not cruelty. She was cynical, yes, but not a monster, not as they thought her to be. Only I saw through the veneer to the woman beneath, could see the beauty others missed in the darkness. The pale gold sheen glinting off her hair when it caught the sunlight. How her thick eyelashes whitened at the tips. The way her lips were several shades darker than was normal.

She was so much more than any memory could ever do credit. I wanted to drink in the sight until she was all I could remember.

I entwined my fingers in her hair, marvelling at how soft the strands were, too smooth for memories to ever do justice. Not even the memori's carefully catalogued records could replicate the tingle across my skin as I tangled my hand in her silky locks.

Hers was an exaggerated, unnatural beauty. Dark eyes

framed by dark lashes. Dark thoughts formed by her dark past. I longed to see inside her, to witness for myself the scorched soil from which love had once grown, from where I hoped it would one day bloom from again.

"How is this possible?" the familiar stranger asked as he peered down at me, worry and hope warring on the face I almost recognised.

Slightly crooked nose. Eyes I didn't dare trust.

Sarilla was too important to risk on a stranger.

"I don't know," she said, shaking her head. "The blackvine had him. It must have, so how...? I don't understand. Falon, can you hear me?"

"Hear, see, smell, touch," I murmured, trailing the back of my hand across her cheek.

I had to suppress the urge to taste her too at the sight of her discomposure. She was so beautiful. I wanted to close the distance between us, to pull her head down and press her lips to mine. How could anyone have ever been blind to the entrancing creature before me now? How much time had I wasted not seeing the match we made? Two bastards against the world.

"His eyes..." the familiar stranger said. "They're still black. Like Cedral's were. But how is he lucid when Cedral wasn't?"

Havric. The name appeared in my mind. I knew him.

"Falon?" Sarilla asked, her gaze still flitting searchingly over me. "Do you know what happened?"

Was she worried for me? I knew I should set her fears to rest, but I instead allowed myself to bask in the sensation for a moment, enjoying the knowledge that she cared for me. From what memories I had, I knew she once loved me. Did she still feel the same?

"Falon?"

"They let me go," I said, enjoying the sight of the

emotions flickering across her face. Confusion. Surprise. Fear.

"They? Who's they?" Havric asked as he frowned down at me, his face far less appealing to look at than hers.

Who was this man and why did he insist on being there? I would have much rather he left me alone with Sarilla. The sight of their camaraderie unnerved me. Who was he to her?

"The memori," I said, causing him to cast a glance at the forest about us

"What memori?" he asked. "There aren't any around here."

"They're everywhere, in the trees, the ground, in my head. They spoke to me."

"How?"

"It has to be the blackvine," Sarilla said. "They must be the ones guiding it through the forest."

Havric nodded, his gaze fixed on something off to my right, his lips drawn tight. What was he staring at? I turned my head to the side to see, but Sarilla blocked me before I could.

"Falon..." she said, her voice breaking. "I... The knife. Cedral must have landed on it in the fall."

"What?" I asked, trying to meet her gaze, but she kept her eyes averted, moving aside to let me see what she had been hiding from view.

Lifeless green eyes stared back at me from a few feet away and surprise coursed through me at the sight of the red streaking the man's face from the many cuts raking his skin. Blood stuck his dark blond hair to his brow as yet more blood soaked through his shirt, staining across his chest and pooling on the stone beneath him. Cedral? That was what she had called him, wasn't it? Had I known him?

Expectation built in the air as they waited for my

reaction. Did they think I would mourn him? How could I? He played no part in any of the few memories I had. Whoever this man had been, he was nothing to me now.

"I suppose we should bury him," Havric said as I turned from the man, returning my attention to the far more pleasing sight of Sarilla.

Sunlight dappled through the lingering leaves in the canopy above, staining her near-white skin a rippling orange that was entrancing to watch. She stared back at me, her jet-black eyebrows twitching in the smallest of frowns as she reached out with hesitant fingers as if to brush her palm across my cheek, but she caught herself and pulled her hand back before she did. Disappointment filled the pit of my stomach.

"I don't understand," she said, staring at my face. "You're not built like a memoria. You shouldn't be able to survive the blackvine's touch. Your mind can't take it."

"They said I wasn't like the rest. That I was empty."

She sat back, shifting away from me and I cursed myself for saying something that had made her worry.

"You mean your memories?" she asked. "They told you that? What else did they tell you?"

"That they've been searching for you."

Sarilla stilled, her eyes flaring as she stared at me.

"Who has?" Havric asked, looking between us.

"The memori have been using the blackvine to scour the Deadwood for you," I said to Sarilla. "For all your family."

"Is that why you've been running from it?" Havric asked, his voice filled with an accusation I didn't like. Why was he angry? She had done nothing wrong.

"Why was it searching for me?"

"They think you have the inherita."

She flinched and I hated that I had caused her such

discomfort.

"The what?" Havric asked. "What's the inherita and why do they think you have it?"

"It's the memori's collective history. A curation of memories. They think I have it because my grandmother had it."

"That's why the blackvine has been attacking us? To find the inherita?"

"When King Lucien stole my grandmother from Oresa, he unknowingly took the only thing the memori cared about."

"You mean you knew this all along?" Havric asked, his gaze cold as he stared at her. "How many people has it destroyed, Sarilla? All while you've known how to stop it?"

"What exactly do you think I could have done? I don't have the inherita."

"Then why not tell them that so they stop searching for it?"

"It's not so simple," she said, raking her hair back from where it fell across her face. "I wish it was-"

"Then make it that simple. If all they want is to know what's become of your grandmother, then just tell them. Touch the ground and do your magic and-"

"Can you promise me I won't end up like the rest of the blackvine's victims if I do? I'm only half memori, Havric. You don't know what will happen if the blackvine touches me."

"It probably won't do anything-"

"You want me to risk my sanity on a hunch? How about you try touching the blackvine and see what happens to you? Maybe you'll-"

"You could have stopped it!" Havric slammed his fist into the ground, his eyes blazing as he stared at Sarilla, all of his earlier camaraderie towards her gone. "The blackvine got Cedral. It got my cousin two years ago too. Do you know how painful it is to watch someone you care about die like that? It takes weeks for the raving lunatics to starve. If Cedral hadn't fallen on that knife then he would have been in for a slow and painful death too, a fate you could have saved them all from."

Tears brimmed in Sarilla's eyes, a muscle in her jaw tensing as she met his rage head-on, refusing to answer him.

"Come with me to Oresa," I said, dragging her attention my way.

"What? No."

"You can tell them what happened to your grandmother. You can explain how the inherita was lost when she died."

"I'm not going to Oresa."

"But... They're your people. You'll be safe there and far away from all the judgement and hatred. You'll be with your kind-"

"I'm a half-breed, remember?" she said, her lips twisting into a bitter snarl. "I'm no more one of them than I am one of you."

"Then go to Oresa for our sake," Havric said. "You can convince them to call off the blackvine. Just think how many lives you could save by stopping the march on Oresa. The king won't attack if the blackvine's stopped."

"There's to be an attack on the memori?" I asked, causing Sarilla and Havric to turn my way again, their brows furrowed in the same confused expression.

"You mean you don't remember?" Sarilla asked.

Before I realised what she was doing, she pressed her hands to the sides of my face, her touch hesitant. My skin hummed and I sank into the sensation as our gazes locked.

"What are you doing?" I asked, lost in the feel of her

hands on my cheeks.

"There's something coating your memories, preventing you from accessing them. That's why your eyes are still black they... Cursen's wrath!"

She pulled her hands back and leapt away from me.

"What? What is it?"

"You're still a part of it! The blackvine. It's still in you. That's why your eyes are like that."

"And?"

Of course I was still connected to it. I could hear the voices whispering in the depths of my mind, hiding in the darkness where it was safe. They were muted, but they would return in full force when night fell.

"But... It's in your mind," Sarilla said as she stared at me, shaking her head without seeming to realise what she did.

Didn't she understand what a gift it was? Through the blackvine, my mind was fully open to the world around me. I could see that which I had been blind to before. There was only one way I would give up the connection now and it wasn't willingly.

"You mean he can communicate with them?" Havric asked. "If that's true, then he can relay a message to them-"

"It's not me they want to hear it from."

"Then you have to go to Oresa," he said to Sarilla. "If you don't, then you'll be to blame for all the deaths still to come from this."

He stared at her, willing her to see things his way, but her gaze was still fixed on me, her thoughts flickering incomprehensively behind her eyes.

"I will if Falon can convince them to keep the blackvine away from us as we journey east."

"They won't attack us," I said with confidence. "They

wouldn't do anything to jeopardise hearing your account of the inherita. It's too precious to them."

"We go to Oresa then," Havric said, glancing across the rocks, his gaze landing on the body beside us. "But what do we do about Cedral? We can't just leave him like this."

Couldn't we?

Havric looked to me expectantly, his expression filled with a pity I didn't understand. He was looking to me to decide what to do about the dead man.

"I'll deal with him," I said, guessing that to be the answer he expected.

I must have guessed right because he nodded, his mouth tightening before he said, "I'll help you."

"No. It's alright. I can manage."

He watched me for a moment, then pushed up from where he knelt. "Fine. I'll go and ready a meal so we don't leave on an empty stomach."

He left, casting one last glance at the dead man before climbing up the rocks and disappearing out of sight. Sarilla followed behind him, leaving me alone with the body of a man I didn't remember.

I don't know how long I sat there staring at the man who might have been my friend. I couldn't know for certain what I had once felt for him, but if my memories would only cause me pain then wasn't I better off without them?

I cleaned him up as best as I could, feeling like I somehow owed it to him. Why, I didn't know.

The ground was too hard to dig him a grave, even if I had a spade to hand. I had a strange suspicion that it was for the best. Perhaps it was only my imagination and not the whisper of a memory ebbing through, but I had the vague impression that this Cedral had not been the type to wish to be laid to rest somewhere so cold. It felt right that he go out in a blaze. Just as he had lived?

The sun was high in the sky by the time I finished collecting enough wood for the pyre. I stacked it and lifted his body, feeling stupid saying goodbye to a man I didn't know. Stupider still standing there until the last flame died, but I was surprised to find my fingertips come away wet as I wiped at my cheek.

CHAPTER TWENTY-FIVE

"I need you to not come with us to Oresa."

Havric's hand stilled as he reached for his pack. A rush of excitement surged through me as I processed what Sarilla had just said. She didn't want him to join us? Why? It didn't matter. I didn't like the way he watched her. His gaze too frequently returned to her and I would have been glad of any excuse to be rid of him.

Havric scowled, crossing his arms. "No."

"You need to return to the army," Sarilla said, not meeting his gaze as she continued to pack up our camp. "You have to speak with Renford so he knows where we're going."

"I'm sure he'll survive."

"And if he continues marching the army on to Oresa?" Sarilla asked, still not looking up. "What if they reach the memori before we do? There's no point trying to prevent a war that's already happened."

"And how exactly am I supposed to stop an army from doing anything?"

"Talk to him. Tell him... Tell him I might have a way

to stop the memori."

"Am I supposed to be alright with leaving you with Falon? For Cursen's sake, Sarilla. Look at him."

I was really starting to dislike that man.

"It has to be you," Sarilla said, throwing his pack at him. "It's not like either of us can go. Falon's connection to the blackvine means he's the only one who knows the way to Oresa."

I nodded in agreement, but Havric ignored me.

"Then we all go to intercept the army."

"We'll never make it in time. We'll only slow you down. Please, Havric. You have to reach Renford."

Havric's jaw clenched and he sighed. "Fine. But I don't like this."

"I know," Sarilla said, taking his hand in hers and squeezing it. Heat rose in me and it was a moment before I realised I had clenched my fists.

"You'll tell him my message?" she asked. "Word for word."

"I will."

"Thank you."

She turned to leave but Havric tugged her back around.

What was between them? It didn't matter. He would be gone soon and it would just be Sarilla and me.

"Promise you'll stay safe?" Havric asked. "You've a worrying knack of attracting trouble."

"Don't worry about me. I'll be fine. It's him I'm worried about."

She bobbed her head my way and I scowled.

"Look after him for me?" Havric asked, casting a worried glance my way. "He doesn't seem to remember it now, but he's the only real friend I have."

I was?

"There's really no talking you out of this?"

Sarilla shook her head and Havric sighed.

"Then I hope Forta is with us all."

Striding over to me, he clapped me on the back. I tensed. I didn't know this man, no matter what he claimed.

"If you've any sway with the memori," he said. "Then I'd appreciate you stopping the blackvine from coming after me. I don't fancy my chances of reaching the army with it on my tail."

"I'll do what I can," I lied, already turning from him, but not quickly enough to miss the hurt that flashed through Havric's eyes.

"Perhaps you should carve out some space in my mind just in case," Havric said to Sarilla before nodding to us. Taking one last look at Sarilla, he disappeared between the trees, leaving us alone at last.

I cast about for something to say, but the words tangled on my tongue and I didn't know where to begin.

"You do know the way, don't you?" Sarilla asked, tearing me from my thoughts.

Did I? I had only been agreeing earlier because it meant getting rid of Havric.

When I didn't say anything, Sarilla sighed.

"Never mind," she said, sitting down and touching the ground, the beautiful marks on her arms moving entrancingly.

"It's this way," she said, indicating through the trees.

***

We journeyed as far as we could before night fell. Sarilla grew more restless the closer sunset drew. As soon as the light had fled, the blackvine rose about us and the voices whispering in my mind were no longer confined to the darkest recesses.

"I thought you said it wouldn't attack us?" Sarilla said, backing up against me, trying to create as much space between her and the blackvine as possible.

"Don't worry. It's here to protect us, not to attack."

"We don't need protecting, so send it away."

The memori in my head heard her request but made no move to recall the blackvine. Reading their decision from their lack of action, I dropped my pack to the ground, happy to stop for the night and rest my feet a bit.

"There's nothing you or I can do about it, so you may as well stop worrying."

As I spoke, the blackvine writhed about us, climbing atop itself in a dark lattice, creating a dome that was either a shelter or a cage depending on how you looked at it. There was enough room within to comfortably move about, and I set to work unpacking our meagre camp.

"We're not spending the night like this."

"At least we won't need to bother alternating watches," I said. "We'll be able to get a decent night's sleep-"

"If you think I'm so much as blinking, let alone sleeping with the blackvine so close, then it's more than just memories the memori took from you."

She crouched down, pressing her hand against the ground, the marks writhing as she connected with the nexus. Was she erasing any memory of our presence from the grass?

She eyed the blackvine sceptically as if she expected an attack at any second. "Start a fire," she said.

"It won't attack us. They gave their word."

"Just start a Gods' damned fire, Falon. Everybody lies. Haven't you learnt that by now?"

To keep the blackvine away? She really was terrified of it. Guilt shot through me at my having added to her unease. I wanted to comfort her, to help her see she had nothing to fear from the blackvine, but what could I say that would convince her? Words held no meaning for Sarilla, they had too often been used as weapons for concealing the truth.

"Would you feel better if I kept watch so you can sleep?"

She spared me a glance for the briefest of moments before returning her attention to the blackvine. "Not really. Can't you just make it go away?"

"They won't agree to that. You mean a lot to them, Sarilla. They want to ensure your safety."

"That's what they told you."

Grabbing every log and twig in reach, she knelt and built up the fire. After several attempts, she managed to kindle a small flame and the blackvine surged away as the fire sparked to life, widening the circumference of our shelter even more. Only when the fire blazed and the blackvine had retreated to enough of a distance that several trees were now contained within our shelter did she begin to settle down. I watched her as she fidgeted, finding any excuse to stay awake despite the exhaustion clearly weighing on her. She was a child of two opposing worlds. The embodiment of black and white, but rather than mixing to grey, the two halves divided her with their territories and battlegrounds, leaving her an extreme in every way possible.

"What do you want to be?" I asked two nights later as she shifted under the blanket, still awake despite the late hour. "Valrorian or Memori?"

Sarilla rolled my way, her face was lined with the evidence of her last few nights of restless sleep. She held my gaze for a moment before her focus shifted past me to the blackvine.

"Do I have to be either? Why can't I just be free?"

"I don't see any manacles on you."

"Not all chains are physical," she said, rolling onto her back and staring up at the bare trees through the gap in the dome above. "I want to be free from judgement and expectation. I already know I'm a monster, but it would be nice not to see the reminder on people's faces for once."

"You're not a monster," I said, making her start. "You could never be that."

She shifted, staring at me with what might have been hope in her eyes before it vanished. "I am what I am," she said. "I just don't need to be constantly reminded of it."

"You'll never find that in Valrora."

"I know."

She rolled over, turning her back to me again, but I doubted she slept. I watched her as she lay there, her body tensed and coiled, ready to spring at the first sign of the blackvine moving. It looked like living smoke with the golden firelight reflecting off it. How could she not see the marvel it was?

I felt rather than saw the lone vine creeping through my shadow towards me. Reaching backwards, I trailed my fingers through the almost unsubstantial tendril, delighting in the cold caress as the vines branched and entangled about my fingers. They climbed up my arm in a creeping coiling motion, but I barely felt it, already lost in the touch of the blackvine in my head as memories danced through my mind. I drifted my fingers through the smoke, revelling in how the memories changed as I did. Many of them were frayed and half-forgotten, but they were still glimpses into the lives of others, doors I could open that most didn't even know existed.

I moved through the memories, exploring first one then another. When I tried to return to a previous one, it was only to find another in its stead. Those close by seemed to vibrate with the same hum, echoing with the same resonance of missing details or focusing on the same things. It was fascinating. I saw the world through the eyes of others, only to realise that it wasn't my world they saw.

Sometimes the differences were subtle, the recollection of scents stronger than I suspected I had smelt in my life. Other times the changes were more obvious.

The colours were all confused in one man's memories. The sky browner. Faces paler. Everything had a strange, yellow hue that was unnerving to experience, but the memories from children were the most disorientating of all. The world was a very different place to those who paid little attention to much above knee height. Had I once seen the world like that?

Disquiet grew in the pit of my stomach and I pulled my hand out of the blackvine, uneasy for the first time about my missing memories. Was I wrong to be so trusting of the memori when they were keeping me separated from so much of who I was?

Don't worry about that, Falon, a voice whispered in my mind as the darkness coated my thoughts, wrapping about the memories of what I had just seen in the blackvine. *You don't need to worry about anything again.*

CHAPTER TWENTY-SIX

Sarilla and I didn't speak much as we travelled. While it was clear that her thoughts were far from empty, mine were hardly less preoccupied. Each night as she slept, the blackvine kept me company, its voices whispering in my mind, their language filling my head as they showed me more about memorian culture than I had imagined could exist. Through them, I saw Oresa in all its glory, its maze of tunnels burrowed so deeply underground that the city lived in permanent twilight.

At first, I couldn't tell the voices in my head apart, their language was too foreign for me to recognise the differences between the speakers, but soon enough it transformed into more than an indistinct whisper in my mind. I began to notice the clipped syllables and the slurring of the vowels, each as distinctive as a memory was in their own way.

Kira was the one who kept me company the most. It was her weaving me tales through the late hours. Her voice filled with a command that expected obedience. The more familiar I grew with her, the easier it became to distinguish her memories from those of the other memori. I learnt to recognise hers just through the details she noticed that others didn't. Hers often focused on the people attending her rather than the food they brought. She had a preference for watching the crowd instead of the speaker and a determination to remember as much as she possibly could that was admirable, even by memori standards.

Kira had taken it upon herself to collect the inherita in the curator's absence, cataloguing her peoples' lives so they wouldn't die without leaving some record of their having lived. She shared with me the first time she performed the rite and I wept at the relief on the dying woman's face as Kira took her memories inside her. Sarilla couldn't realise how important the inherita was to the memori. If she did, then surely she would do everything she could to give them closure for its loss. Her account wouldn't recover what the memori had lost, but it would help them begin anew.

As the blackvine coiled about my arm on the fourth night, I expected more images of Oresa to fill my mind. I was already eager to learn more of their culture. I wanted to delve deeper, where there was more to life than living and eventually dying. To the memori, touching was a far less intimate act than it was to my own people. To do so allowed the exchange of memories in the place of conversation, the sharing of hopes, dreams and the expression of that which had not come to pass. To them, language was more of a necessity, one driven by the rare situation when the sharing of memories wasn't appropriate or feasible.

The underground city existed in a strange hush too despite being filled with memori, so quiet that you might think sound was as harmful to their way of life as the light. Some aspects of their culture were so astonishing that I still couldn't quite think them true. Despite the number of memories Kira shared with me of mothers communicating with their babes before they were even born, I still couldn't believe it. They helped their infants develop before they could even lay eyes on their offspring, communicating with them as they grew up, able to understand them while ours were only frustrated by their inability to make their wishes known. If nothing else, the ability of the memori children to be so easily understood seemed to make for a much happier childhood.

I waited for Kira to show me more memories, but instead, I found myself watching some that were far more faded than a memori memory ever was.

I didn't recognise where the memory was of. It seemed to be in a tunnel, the ceiling of which had been carved to resemble a forest canopy, with pinpricks of light twinkling between the leaves, recreating the effect of the stars. The light was dim, but enough to see a short way down the tunnel.

It's beautiful, is it not? Kira's voice asked in my head. *Much of our memories of this place were lost when we fled to Oresa. The sunlight poses many threats to my people, and the Deadwood forest could only protect us so far.*

"These are the tunnels beneath Dranta?" I asked, turning through the memory filling my mind. "You left all this behind?"

We had to. Your armies drove us away. We would not have relinquished our home willingly had we any other choice.

"It can't have been easy for you to leave."

I wasn't alive then. We have long lives in comparison to yours, but not so long as that. It was my grandmother who made the decision for us to leave. She led those who were willing away. And some of those who weren't.

"The curator?"

Kira hummed an affirmation, but no thoughts

accompanied the sound.

"Why didn't she wish to leave?"

I'm sure she had her reasons. Fear of what journeying outside might do to the inherita, perhaps? But I think not.

"What do you mean?"

Only that there's no telling why she fought so hard to stay in Dranta now, not with the inherita gone. But sometimes I wonder about what the inherita contained. A thousand years is a lot of secrets for one person to have stored inside them.

"How did you manage to get away without damaging it?"

The tunnels helped us for a lot of the journey. Then the forest shielded us where the tunnels could not, but... it wasn't enough. Beyond the Deadwood, we were exposed. We did what we could, but sacrifices had to be made. Only the curator made it to Oresa without suffering the effects of the sun, and that was achieved at great cost to the rest of our people. My grandmother had almost no memories of her own to offer for curation when her time came. I should know. This was one of hers.

I glanced around with renewed interest, this time staring at what was missing rather than what was there, trying to imagine what had been lost to the sunlight. The colours were faded in an unnatural way I had failed to notice before, worn away to grey entirely and creating a patchwork effect.

The curator elected not to take it when my grandmother's time came. I'm sure she had plenty of other memories stored within her that were far better, but after everything, the rejection still hurt. My grandmother gifted the memory to me instead. It's good she did. If she hadn't, then we wouldn't have any memories of Dranta since the curator was stolen from us.

The bitter sorrow in Kira's voice almost broke me. I tried to think of something comforting to say, but before I could, Kira swapped the memory for another. The sudden change was disorientating. The new memory was so thread thin that it barely held an image any longer. Just enough remained for me to make out the familiar pale eyes shattered with shards of green. I recognised the gaze. Where did I know him from?

You see now why it's so important that you bring her to us? Kira asked, dragging my attention away from those all too familiar eyes. *Memories have a power few truly comprehend.*

"But... She says she doesn't have the inherita. What good will her being in Oresa do you?"

There was a long pause. I thought for a moment that Kira had released the connection, but I could still feel her moving through my mind.

Do you believe her? It wouldn't be the first time she concealed memories inside her.

"What do you mean?"

The memory shifted again and the man with the green-flecked eyes appeared before me once more, this time joined by the sound of his name in my head. It trickled through my mind, along with a strange pain I couldn't explain.

Ced.

Do you wish to know what she hid from you?

"What do you-?"

Pebble thoughts rippled through the black depths of my mind, shimmering the surface as one memory after another was released to me.

I knew him. I had travelled with Ced to Dranta. This man was my lifelong friend.

No. We were far more than that to each other. He had come with me when I had gone to assassinate the king, but he hadn't finished the journey, instead turning back for Arvendon and leaving me to go the rest of the way alone.

This is just one of the memories she took from you.

I shuddered as Kira passed me the memory. It slotted with ease back into the void Sarilla had carved in my mind, and I reeled from the return of what I had lost.

Slapping flesh and lusty groaning filled the air as the image of the bedchamber in the Claw and Paw tavern suffused my mind. I felt my hesitation as I pushed the door open, staring into the room and the two men tangled together atop the bed.

Ced's face dropped at the sight of me in the doorway and he stilled mid-drive into the young man he had been ploughing, an apology already spilling from his lips. I felt how annoyance had stabbed through me at the sight, and the sensation struck me as odd. I had known Ced wasn't the monogamous type, but why wasn't I more hurt by his blatant betrayal?

"We should get going," I had said, ignoring the other man's presence as I strode into the bedchamber and grabbed my pack, Ced's expression transforming into a scowl as he watched me.

"That's it? Cursen's wrath, Fal. Is that the only reaction I'm to get out of you?"

"You want me to yell?" I asked, spinning about, my pack swinging as I rounded on him. "You want me to be angry? Is that why you did it? You're angry because I was flirting with her downstairs, but I was trying to get information. What exactly were you trying to do here other than prove that you're a spiteful brat? Now get your stuff and get moving. If you want me to yell, then I'll be more than happy to oblige on route."

"And we wouldn't want to delay you, would we? Look out everybody, Falon the Bastard is on a mission to prove himself."

My hand had frozen on the doorknob as I struggled to process what he said. There were few people in my life who never referred to me with such derision. I had counted Ced among that meagre number and loved him for it. Even when the rest of the world mocked me, he had never seemed to care about the failings of my birth. If anything, he had used to act out just to be a bastard too and make me feel less alone.

"It takes one to know one," I said, ignoring the guilt that flashed across Ced's face as he realised what he had done. "If you're so unhappy about going to Dranta with me, then don't bother. I've had enough of you."

The memory faded as I stormed from the bedchamber, my vision returning to that of trees and the blackvine as my emotions rioted inside me.

"He… He kept that from me?" I asked as small tendrils of my memories returned to me, wading out of the blackness in my mind, providing me with the context that had been missing moments before. "He wouldn't tell me what happened, so I thought… I thought…"

Ced hadn't told me what had happened because he was afraid of how I would react to his having slept with another man. He had been trying to hide the fact that what had been between us was over. Had he been hoping to trick me into giving him a second chance?

That was all we could salvage, Kira whispered, her voice filled with apology. *She may yet have the rest of your memories.*

"Let her keep them. I don't want to know them."

I wasn't that man anymore. I didn't ever want to be that man again.

Sarilla stirred. She rolled over to stare at me, her gaze taking in the blackvine wrapped around my arm, but she didn't react. The embers of our dying fire reflected in her eyes as she studied me, looking as if her soul was aflame inside her. The orange glow suffused her face, deceiving the eye and making her look almost normal, but she wasn't.

I knew that now my memories were trickling back into me, yet she wasn't quite the monster I had used to think her. I couldn't push through the affection I had begun to feel towards her enough for that.

Clarity finally dawned as we stared at each from other across the fire. How long had I blamed the evil Sarilla created upon her heritage? I had assumed she acted as she did because of what she was born to be, judging her as evil while failing to realise that it was her own actions that made her such.

"You really are a piece of work," I said as I withdrew my hand from the blackvine.

I expected her to be indignant, to try to defend herself, but clearly I had yet to learn that there was little point expecting anything when it came to Sarilla.

"Got your memories back, I see."

"And some."

"They gave you Cedral's too?" she asked, rolling onto her back and staring up at the stars.

"You knew they had them?"

"Where else would they have gone?"

Her indifference took me by surprise and riled me.

"Why don't you care more that I have the memory? You were trying so hard to keep it from me."

"Because he's dead," she said, shrugging under the blankets. "What does it matter what you know at this point? It's not like he can earn redemption now."

"Dammit, Sarilla. You've no right to play at being God with my memories."

"Isn't that what the memori in your head are doing right now?"

"They concealed my memories to protect me. For who's benefit did you do it? I was wrong to blame how you are on the memori. It has nothing to do with them. You're a monster all of your own making."

She rolled onto her side and stared at me, her black eyes concealing the darkness within.

"I know exactly what I am. Which is more than you can say."

I grabbed her hand, stopping her as she tried to roll away. She tried to push me off, but I held my grip, her cheeks flushing as she kept her gaze averted, determinedly not meeting mine.

My emotions were a riot inside me, a war of two extremes that could never mix. Even with my memories coming back to me, I could still remember the desire that had filled me, my urge to protect her. I loved and hated her in that moment, and I didn't know which to believe. The creature who had stolen my memories, or the one who had done it to protect me from the king?

Her breath hitched as I brought my other hand up to touch her face. Her gaze met mine and I no longer cared that her eyes were black or that she had a propensity for deception. She and I were entwined by more than I could even remember and I couldn't stop myself from pulling her lips to mine.

I don't know what I expected, but as she kissed me back, need rose inside me, so strong that I could hardly believe I had ever forgotten it. The familiarity of her touch stoked my desire and it didn't matter that I had no memory of kissing her before, I knew I had felt her lips on mine as sure as I knew that night was dark.

Pressing her back, I pushed her to the ground, pinning her with my weight in case the moment passed too soon. I gripped her to me, wondering how even losing my memories could have robbed me of the sweet ache of her body against mine and the warmth of her legs wrapped around me.

"I thought I was going mad," I said, breathing in the smell of her hair. "When I found you outside Arvendon, it was like my body knew you even when my mind didn't. Even when I thought I hated you... you knew what was between us. You've always known. Why would you keep that from me?"

"Because there's nothing between us," she whispered, trying to break away even as I drew her mouth to mine again.

"Liar," I murmured, slamming our lips back together.

I kissed her neck, my hot breath tickling her and causing a groan to slip from her. Her lips might be liars, but there was no way her body was too. She still cared for me.

I lost myself in the feel of her as I grazed her skin. After weeks of fighting my desire, I was only too happy to be adrift in the heady rush her presence invoked. If she wanted to keep my memories of our past from me, then that was fine, I would force her lips into a different kind of admission.

Pleasure suffused me as she kissed me back, squirming beneath me and pressing her body against mine, forcing all thought from my mind. My hands roamed lower, retracing contours at once new and so achingly familiar. How did my body remember what my mind could not? Her groan turned into a gasp as I relinquished control, letting my hands roam instinctively. I splayed my fingers across her hips and she clung to me in answer.

She loved me. I could feel it to be true, even if she couldn't bring herself to say it. Was that my true crime, perhaps? Not that I had tried to kill the king, but that I had been loved by the one he could only fear to touch.

Sarilla pulled back from me, and I was suddenly bereft. She trailed her hand down my cheek as a tear trickled down hers.

"How do you think this ends, Falon?"

"However you want. We can go wherever you want. There's nothing left for me in Arvendon now. We can leave behind the prejudice and go somewhere nobody has heard of memori or of bastards of Arvendon. We can be free. Like you wanted."

Her lips twisted into a not-quite smile.

"Our pasts would always haunt us."

"What are you seeking redemption from? For the crime of being born? It wasn't our sins that made us what we are."

"You're sure about that?"

She rolled out from under me and turned away. Behind her, the blackvine writhed, encircling us protectively as I stared at Sarilla long after she fell asleep, unable to shake the feeling of her lips on mine. Nor the nagging suspicion that there was far more she was keeping from me than just my memories.

More memories of Ced returned to me as the night slipped by. They emerged from the blackness, confusing my emotions as they filled my head. Ced laughing in my arms as we lay in bed, staring out over the treetops about Arvendon. Ced gambling at the cards table, his gaze always meeting mine for the briefest of instances whenever he bluffed.

Ced's dead eyes staring sightlessly at me as I lowered him atop the pyre.

Oh, Gods. It hurt.

My chest ached more than I had thought possible, and I didn't want to feel anything anymore.

You see now why I kept your memories from you? Kira said as the twilight brightened about me. *You have much pain to process, Falon. I hoped I might spare you some of it.*

"Can you take them from me? I don't want to feel this

way anymore."

Hiding from them won't lessen the pain, it will only delay it.

"Please, just do it."

As you wish. I can release them whenever you want. You need only ask.

One by one, the memories of Ced slipped from my mind, taking the pain with them until there was only Sarilla.

I would convince her to give us another chance. I had to. There was too much between us to let what we were die.

CHAPTER TWENTY-SEVEN

After travelling beneath the forest's shelter for so long, Valrora's plains were strangely exposing. Leagues of uninhabited grassland stretched before us in every direction, those few pioneers who had dared to colonise the kingdom's easternmost reaches were either dead or had fled. Remains of the homes they left behind littered the plains, weeds sprouting from the roofs and most of the front doors hanging crooked. They stood as monuments to the blackvine's reach.

"We have to be getting close, right?" I asked after we had been walking for a while along the road east.

"Another day or so, I should think," Sarilla said. "I didn't realise it was so bad out here. None of the memories I took were from anyone who lived this close to Oresa. These homes have been this way for a while. Why did Renford not do something about the memori years ago?"

"My father started asking that question a long time ago, ever since blackvine refugees started pouring into Arvendon. He sent hundreds of reports to the king on the subject."

"And Renford ignored him?"

"You expected better from a man who forced you to take memories from his people?"

"It isn't hatred that drives him, you know."

"If you say so. You know him better than I do. What is it then?"

Sarilla fell silent for a moment, her gaze lingering on the abandoned house.

"Fear."

"There's a difference?"

"When it comes to Renford there is…" she said as she stared behind us. "What's that?"

I followed the direction of her gaze to the dust cloud in the distance. "Looks like riders."

"The army?"

"There's only a few of them. A scouting party? Unless that's all that's left after the blackvine attack."

The silver and green uniforms flashed in the distance as the party rode for us.

"What do we do?" I asked as I grasped my sword by the hilt. "Hide in the house?"

"We wait."

"But-"

"We wait," she said again, her jaw set.

Resigning to her decision, I repositioned myself so I stood just ahead of her, my unease growing as the riders drew closer.

They brought their horses up as they reached us, encircling us as they glanced about the empty countryside while one of the men leapt down from his horse and hurried over to us. Relief surged through me as I recognised Havric and I was more than grateful for the chance to apologise to him for how I had treated him when we last parted. He hadn't deserved that. If he cared for

Sarilla, then it was only because he wanted to keep her safe. Did he resent me for how I acted towards him?

Would he forgive me now?

He looked my way, his gaze lingering on my eyes before he nodded to Sarilla, offering her a quick grin before asking, "Is it still in him?"

"Yes, but I've got my memories back," I said, giving him a half-smile, unsure how to act about him.

"That which he remembers," Sarilla muttered, ignoring the scowl I shot her way. "I take it you found the army."

"You doubted me? You should have seen the king's face when I mentioned where you were heading."

He gestured behind him. I followed the motion and startled as I spotted the king where he sat atop a horse, staring down at Sarilla. Rage rose in me at the sight of him, this man who had forced Sarilla to endure so much and would happily inflict it on her all over again. He couldn't be allowed anywhere near her.

"This man tells me you're journeying to Oresa," he said, idly running the reins between his fingers. "And that you intend to end the animosity between Valrora and Oresa. Is that true, my dear?"

Sarilla opened her mouth to speak, then glanced my way, her forehead creasing as she struggled over something I couldn't understand, but still felt the need to protect her from.

"You don't need to fight them," I said, drawing the king's gaze my way for the first time. He flinched at the sight of my eyes, jerking back in the saddle.

"What is this corruption? Is he a victim of the blackvine?"

"Yes, but he's lucid," Sarilla said, sounding only half convinced by what she was saying. "We think it's something to do with the memories I took from him, that

I somehow made enough room in his mind to protect him from the blackvine."

The king studied me, his disgust at my condition written for all to see in the crinkling of his nose. I could almost see his mind at work as his expression turned calculating.

"And what of your plan?" he asked, returning his attention to Sarilla.

"They want a peaceful resolution," I said instead. "You have to stop the army from attacking Oresa-"

"Do you see an army here, Bastard?" the king asked, spreading his hands wide as his lip curled. "This retinue is here to guard my person. It's hardly a force to be reckoned with now, is it?"

"All I meant was that there's no need for you to journey to Oresa."

"You think so, do you? And here I was thinking that I had travelled all this way to speak with those wishing to act as my envoys."

He slid down from his horse, throwing the reins to one of his guards.

"My apologies. That's not what I meant. I was only pointing out-"

"If you've finished questioning your monarch, I've direction to provide concerning my interests in Oresa. Or do my self-elected envoys object to hearing such guidance?"

"We'll listen," Sarilla said, placing a hand on my shoulder and squeezing it.

Something flashed in the king's eyes as she did, and I gripped my sword's hilt tighter. There was nothing comforting about the way he looked at her. His gaze was so possessive that it was a wonder he hadn't branded her to prove to everyone who she belonged to.

"What I have to say doesn't require two pairs of ears to

hear it," he said, giving me a pointed stare before gesturing Sarilla forwards. "Come, my dear."

Hands gripped my arms and somebody snatched my sword, wrenching it from me along with my other weapons. I struggled with the soldier, trying to shake him off, but another grabbed me and together they held me fast.

"Get off!"

"I would advise you not to resist, Bastard. With eyes like that, it would take little for you to be deemed a credible threat to my person."

"Renford, please," Sarilla said, laying her hand on the king's arm. "He's only trying to protect me."

The king and his soldiers tensed, their gazes fixed on Sarilla's ungloved hand. She glanced down and only then seemed to realise what she had done. She quickly pulled her hands back, trying to hide them like it would do any good.

"How can anyone be sure what his motivations are with such corruption inside him?" the king asked as he cast another disgusted glance my way. "No. Come, my dear. We must talk."

"Sarilla-"

The soldiers' grip on me tightened as I tried to shrug them off. Sarilla glanced back at me, something unreadable passing across her face, then she turned her back on me too, walking away as betrayal sliced through me.

"Don't worry," Havric said as I renewed my struggles against the soldiers. "I think he's on board with the plan. He was just adamant that he talks with her first."

I raised an eyebrow but didn't say anything as I watched Sarilla speak to the king, too far away to make out what she said. She glanced my way a couple of times, but quickly looked away again.

"Are you sure you're alright?" Havric asked, motioning for the soldiers to relax their hold on me.

"Never better," I said as the men released me and stepped back, keeping a wary eye on us. "Hey, Hav. I'm sorry…"

"Don't worry about it." He flashed me a grin. "I'm just glad to have you back."

He fell silent as Sarilla and the king made their way back over to us.

"Thank you for everything you've done, Havric," Sarilla said, smiling at him as the king climbed atop his horse, nodding for his men to return to theirs. "If we don't meet again-"

"What do you mean if? I'm coming with you."

"You can't." She glanced over his shoulder at where the king watched us, his gaze fixed on Sarilla. "You're to go with Renford. You're his… insurance."

"Against what?"

"He needs leverage, assurance that we'll act in Valrora's interests. Since Falon's connection to the blackvine makes him suspect-"

"You think I would betray my own people?"

Her gaze flickered to mine, but she quickly averted it again as Havric grimaced, shaking his head.

"Consider me reassured," he said.

"Havric-"

"No, it's alright. I'll be fine. It's you two I'm worried about." He glanced across the plains in the direction of Oresa. "Just… take care, alright?"

Gripping my shoulder, he bid us goodbye and we watched as he left with the king and the soldiers, leaving only a dust cloud in their wake.

"What did the king say to you?" I asked when they were gone.

"Nothing of consequence," Sarilla said, setting off.

"Sarilla?" I called after her. "Sarilla!"

But she didn't turn back around, instead continuing to make her way towards Oresa, a determination in her step that hadn't been there before.

CHAPTER TWENTY-EIGHT

The blackvine rose again when night fell, writhing up like worms out the dirt. Sarilla's hand found my arm as she stared at a break in the darkness that was only just discernible in the fading twilight.

"It's a path," I said, taking a cautious step forward. "I think the blackvine's showing us the way."

"Then we must be getting close," she said, moving hesitantly along the path.

We walked in silence, the whisperings and the crunch of our footsteps the only sounds in the night. After what felt like hours, Sarilla slowed and came to a stop, staring at something ahead that I couldn't see.

"What it is?" I asked, moving around her.

"Not what. Who."

I frowned, not understanding her meaning. Shapes resolved in the darkness. The faces of the three memori men were so pale that they could have been carved from snow as they watched us, their expressions devoid of emotion.

"We have come for you," the man in the middle said in

broken Valrorian.

As he spoke, the blackvine swarmed my head once more, filling my vision with images from another. I stumbled, the change disorientating. I started at the sight of myself, my face slack jawed as I stared sightlessly at my surroundings. No longer was the night so dark when seen through the eyes of one of the memori men before me.

"What is this?" I asked as I turned my head, unnerved by how my vision remained as it was.

It is for your safety, Kira's voice said in my mind. *Oresa is darker than your eyes will tolerate.*

"You are to come with us," the man said as he turned, making his way along the path.

I hurried after him, Sarilla's lighter footsteps following in my wake as the other two memori walked behind her. It was disorientating to move under the directions of another's vision, but fortunately the path was straight. Even so, I still tripped up a few times as the memori led us to a small stone tower. There were no windows, only a small door that the first memoria knocked on. He spoke something through a small opening and the guard on the other side opened it, standing back to permit us entry.

I reached out, trying to feel for the entrance as the memoria disappeared inside, his sight abandoning me as I shuffled forward.

"What are you doing?" Sarilla asked from somewhere off to my right.

"I can't see anything," I said as my fingers met cold stone. "The blackvine's taken my vision."

"What?"

Finding the door, I made my way inside. My stomach lurched as I dropped for a moment, flailing into the darkness in the second before my foot found something solid.

"It's a staircase," Sarilla said, grabbing the back of my shirt and holding me steady. "Be careful."

"I'll be fine," I said with more confidence than I felt as my vision shifted again. I couldn't tell who it belonged to this time, only that it was from someone far below as they stared up at where we stood at the top of a spiralled staircase.

I took my first hesitant step, my hands cast out uncertainly to help protect me should I fall. Relief washed through me every time I made it safely to the next step.

It was more than a little unnerving to see myself through another's vision. My black eyes were disturbing to behold, adding to the general slackness of my features as I stumbled down the stairs. No wonder the king and his guards had reacted to me as they did. I looked downright sinister.

Sarilla moved to walk ahead. Mistrust filled me as the vision I was borrowing focused on her. It was a moment before I realised that the emotion wasn't my own, instead belonging to whichever memoria was feeding their sight into me through the blackvine. I tried to figure out whose vision it was, but the image shifted to another's on the other side of the room.

I stumbled from the change but didn't fall. The new viewpoint offered me a better vantage and I continued to make my way down, my vision shifting a few more times before we reached the bottom, but no matter how many different memori I was passed between, they all stared at Sarilla with the same unease as her gaze swept back and forth over the onlookers, still wary of them. Didn't she realise they meant her no harm?

My vision shifted again as we reached the bottom of the stairs. Everything went black and it was a moment before I realised that it was my eyes I was seeing out of once more as we walked across the dirt floor, moving to the centre of the gathered crowd. If I had thought it dark before, it was nothing to how blind I was without the memori's help. The only light source was the distant flicker of faint firelight behind screens in the shadowy alcoves of the chamber. It was barely enough to make out the female memoria stood before us. Her slanted eyes gave her face a pointed look where they pinched about the nose, and she seemed to watch everyone at once with her all-consuming gaze.

Kira. It had to be her.

She studied us intently, her long, unadorned black gown sweeping the floor, a darker shade than those worn by the others standing beside her.

If she shared the other memori's mistrust, then she concealed it well.

Had this been a mistake? What if I had I been wrong to encourage Sarilla to Oresa? I had brought her there believing Kira's promise to keep Sarilla safe, but what if…

Kira's lips pursed a fraction, her studying gaze flickering to me as darkness lapped through my mind. My fears melted away and I couldn't remember what I had been worrying about.

We had made it. We were in Oresa. Sarilla would be safe now.

"You came," Kira said in memorian, her words filling my mind.

"Don't pretend you haven't mastered their language yet," Sarilla said in Valrorian, her tone sharp. "We all know you've stolen more than enough memories for that."

Kira cocked her head to the side slightly. "Enough?" she said in Valrorian, her mouth struggling with the shape of the words. "Can an inherita ever be enough?"

"It can when it's made of that which you've stolen."

"What we did was a gift, one they never would have

been capable of receiving without our intervention. Through our actions, their memories will outlast them all."

"It's a gift no-one asked for."

"Yet it's a gift nonetheless," Kira said, her lips drawing tight. "You are welcome here, lost daughter. If you wish it, you are welcome home."

Sarilla flinched. Home. Had she ever thought of anywhere as such before? Or was she so disgusted by the prospect of finding her place among the memori?

"Even if I don't have what you've been searching for?"

"Even then. We accept where others reject."

"Why?" Sarilla asked, hurling the word like a challenge. I cast a sidelong glare at her, but she ignored me, her attention fixed on Kira.

"Why wouldn't we? With or without the inherita, you are still welcome among us. As your family would have been had they made it here as your father intended. When he spoke of your plight, we had not thought your path to our protection would be quite so treacherous-"

"What do you know of my father? You never met."

"On the contrary. He sought us out, seeking a home for his children that was safe from your uncle. That's what you are here. Safe."

"And you won't set your blackvine on me?" Sarilla asked, mistrust lining her voice.

"It is not our custom to force memori to reveal what is sacrosanct. Memories are to be gifted or not shared at all."

"Except from those who don't share memori blood?"

"Would you deny a dog a roasted shank because it has not the ability to start a fire? No. I only ask that you share your story with us. My people would know what became of the child and the memories stolen from us."

Sarilla hesitated, her gaze flickering from Kira to the others watching us from about the room. "I won't join my mind to the blackvine."

"In words then," Kira said. "If it must be. But you have travelled far and I know you must be exhausted. We have waited so long, I am sure a little longer won't hurt. A chamber has already been prepared for you and your mate. If you would follow-"

"Mate?" Sarilla asked.

"My apologies. We assumed from what we witnessed…"

Heat flooded my face as I understood her meaning. Was there nothing Kira hadn't been privy to in my memories? Her gaze prickled my skin as she glanced my way again. Did she know my thoughts even as I stood there?

I looked down at her feet, unsurprised to find them bare. If a connection to the nexus was all it took to link a memori to the blackvine, then could Kira be connected at any time she wished? It was a good thing I had no plans to betray the memori. I doubted I would get far if I did.

"You are the bridge between our two peoples, Falon. We honour you greatly in sharing our memories in this way. Come. You must rest now from your journey," Kira said, addressing me for the first time as darkness lapped at my mind and I couldn't remember why I had felt so uneasy only a moment before.

CHAPTER TWENTY-NINE

Kira gestured for us to follow, leading us further into the darkness to a set of rooms deep underground. A damp, earthy scent filled my nose as I stepped inside to find a brazier of gently shimmering coals burning behind a screen in the far recesses, permitting just enough light to see by. Water trickled soothingly from somewhere nearby, but I couldn't see where it came from. The chamber was certainly nothing like the exquisitely carved tunnels of the memori's home under Dranta, but it was still elegant for all its simplicity.

"This is where you shall stay," Kira said from the doorway, her gaze fixed on Sarilla as she made her way cautiously about the room.

"Both of us?" Sarilla asked, turning to examine the bed.

"This will suit fine," I said before Sarilla could protest. I didn't feel comfortable leaving her alone down there, even with Kira's offer of protection. Perhaps it was only Sarilla's wariness, but I couldn't bring myself to relax and let my guard down.

"There is a heated pool," Kira said, gesturing towards

the darkest part of the room. "Changes of clothes have been prepared for you both. Rest. Recover from your journey. Take as long as you need. Guards will wait outside your door. Let them know if you require anything. You may rest for as long as you choose-"

"Fetch us before dawn," Sarilla said, staring at the dimly glowing brazier as if fascinated by the shaded embers.

"That is not long away. You will not have had the time to properly rest-"

"That doesn't matter. Fetch us before dawn. You shall hear my story then."

Kira hesitated. After a moment, she nodded. "If that is what you wish. I will have you summoned when night's shade is almost over."

She left, backing through the doorway and leaving Sarilla and me alone.

"You alright?"

She didn't answer me, instead she made her way through the room, examining the walls and furnishings with hesitant fingers.

"I can't imagine this is easy for you. The memori-"

"Are acting no differently than I expected. I'm a half-breed, remember?"

"You really think they care about that?"

"Is your eyesight that poor or are you just willingly blind to the truth?"

"Sarilla... What reason have they given that you should mistrust them now? Give them time."

Sarilla lifted her gaze to meet mine, looking away again quickly. "I'm a half-breed, remember? They think me unworthy of their culture, just as Valrorians do theirs. I'm as tarnished here by my birth as I ever was in Valrora."

"Sarilla-" I grabbed her arm, spinning her about. "Stop this. You're not a monster, but you are if you choose to act like one."

A tear trickled down her cheek and I wanted to tell her that she was being stubborn, that she was clinging to a self-hatred that was as stupid as it was destructive, but I couldn't find the words.

"Stop making assumptions about how they feel towards you. You've never been here, so you can't know their opinion. If you had the inherita, then at least you would be able to claim some insight into their culture, but-"

Sarilla's eyes flared and she turned her back to me. Realisation hit me and I cut off the thought, trying to think about something else. Anything else. Any thought that would hide the one that I didn't want the memori finding in my head. I didn't know why Sarilla was keeping her possession of the inherita a secret, but whatever her reasoning, I wouldn't be the one to betray her.

She made her way to the back of the room and the sound of lapping water soon echoed into the chamber as she submerged herself, washing away the accumulated grime of travel. Her sigh rang through the darkness and memories of when I had bathed her in Arvendon rose in my mind. The image of her naked figure filled my head, and I had to fight back the urge to follow her into the chamber. Instead, I sat down on the bed, enjoying the darkness. There was something protective about how it wrapped around me. Where before I might have viewed a shadowy alcove with suspicion of what might lurk within, now the dark was a place of reprieve, somewhere I might seek protection from the light and all the dangers it brought.

My eyes weighed shut and I drifted off, lulled by the soft splashing from the next room. I awoke to Sarilla's hand trailing up my arm, her touch warm and damp. I opened my eyes to peer at her, but only her silhouette was visible in the darkness.

"You trust them, don't you," she said, her tone making me wish I could see her face.

Stretching, I woke up my sleeping muscles, enjoying the pleasant strain and protest.

"I do," I said, gripping her hand. "As can you. They want to accept you, Sarilla. You just have to give them the chance."

I stroked her palm with the pad of my thumb. Her skin was silky soft except for the cuts she had accumulated in her weeks of journeying across Valrora.

"You'll learn to not be so trusting soon enough," she said, her hand leaving mine as she grazed my cheek.

My breath caught in my throat as she brushed my eyelids closed. My heart thundered as I waited, not daring to move or breathe lest I frightened her away. Her lips brushed mine and I couldn't stop myself from drawing her to me, I needed to make it so she couldn't slip away again. So I could never forget her again.

I craved the sweetness of her touch even as I breathed in the clean scent clinging to her, revelling in how it teased my senses as she kissed me back, stoking the fire between us and sealing my fate. I groaned when she pulled away, wanting to draw her back to me.

"Why do I feel like you're always running from me?" I asked into the darkness, kissing her fingers as she pressed them to my lips, silencing me.

"I'm not the one who should be running."

"You know you're as maddening when you're being honest as you are when you're lying?" I asked, squeezing her hand before letting her go.

"I know," she said, slipping away and leaving me bereft without her touch.

Deciding that a bath wasn't a half bad idea, I made my

way into the other chamber. It was so dark that I had to feel my way into the water. I sank into its soothing warmth, my body surrounded by its reassuring embrace. It was only a fear of dozing off in the pool that eventually dragged me out. I groped about on the side for something to dry myself with, eventually locating a soft bit of fabric and rubbing myself down before moving towards the doorway, stopping at the sight of the figure blocking my way.

"Here," Sarilla said, holding something out.

I took what she offered and shook it. How long had she been watching me?

"This is a dress. It must be meant for you."

"Everyone wears robes here."

"I noticed. I think I'll stick with my clothes though."

A soft tapping echoed through the room and Sarilla turned about. "Either way, choose quickly. Unless you want them all to see that mole on your backside."

I blinked, then cursed, realising her meaning and scrambling to cover myself up. The darkness had lulled me into a false sense of security and I had temporarily forgotten that just because I couldn't see much in the darkness didn't mean Sarilla couldn't either.

"Don't worry," she said, making her way into the other room. "I've seen it all before."

I stilled, her meaning crashing into me. "Did we…?" I asked, uncertain if I wanted to know the answer. A sense of loss tore through me at what might have been taken from me. That I couldn't remember having loved her in that way…

"I have six months of your memories, Falon," she said over her shoulder. "Believe me when I say that your nudity isn't the only thing I've seen."

I didn't even have the solace of knowing that the darkness concealed my embarrassment as my cheeks heated, my mind guessing at the many no doubt embarrassing moments she must have witnessed in my memories.

"Sarilla," I called after her as she made her way towards the door. "You're doing the right thing."

She hesitated before turning back around.

"I know."

She opened the door, letting the guards into the chamber as I hurried to finish dressing, unable to shake the uneasy feeling that Sarilla and I had been speaking about two very different things.

CHAPTER THIRTY

Sarilla's robes swished as she walked ahead of me, the noise of the fabric a useful guide through the darkness as our escort accompanied us down the corridor, leading us deeper into the maze that was Oresa. I was as lost as I could be, convinced that even Havric would have struggled to find his way about down there.

Even if I had been able to see further than an arm's length in front of me, I doubted it would have helped much. The memori seemed to have created their tunnels to confuse those trying to navigate them, but considering the massacre they had faced twice now from Valrora, I couldn't say I was surprised. If I were them, then I would have gone one step further and set traps to catch unsuspecting invaders.

I was starting to think the tunnels would continue forever when we eventually stopped and our escort led us into a large chamber. The sides sloped steeply, meeting in a single point above us with shaded light flickering from fiery veins criss-crossing the ceiling, casting a dim glow down on us and the dirt floor. Memori gathered upon the concave shelves above, each shelf hanging out further than the one underneath. Pale faces peered over the rails, staring down at the dais we stood on as they jostled for a better view. Kira and several other memori waited upon the dais, their gazes fixed on Sarilla.

"We thank you for this, lost daughter," Kira said, her voice ringing clear through the chamber as the dirt walls absorbed any echo. "Words are insufficient to convey all that this means to us."

Sarilla glanced my way, something unreadable in her eyes as all around us, memori leaned forward, staring eagerly at her, no doubt recording the moment with the exquisite detail only memori could capture. Expectant silence filled the chamber as they watched, seeming to barely dare to breathe lest they missed a single word she said.

Catching Sarilla's eye, I smiled encouragingly as she fidgeted, grasping and pulling at her robe as she kept her gaze focused on the dirt floor.

"It's alright," I said, squeezing her hand. "You can do this."

Meeting my gaze, she searched my face, pulling her hand away as she turned to address the chamber.

"I never had the chance to meet your curator," she said, her Valrorian words seeming insufficient to fill the expectant silence. "My grandmother died before I was born. My mother, her daughter... she was the child of King Lucien Denvard, the father of the current King of Valrora. It was King Lucien who raided Oresa. King Lucien who stole your curator from you. King Lucien who took her back to Dranta to live among his people and warm his bed."

Silence greeted Sarilla's words, but something shifted in the air. The change was subtle but impossible to ignore. Mouths pursed as abhorrence suffused the faces of the onlookers. Had Sarilla been right? Did the memori care about the distinction between our races as much as Sarilla thought they did?

"As a child, King Lucien cared for her, keeping her safe even though others called for her to be destroyed. For many years, she was thought to be the last memoria alive. King Lucien... I don't know why he took my grandmother to his bed, but I was told he was fascinated by her. Perhaps he thought to preserve her ability for his own ends, to give his bloodline a power over others. Although already married and with an heir, he created a descendant with a power he thought would belong to his family alone."

Murmurs broke out among the memori and I knew for sure that Sarilla had been right this time. Disgust poured from them, the words half-breed, impure and polluted whispering through the chamber.

"Against her wishes, my grandmother bore him a child. In return for granting him that, she stole his memories, robbing him of his reason even though her body rejected his memories. She sickened a little more with his every visit, robbing him of more of his wits every time he returned to try to sire another. He soon became a shadow of himself, his memories so riddled that his mind was too confused. It caused him to trip on the stairs and fall to his death. That was the day his son ascended to the throne and ordered your curator's death."

"And the inherita?" Kira asked.

"Renford hated what his half-sister represented, but he couldn't bring himself to kill her too. He allowed her to live, unknowingly permitting the inherita my grandmother passed to her to live on too."

Excitement rippled through the room and I could feel the desperate curiosity that had united the memori since the curator's loss. Sarilla paused her story, waiting for the chatter to die down again before continuing, her gaze focused beyond the crowd, resting on the doors we had entered through.

"My mother lived in the palace her whole life long. After a few years, she fell in love with the ambassador from Frioca. Having grown up knowing nothing of the memori, he didn't know to fear her as the young king did. They kept their affections a secret and my mother bore him three children before he was sent away, banished back to Frioca. That was the last I saw of him until four months ago when he returned to Dranta, his head full of plans to steal his family away."

"And your mother? What of her?" Kira asked, her gaze fixed on Sarilla with an intensity that scared me.

"My father returned too late for her," Sarilla said. "King Renford had used her to steal memories for too many years. She died with her mind corrupted by all the memories she had been forced to take."

"And the inherita?"

"That's all you ever cared about, isn't it? You're incapable of looking to the future without clinging to the past and the secrets you hope to dig up. You think it excuses everything you've done, but it doesn't." Sarilla raised her gaze for the first time, meeting the ardent stares of the memori peering down at us. "The Valrorians should never have attacked your people. They were unprovoked each time, but you should never have sent the blackvine out in retaliation."

"It was no retaliation. We were only searching for what had been stolen from us."

"You were showing your strength, warning Valrora of

what you could do, but all you did was prove what you are. Monsters that cannot exist peacefully with those they consider so inferior." Sarilla hesitated, glancing again towards the entrance, her jaw clenching as a resolution passed over her face. "You should know that this time you brought this fate down upon yourselves."

A deep rumble tore through the room. Dust and dirt tumbled from the ceiling, scrabbling down about us and filling the air with the scent of soil as something far off clanged. Confusion broke through the chamber as the memori stared about, the panic in their voices reaching a strained pitch. Some memoria on the upper balconies disappeared from sight, rushing away and racing down tunnels to who knew where, as others leaned forward, calling down to Kira and begging for her instructions.

Footsteps pounded down the corridor and Kira turned to the chamber entrance as a man raced into the room, his robes streaming behind him as he ran for Kira, barrelling past Sarilla and me.

"It's an attack, Majestic," he said in Memorian, his words half-garbled as he hauled in panting breaths. "Valrora's forces are invading the tunnels from the surface. They're already inside."

Kira's eyes widened in terror as her gaze snapped to me, her black eyes pinning me with the full weight of her stare as her mouth moved silently and images flashed through my mind.

Memories of the king and Sarilla conversing together, standing too far away to hear what they said, but not to miss the gleam in the king's eyes as Sarilla spoke to him, explaining her plan.

Kira's eyes widened, her attention snapping to Sarilla, fear in her expression over the consequences of what we had both failed to realise before. Sarilla was here to end the animosity between her peoples, but not peacefully.

"You did this," Kira said, her voice breaking at the betrayal. "You led them here. You brought their army down on us when you know what they'll do. Why? We offered you sanctuary."

"You think that makes you any less monstrous? I know what I am, and I know that the world will be a better place when it's free from memori-"

"Sarilla!" I called. "Stop this. You can't… You're wrong about them."

"What do you know of anything, Falon? Your memories have been so messed with that you don't even know who you are anymore."

"But you stopped the king," Kira said. "The army was halted. There was to be peace between us."

"Renford was always going to come for you. He would never have suffered you to live after what you did to his people. I couldn't have stopped him even if I wanted to. Your blackvine has destroyed too many lives. There was never any other way this could end."

"But we called the blackvine back! We stopped the assault! We are defenceless now!"

Screams tore down the corridor, filling the chamber and drowning out everything else as I realised with a lurch that they weren't the hardened voices of soldiers, but of civilians caught in a war they hadn't seen coming.

"Majestic? What are your orders? We must defend ourselves."

Kira turned to the adviser who had spoken, groping for words, but nothing came out.

"Majestic! The blackvine, it's our only hope!"

He grabbed her arm, shaking her until the dazed look on Kira's face crumbled away. She nodded and her gaze sharpened as she swept it across the chamber, meeting the stares of those who had yet to flee into the tunnels.

"Summon it," she said, her expression slackening as the blackvine surged to life in my head once more.

CHAPTER THIRTY-ONE

Whites of the eyes turned black as the memori about us connected their minds through the blackvine, pouring their memories into the dirt to bring forth their greatest defence. In the recesses of my mind, I felt the blackvine taking shape from the memories they fed it. Memorian, Valrorian, plant, animal, it didn't matter. All were used to bring the blackvine back to life again.

Kira's presence filled my head even as thick smoke-like vines writhed up from the ground, spilling out into the tunnels. The Valrorians wouldn't stand a chance. What good was steel against smoke?

Hold her.

Kira's voice rang through my mind as the darkness consumed me, it tugged me down into its black depths, stealing everything from me until I was Falon no more. All that was left was Kira's instruction and I could but obey it.

I reached for the white-haired creature beside me, needing to contain her as I was bid, even though I didn't understand why.

Hold her. She's dangerous to all of us.

Hold her. I would do as I was told.

My grip tightened about the white-haired woman's arm as a sad smile formed on her face. Recognition speared through me at the sight and I faltered. I knew her. Sarilla. Why was I seizing her like that?

I pulled my hands back, staring at them without understanding how they had been made to move without conscious thought on my part.

She's dangerous! Hold her!

Black fog filled my mind again, but this time a wave of memories accompanied it. Terrified memories of memori being chased through tunnels. Agonised screams as steel pierced flesh. Desperate hands gripping the soil where they fell, bleeding memories and blood into the dirt. One by one the connections to the blackvine snuffed out.

Even though the blackvine surged through the tunnels, cleansing Oresa of soldiers, it was already too late. The memori were trapped, pinned down by the soldiers who had poured into the city through secret entrances that had somehow been compromised.

Memori frantically pushed their memories into the ground, filling the blackvine with the last vestiges of themselves as their lives drained from them. How many had already died? How few of them had there been left to begin with?

My hand clamped down on the arm of the woman beside me and I hauled her roughly away from the memori, barely aware of what I did through the blackness and the confusion of the memories.

My head was filled with hate for her, she who had done this to us. She was dangerous. She had caused so many deaths already.

Abomination.

The half-breed must die for her betrayal!

"Steel can't kill all of us," Kira said, her voice ringing through my head and my ears together. "Already our blackvine purges our lands of your soldiers once more. It will take just one of us to survive and I promise you that will be enough to destroy every man, woman and child in Valrora!"

"I know," the woman in my arms said as she kicked my leg, knocking us both off balance and throwing us to the ground. We hit the dirt floor with a thump and the air was knocked from me. The woman landed atop my chest and I heaved in a deep breath, fighting back the pain as she cupped my face with one hand, pressing her other into the dirt beneath us.

"I'm sorry," she said, staring into my eyes with a pain and guilt I couldn't understand.

In a blast of awareness, her mind invaded mine, driving the blackness back into the darkest recesses, hastening its flight as memories filled with light surged into me. I could taste Sarilla in my mind. Her stubbornness. Her determination. Her obstinacy. Her conviction. Her hatred. She loathed the memori and as I felt her in my head, I understood why.

I felt her shame at Renford's disgust in what she was. Her bitter and twisted self-loathing at what her family had been. Renford might have brought the army, but she had brought the resolve to see this genocide through. In that moment, I knew she would see them all dead or die trying.

I flinched, trying to break away as the light speared into me, but not knowing where there was left to run to as the memories of fire and sunlight poured into my mind, dissolving the darkness coating my memories, layer by layer.

STOP HER!

I distantly registered Kira's panicked scream and felt my

hand unsheathe my knife as I moved without thought.

The blade pierced through the robe and drove through fleshy resistance, stabbing in as the darkness retreated further in my mind, leaving me reeling as Sarilla drew forth a thousand sunlit memories from the dawn outside, channelling them from the nexus and into the blackvine through me.

The blackvine burnt about us, the memories sustaining it destroyed one after another by the sunlight, disintegrating the minds of the memori still connected to it in one destructive blow.

I think I screamed. I know I clung to my head, trying to stop it from bursting open as the blinding light in the memories consumed my consciousness, blotting out all thought streaming through me and into the blackvine. There was only one place in my mind that was safe. One place shielded by Sarilla from the light and I hid there until the blaze stopped, the link between the memori as severed as their memories were annihilated.

Sarilla released her grip on my mind and the dam blocking my memories was broken. They flooded my head, filling me with everything I hadn't realised the memori had been hiding from me.

Sarilla. Ced.

Oh Gods. Ced.

What had I done?

Sarilla released me, but I reeled too much from the return of my memories to care. Ced was dead by my hand and-

A whimper escaped Sarilla as she shifted off me. The noise was filled with a pain that dragged me out of the past, even as my mind still struggled to readjust.

Memori screams filled the nearby tunnels and I knew the soldiers were renewing their assault on Oresa now

Sarilla had burnt the blackvine from existence.

The cries of the memori had changed, morphing into a disjointed dirge that rang through the chamber, the sound filled with a new kind of terror now their memories had been taken from them.

How could she have done this? I had known Sarilla capable of a lot of monstrous acts, but not this. Not the murder of hundreds. Not the snuffing out of an entire race as dispassionately as you might extinguish a candle.

Something heavy fell from my hand. It thudded against the dirt, but the noise barely registered above the screaming.

"Are you alright?" Sarilla asked, the sound of her voice raking through my guts as rage and love warred inside me.

I felt like my head had been scoured raw from the inside out, but what was that to the agony of the memori dying in the tunnels about us? What use was her misplaced concern now? Where was her compassion for those she had just fated to die in pain and confusion?

She had done this to them.

Those still in the chamber with us groaned, slowly regaining awareness, alive after what Sarilla had done to them, for now at least.

"What did you do?" I asked, staring about the room as I struggled to process it all.

"I had to, Falon. I had to stop them."

The pain filling her voice set me on edge. I blinked, trying to focus on her in the gloom, needing to understand the instinct telling me that something was wrong. Terribly wrong.

At first, I didn't see anything. The room too dark and my mind too confused. Then it caught up with me, as did the images I hadn't been able to process while Sarilla forced the sunlight through me. The heavy blade falling from my hand. The resistance of her flesh as I forced it into her, just as I had done to Ced.

Sarilla cradled her stomach, her weak smile failing to hide the pain etched into her face. Blood coated her hands as she pressed them against the wound, her whole body giving in to the shakes as her life slipped out from between her fingers.

"Sarilla? Oh Gods. What have I done? I didn't mean to. I didn't know-"

"Shhh. Falon... It's alright."

"It's not alright! How is any of this alright?"

I pressed my hands against her stomach, trying to stop the bleeding, the warm liquid leaking out despite my best efforts.

She needed a healer. Even then... Even that might not be enough. If the memori had a healer then they were likely dead already, but what about the army? There must be a surgeon in their ranks, someone who would know what to do.

The soldiers would be upon us soon. Screams filled the chamber from the tunnels, announcing their approach. She just had to hold on a little longer. That was all.

"I don't blame you," she said, her voice weaker than it had been before.

"I didn't mean to do this. Sarilla... I'm sorry. I'm so sorry. I should have been able to break Kira's control-"

"Shh. This is for the best. You'll see that soon."

"How? How can your bleeding to death possibly be for the best?"

I strained my neck, trying to see the doorway and the soldiers I expected to come bursting through it at any moment. What was taking them so long?

Sarilla's bloodied hand pressed against my face, turning my head until our gazes locked.

"Because I'm just as much a monster as they are, Falon. Kira was right. If even one of us lives, then it's one too many."

"Stop. You aren't. None of the memori are. Don't you see? It's just the twisted prejudices you've been made to believe that's making you think that."

She smiled weakly, her voice frail as she fought to keep her eyes open. My cheek tingled from her touch and I wondered at the familiar sensation as she glanced over my shoulder, her eyes widening.

She forced a memory into me, flooding my mind with her near-perfect vision. I saw my face as I stared at her through the darkness, love and hatred warring on my features as the figure behind me picked up my discarded knife. Kira raised the blade as Sarilla's fingers slipped from my cheek and I spun about, my vision returning to me as the blade glinted, stabbing through the air.

CHAPTER THIRTY-TWO

Pain seared my shoulder as I twisted, landing atop Sarilla as the blade sliced along my back, raking the skin without sinking in. Kira screamed as she clung to the weapon, lunging for me again and slashing wildly. She nicked my hands and arms in her frenzy, cutting me half a dozen times before I managed to grab her wrists.

Her grip on the dagger slipped as we struggled, and it fell from her clutches. She whimpered, confusion and terror filling her gaze as she shook in my grip, her fear having driven her to attack me. Did she even know what she was anymore?

I had a sense of what she must be feeling, but even when the blackvine blanketed my memories, it had never robbed me so completely of my past, leaving me empty like Kira was now. Where I had only been separated from them, hers had been eradicated. I could only guess what that would do to a person.

Sarilla had done this through me. Without my connection to the blackvine, she wouldn't have been able to break their minds as she had.

Kira struggled to free herself and I let her go. She wasn't Kira anymore. The Kira who had hoped for peace and restitution was already gone. The memoria before me was no more than a scared and broken shell of the woman she had been.

I stared after her as she fled down a tunnel, wishing her luck, even though I knew she wouldn't make it out of Oresa alive, not with the soldiers already inside.

It didn't take long for them to find her. Screams filled the air from the tunnel Kira had run down, and the clanking of armour grew as the footsteps drew closer. The memori still in the chamber fled as the soldiers stormed inside, slaying any they came across on the way.

I tore Sarilla's robe with my teeth and pressed the fabric to her wound as the tang of iron filled the air.

"Hold on, Sarilla. Hold on."

A group paused as they made to chase after a memori man darting down a tunnel. I shielded my eyes as a soldier pointed a flaming torch in our direction, holding it as if to ward away the blackvine. He spotted us and motioned to the other soldiers, their gazes raking over Sarilla.

"Is that her?" one asked, waving his torch in her direction. "The king's pet? Is it her?"

"Yes. Sarilla. His niece. She's been stabbed. We have to get her to a surgeon."

"We could just leave her here," one of the soldiers muttered, glancing about the room as if expecting a memoria to jump out at him from the shadows at any moment. "Say we got here too late and that she was already dead. It won't be long now anyway by the looks of her-"

"You heard the king's orders," another said, brushing past the first man to take a closer look before gesturing at the three other men in their group. "Get her out of here. And hurry about it. He won't thank you if you present him with a corpse."

The men moved hesitantly as they obeyed his orders. They hefted Sarilla up, carrying her limp body from the chamber and leaving me with only her fading warmth and the blood seeping into the soil beneath me.

I wanted to follow, to make sure she was alright. It was easy to guess what blood-crazed soldiers might do when they caught sight of her pale complexion. That she was still wearing the memori robes wouldn't help matters.

"And you," the soldier in charge said as I stumbled to my feet. "You're Arvendon's Bastard?"

"I am."

"Alright then. Hold him," he said to the two remaining soldiers.

Hands grabbed my wrists and they wrenched my arms behind my back. I winced as I was pushed down onto my knees, the soldier who had given the order drawing his sword.

"Get off me-"

Something thumped and the soldier frowned. He glanced down at his chest, seeming as surprised as I was to find an arrow tip protruding from it. He slumped forward, landing beside me in a heap, the arrow shaft sticking from his back.

I stared at his body, unable to process the sight of it. The other two soldiers recovered from their shock faster than I. One ducked, narrowly avoiding an arrow that instead shot over his head, but the other wasn't fast enough. The tip pierced through his neck and he dropped, his body twitching death spasms as Havric emerged from the shadows across the chamber.

He notched another arrow, aiming it at the final soldier, but his shot went wide as the soldier dodged again. I stared at Havric, dumbfounded to see him there as the third guard charged him, his sword already drawn. The sight finally wrenched me out of my reverie and I threw myself after him, too close to draw my sword. Instead, I tackled him to the ground.

He rolled up, quickly gaining his feet and kicking me in the stomach. I groaned as I curled inwards, catching sight of Havric behind the soldier as his blade sliced across the man's neck and warm droplets splattered my face.

Havric wiped his dagger clean on the crook of his elbow, raising a wry eyebrow to me.

"Looks like I found you just in time."

"Don't suppose you know why they were about to take my head off?"

"The king ordered it. Apparently, he thinks you'd look better without it. I'm almost of the same mind."

"What? Why does he want me dead now?"

"Why do you think? He even mentioned a reward for whoever brought him your head. I didn't think I'd make it to you in time. We need to get out of here. Where's Sarilla? I thought she'd be with you." He glanced about the chamber as he spoke. He must have noticed something in my expression to alarm him because he asked, "What is it? Is she alright?"

"She... She was stabbed." I gestured at the blood at my feet. Most of it had already seeped into the dirt, making it gleam red gold in the light of the torch one of the soldiers had dropped.

"Will she be alright?"

"I... I don't know. The soldiers took her away to be tended to, but... I don't think she means to survive this place."

"What's that supposed to mean?"

"She did this, Havric," I gestured about the chamber to the destruction Sarilla had brought to Oresa. "The army might have wielded the swords, but Sarilla struck first and she struck deepest."

"What? Why would she do this to them?"

"I don't think it was the memori she was attacking. They just got caught in the crossfire of her own self-hatred."

"Whatever her reason, the king won't let her die. He loves her as much as he hates her," Havric said as shouts rumbled through the tunnel towards us. "Come on. We need to focus on getting you out of here. Don't worry about Sarilla. The surgeons will do what they can. And with the king breathing down their necks, they'll be sure to do their best."

"Hav, listen. Oresa's a maze and right now it's one that's swarming with soldiers. Don't sign your own death warrant by throwing your lot in with a dead man."

"Stop fretting. You sound like my ma. I can get us out, though not with you looking like that." He grabbed the nearest soldier and divested the man of his uniform. "We just need to reach the surface. Once we're there, we can disappear among the chaos. Queen Meradia of Evaleon has arrived with her army to aid King Renford's efforts. The two armies aren't mixing well. We'll be able to use it to our advantage."

"What are you doing?" I asked as he shrugged the dead man out of his breastplate.

"Take this," he said, handing me the soldier's armour. "If you look like a soldier, then we've a better chance of getting out of here alive."

He had a point, I thought as I glanced at the uniform he was wearing.

"We should hide them," Havric said, grabbing one of the soldiers and dragging him towards the side of the chamber.

A heavy pounding echoed down a tunnel as I reached

for one of the other bodies.

"No time."

Havric's gaze met mine and we darted into the nearest tunnel entrance, leaving the torchlight behind as we plunged into the darkness. I couldn't see a thing. There might have been anything in the tunnel with us as we ran. Memori, soldiers, a spine-snapping hole we might fall into at any moment. All I had to guide me was the light tapping of Havric's footsteps ahead, but the sound was almost entirely drowned out by my own heavier tread as I chased behind him, racing to keep up. I didn't even realise that there was another tunnel connecting to ours and flew past it, only for Havric's shout to pull me up short.

I followed the sound of his voice into the side passage and hoped Havric was as confident about finding his way out as he seemed. The dark wasn't as comfortable to me now the blackvine no longer filled my mind.

"We'll end up in Dranta at this rate," I said between gasps. "You don't reckon the two sets of tunnels are somehow connected?"

"We're going the wrong way for Dranta. These tunnels are heading in the direction of the eastern mountains."

"How for all of Forta's grace do you know that? It's blacker than death down here."

"Just because your sense of direction is broken, doesn't mean mine is," Havric said, hurrying away again.

The tunnel began to lighten eventually and Havric slowed down. We emerged into a brightly lit chamber and I was surprised to spot the staircase I had come down when first entering Oresa. It bustled with light and activity as soldiers hurried about, their armour glinting and reflecting the golden glow of their torches. Some made their way back up to the surface while others poured into the tunnels, ready to take on what little must remain of the memori.

The tunnel Havric and I stood in was hidden among the sheer quantity of other tunnels leading from the chamber, which must have been how it had gone unnoticed by the army.

Emerging from it, Havric and I fell in behind a group of soldiers who were returning to the surface. They carried a fallen comrade between them. The man stared about, seeming dazed even though he appeared physically unharmed. Had he been a victim of the blackvine before Sarilla destroyed it? What of the memories of all those connected to the blackvine? Had the sunlight annihilated those too?

As we reached the top of the staircase, we made our way out of the tower and through the small doorway, passing the many soldiers waiting eagerly to get in and join in the easy victory.

I glanced about, immediately lowering my gaze at the sight of the horses and riders gathered nearby, the king among them. He gripped the reins tightly, worry lining his brow. For the fate of his war or for Sarilla?

"There's no sign of him yet," a young soldier said to the king, speaking up from in front of the king's horse. "But there's still a lot of tunnels to clear down there."

"And the blackvine?" the woman sat on a horse beside King Renford asked as she peered down from her impressively pointed nose.

"Still no reported sightings since it disappeared, Your Majesty. We think it's gone for good."

"If I ask for your speculation, you'll know it," the woman said. I guessed her to be Queen Meradia as she reached over to rap on the king's clenched fist with her knuckles. "Purge the tunnels with fire if you have to. There's nothing down there of value to us now you have the girl back."

I froze. Was she speaking of Sarilla? The guards must have got her to the surgeon already.

I stared out at the hastily erected camp. Soldiers we had followed up the staircase were supporting their fallen companion outside a tent a short distance away. They stood waiting at the end of a queue of soldiers with various injuries. Tapping Havric's arm, I gestured their way.

"Let's go," I mouthed to Havric before making my way across the camp towards the tent.

I had to make sure she was going to be alright. No matter whose voice it had been in my head, it was still my hand that wielded the knife, my skin coated red with her blood. I didn't think I could cope with Sarilla being dead by my hand as well as Ced.

Moving through the queue, we made our way inside the tent, only to find it divided within. We set to searching the compartments, finding restrained soldiers in most of them, many lashing out, their memory loss fuelling their fears as surgeons raced about the tent.

We moved through the chambers until we happened upon one that was empty except for the figure tied to a post in the centre. Blood had spread on her black robes and red smears had dried across her arms and face. She bent forward, her hair falling about her and shielding most of her face from view.

Where were the surgeons? Why weren't they attending to her?

"Sarilla?" Havric asked, making his way over to her, his voice unsteady.

He touched her shoulder gently and relief flooded through me as she shifted, responding to his presence as he knelt beside her.

"Havric?" she asked, her voice so weak that I might

have imagined the sound.

"I'm here. Don't worry, everything's going to be alright, I'm just going to have a look at the damage." He moved her hands aside so he could inspect the wound. "This isn't so deep. It doesn't look like it hit anything major. Why aren't they in here fixing you up?"

"I sent them away," she said softly, her voice breaking as she spoke. "Didn't take much to get them to leave me be."

"The king will have their heads when he finds out."

"He won't like it, but I don't anticipate having to suffer his displeasure for long. You should go. He could be back any minute."

"We're not leaving without you," I said.

Sarilla's eyes flew open as she sought me out, seeming to struggle to focus on me.

"Hav, do what you can to fix her up. We'll get her out of here, then get someone to attend her-"

"No. Please, Falon. Just go."

"Sarilla-"

Something moved in the corner of my vision and I spun, catching sight of the king as he entered the small confines of the chamber. He froze at the sight of us, his gaze sweeping through the room even as I moved, grabbing him and hauling his back against my chest, my dagger already pressed against his throat.

"Falon- no!" Havric hissed as I dragged the king away from the entrance and forced him onto his knees before Sarilla.

"What was I supposed to do?" I asked as a small trickle of blood tumbled down the king's throat.

"Not that!" Havric hissed back.

"Quiet a moment. Sarilla... He did this to you," I said, holding her gaze with mine as I shook the king. "Don't you see that? His hatred is what's made you act as you have. You're not a bad person. You never were. You're only what he made you. If anyone understands that it's me. I know what it's like to be despised for my birth, but that's not my fault. It's not either of our faults, but it will be if you let it define who you are-"

"Stop, Falon. Just stop," Sarilla said, a tear rolling down her cheek.

"No! I won't let you lay down and wait for death. I love you. I love your fire and your determination. I love your-"

"But you don't, Falon. You never did."

Raising a shaking hand, she touched her fingers to my cheek. My skin tingled as the marks on her hand began to ripple, the darkness pulsing as memories filled my mind.

CHAPTER THIRTY-THREE

The rush filling my mind was too much for me to make sense of. I could barely register one memory before another swept it away.

I still recognised the inherita for what it was though and hated Sarilla for pushing the last vestiges of the memori into my inadequate mind. Was my body already purging them? After everything she had already done to them, this final blow was far worse.

Echoes of memori long dead and all but forgotten flashed through my mind. I tried desperately to cling to as many of the details as possible, even as they slipped away. Families living in darkness. Children playing strange games I almost understood. Something powerful buried beneath stone trees and hidden from the world. Strangers who wanted nothing more than to provide for the future of their people, but all for nothing as they were forgotten forever.

More memories filled my mind, swarming me in a rush that was both strange and familiar all at once. Were they my memories? They certainly felt like they were, but after having spent the last half a year searching for them, I couldn't quite believe it as they slotted back in place, my two halves finally reunited as old warred with new, too different to mix, let alone blend to grey.

If it was odd to have woken up without them, then it was nothing to how unnerving their return was. Some were so wrong that I was half-convinced they weren't my memories. I relived them, needing to be certain they were mine, but how could I mistake the pride that had surged through me at my father asking me to be his agent in Dranta? The excitement as he had handed me a small black vial that glinted in the firelight, along with the goblet I was to coat with the poison and present to the king as a gift.

"It works through the skin so you'll have to be careful not to touch it. You take a great risk by doing this, but you will earn your place as my heir if you do."

I had been so sure of myself as I journeyed to Dranta, so certain I could accomplish my father's wishes and rid Valrora of a king who was destroying his own country.

My astonishment when I happened upon the memori half-breed wandering the palace unguarded had been immense. I had taken a hasty step back from the monster with the sharp, unnatural features, finding it easy to believe her capable of all her kin had been rumoured to have done over the years. All I could think was that my father had sent me to Dranta to rid us of the king, but what if I could also save us from the half-breeds he used to terrorise his people?

How many lives had her kind destroyed? How many memories had her people stolen? How much would she steal if I let her live?

My bastard blade was already freed from its scabbard as I closed the distance between us, ready to plunge it into her gut and bring Valrora one step closer to freedom. Then she raised her charcoal black eyes and they fixed me in place, the darkness practically seeping from her, tainting everything in her vicinity.

A blush stained her cheeks and she broke the stare. The sudden flush of colour took me by surprise. It tempered the unnatural darkness of her features. She looked so normal, so youthful. I didn't know what to think as her gaze flickered back up to mine, the blush spreading as she glanced away again, her embarrassment apparent.

"Sarilla!" a voice called from down the corridor. "The king has asked for you."

"Coming," she said, her blush deepening as she glanced my direction one last time before darting away.

A monster she was, but a naïve one at that. I had decided to use her innocence to my advantage to make her fall for me. To convince her to trust me so that instead of killing one memoria now, I could see them all off at once.

The memories changed, replaced by one far clearer than my own had been. I stared at myself as the guards dragged me into the throne room, the doors clanking shut, barring my escape. Fear coursed through the memory owner as the guards hauled me before the king.

"Renford, please, I beg you," Sarilla said as I watched the memory through her eyes as she knelt before the king. "Let him go. Please don't hurt him-"

"If he's innocent, my dear, then he has nothing to fear, but I suspect not."

"You can't do this!"

The king cocked an eyebrow at me, a small smirk forming about his mouth. "And why is that, Bastard? I was appointed to rule by the Gods themselves. I find it interesting that you question my motives when I have every right to suspect yours."

"I've done nothing-"

"Do not lie to me! Your rooms have been searched. We found the poison." He pulled out the small vial, looking for a moment like he was seriously considering uncorking it and pouring the contents over me. "So you can choose to admit your guilt or Sarilla can discover the truth for herself."

"I won't. Renford, I won't do that to him."

"You would take his side in this?"

"Please, Renford. I know Falon. He wouldn't betray you like that. He's loyal, I swear it!"

"No," the king said, motioning a guard forward. "Either search his memories or stand aside for his execution. It's your choice, niece."

Sarilla took a shaky step back, revulsion and fear flowing through her. She hated the thought of stealing memories, but the idea of taking them from me made her want to be sick, yet what other option did she have?

She tugged off her glove, hot tears spilling unchecked down her cheeks as she reached for me, a sob catching in her throat.

"I'm sorry," she whispered as her fingertips hesitated a hair's breadth from my cheek.

I flinched before her, my eyes wide with terror as I tried to avoid her touch, but the guards behind me held me fast and I couldn't escape.

Warmth filled Sarilla's fingertips as my memories surged into her. They vibrated with an intoxicating hum that coursed deliciously through Sarilla, all her objections from only a moment ago fading away. Her fear of becoming like her mother. Her hatred of what she was doing to me. She was lost in the way my memories teased her senses as she rifled through my mind, turning over what should have remained mine alone, delving into my memories until she reached the one of my father sending me to Arvendon. Shock tore through her as she learnt the truth and she almost broke the connection. I relived her disbelief as she searched my memories, trying to find evidence of my having changed my mind, for anything she might use to convince the king not to execute me, but there was nothing.

She saw every lie I had ever told her. Knew the monster I thought her to be.

She was right. I didn't love her. I never had.

She pulled her mind out of my memories, stumbling away from me. No-one reached out to steady her. Their gazes were fixed on the thin black lines that had sprouted at the tips of her hands. My memories. The ones she had taken from me of my father laying out his plans.

"Well?" the king asked. "What did you see?"

I waited for her to condemn me as the king leaned forward atop the throne, but she didn't.

"There was a plot," Sarilla said, determinedly looking anywhere but at me as she fought back the tears stinging her eyes. "But Falon had no intention of carrying it out."

The king's jaw clenched, his eyes narrowing to slits. "If you're lying to me-"

"I'm not. I swear. It's the truth."

"Even if that's the case," the king said, pressing a hand to his temple and letting out a slow breath. "His loyalty is still in question. He cannot be permitted to go free when-"

"I'll take his memories."

Sarilla's voice rang through the room as all eyes turned her way.

"What did you just say?" the king asked, leaning forward, his forehead creasing into a frown.

"I'll take his memories from the moment his father ordered him to kill you. He won't remember it, nor anything else since then, all on the condition that you let him live. You can't order his death, Renford. Not now, not ever. He lives and you send him away."

She couldn't let me die. After everything she had learnt from my memories, she couldn't let the king kill me, but nor could she bear the thought of existing in a world where the man who tricked her into loving him was still alive and aware of the fool he played her for.

"I'll agree to your terms if you agree to act in your mother's stead," the king said, a shrewd glint in his eyes as he bled her bargain for all it was worth. "She's less reliable of late and I need another memoria to step into her shoes."

Hot tears tumbled down Sarilla's cheeks as she nodded, agreeing to be what she hated in exchange for my life.

"Please, Sarilla. Don't do this," I begged, struggling uselessly against the guards, my body shaking as I fought to get away. "I'm sorry. I-"

She touched my cheek again and I watched my eyes glaze over, my memories slipping from me.

CHAPTER THIRTY-FOUR

The memories faded from my vision, but not from my mind. Months might have passed since they were formed, but in my head, they were as fresh as if they happened only minutes ago.

Everybody lies. I just hadn't realised she had been talking about me.

It was my corruption that stained her hands black. My deception that had set her on this path. She hadn't been keeping my memories from me to keep me safe. She had done it because she hadn't wanted me to know the truth. Had she hoped for a second chance at making me fall for her?

I was responsible for turning her into the monster and I hated myself for it, but I wasn't alone in my guilt. There was someone else whose actions had brought Sarilla to this.

No-one had forced the king to use his half-sister and her children as he had. Nobody had made him groom them with his mangled mixture of love and malice. He was worse than any memori had ever been.

"Release me now, Bastard, and I won't have you executed for your treason," the king said as he strained under my blade.

Sarilla whimpered and flinched back, her eyes wide as she scrambled to get away from us.

"Can't do that," I said into the king's ear as he struggled against my chest, my grip too strong for him to break away. "I should have Sarilla take your memories from you as punishment for what you've done, but just because you're depraved enough to force her to do that, doesn't mean I am."

"Falon-"

"The Gods will decide your fate," I said, dragging the blade across his throat.

Hot blood spurted from the wound as Havric moved too late to stop me. I had done as my father had asked of me, even if he wasn't alive to know it.

I held the king tight as he jerked his death spasms, my gaze locked with Sarilla's as he stilled. I let his body fall to the floor, still not glancing from her and the confusion in her eyes.

"We need to get out of here," Havric said, moving to stand beside me. "Gods. Falon… You didn't think that we might have been able to use him to bargain for our freedom? Now we have to pray no-one realises he's dead until we get out of here."

"Get Sarilla. I'll draw the guards' attention so you can get out of here."

Havric flinched and spun about, his eyes narrowed. "What are you talking about? I'm not leaving you to get caught."

"You have to otherwise there isn't a chance any of us will make it out of here alive. Please, take her, Hav. I owe her that much at the very least."

"Don't be ridiculous," he said as he reached for the rope binding Sarilla to the post. "You haven't done anything-"

"Get away from me!" Sarilla yelled as Havric cut her free. She scrambled away from us and Havric jolted back in surprise.

"What?" He looked between Sarilla and me like we were both mad. "Sarilla… We need to get out of here-"

"She's not Sarilla anymore," I said, drawing both their gazes my way.

"What are you talking about? Of course she is."

"She gave me her memories. There's nothing of Sarilla left in there now. She's pushed them all into me."

"She… She can't have."

"She has, Hav. And after what I've done to her, this chance at a fresh start is the least I owe her."

I glanced out through the tent door, peering about for the king's guards as Havric crouched down beside Sarilla, trying to calm her down.

"Goodbye, Havric. I hope Forta's with you. She'll need to be."

"Fal… You're not serious?"

"Deadly," I said as I managed a half-smile. "Go. You'll need as much of a head start as you can get."

Realising he couldn't change my mind, Havric reached for Sarilla. Speaking soothingly to her, he convinced her to take his hand in hers and helped her up, promising he was going to keep her safe.

With one final look my way, he nodded to me then used his blade to cut a hole in the outer wall of the tent and helped Sarilla through it.

"Good luck, Falon," he said before he disappeared through the gap after her.

"Good luck," I said, making my way out the tent after them, my red-stained hands held aloft as Havric and what was left of Sarilla disappeared from view.

The Sarilla I had known was a monster I helped create, but in her memories I could feel her hope to be free. If I could only manage one thing now, it would be to give it to her, no matter the cost.

Some say it's a gift to walk a day in another's shoes, but have they ever had the misfortune of trying? Doing so only draws attention to our differences. It exposes the unevenly worn soles, victims of the previous owner's lopsided gait. Sarilla had walked in the wrong shoes for so long, her feet had contorted to a different fit, moulding into something unrecognisable until it no longer mattered if she wore the shoes or not. She couldn't escape the effects of the memories she stole, so she escaped the memories instead.

Now you see the monster she truly was. One I created from my hatred. I carved her out of my disgust, shaping her with my lies. It is little wonder she ended up as she did.

I don't know how many weeks I've been locked up awaiting my execution, only that I've had one long headache this entire time, even while I sleep. The memories crowd my mind. If you were to crack my skull open, I'm convinced they would come pouring out. Some days I let them take me, even though I know it will be hard to fight my way back out of them later. I don't even care whose I get lost in. Mine. Hers. The fragments of the inherita not yet purged by my mind. I've tried to write down what I could, paper and ink being the only luxury my jailers have permitted me. I suppose my account is an inherita of sorts, even if only a poor mimic of the original. I thought that by recording it, by separating her memories from mine, it might help provide clarity, but all it has done is smear grey over the lines separating monster and man, if there ever were any to begin with. I find it hard to know what thoughts are my own.

Strange though it is, I don't believe I am truly myself anymore, even less so than when she stole my memories. If I've learnt anything, it's that forgetting is freedom, but that remembering weighs heavier than chains. I look forward to my own mind being released from its cage. It will come soon, no doubt. Then we will both be free.

ABOUT THE AUTHOR

Rachel Emma Shaw has a PhD in neuroscience and a fascination with identity. She began writing fiction during her degree because she needed a creative outlet amidst the science, but she was soon swept up in her stories. Although she still works as a science communicator, her fiction writing now consumes the rest of her life. She's an infamous presence in the London writing community and loves sharing insight gained over the years on the wonders of storytelling with her fellow writers. Last Memoria is her debut novel, but it won't be her last.

Printed in Great Britain
by Amazon